MARGAR

LOVE ON THE EDGE -

the Castle *in the Bay*

Margaret Amatt x

LEANNAN
PRESS
INDEPENDENT PUBLISHER

First published in 2025 by Leannan Press

Cover designs, Margaret Amatt 2025

eBook ISBN: 978-1-914575-35-8

Paperback ISBN: 978-1-914575-33-4

Chapter One

Monty

Monty MacNeil took a deep breath and peered out the window of the plane. *Ok, should not have done that.* He pulled his head back so it was jammed against the headrest, and pushed his glasses up the bridge of his nose. Flying had never been a problem for him before. Business class flights were pretty decent, but this. How could this even be classed as a plane? Utterly baffling. It had wings, but that was about it.

The seven other passengers onboard oohed and ahhed as the plane banked. The pilot looked like he knew what he was doing, which was about the best thing that could be said for having the cockpit visible. But none of that was the main problem. Monty's eyes screwed up as he looked towards the window again. Holy crap, that was a lot of water. Other passengers had their phones out and were chattering excitedly about how clear it was, how blue, green, turquoise... Almost tropical.

No doubt it was all that, but Monty couldn't bear to look. If the engines failed, they'd plunge to their doom in that sea. Clutching the armrest, he sensed the drop in altitude. Landing on Traigh Mhor beach on the Hebridean island of Barra featured on several people's bucket lists. Tourists worldwide would have paid good money for weather like this to do it in, but Monty just wanted to get his feet on dry land. Maybe an island wasn't the best place for that, but he had a job to do. And when Monty was given a job, he liked to do it properly. It was how he'd gained his reputation as a trustworthy banker and a dutiful son.

His hand darted to the seat beside him, and he gripped the bag containing what was left of his father. The ashes of Hector MacNeil were on their way home. Monty closed his eyes. A thud followed by some squeals and chat told him the plane had landed. He let out a breath. *Made it.*

Time to get off this glorified minibus and explore the island his father had told him so much about. Apparently, Monty had been here as a child, but he couldn't remember. Maybe at thirty-six, a visit was long overdue.

He stopped as he crossed the beach runway, heading for the 'airport'. The turquoise waters murmured gently on the pale golden sands in a rhythmic lullaby. Stunning really. As long as he didn't have to get too close. He didn't understand people who wanted to swim in there or do water sports. Getting wet and cold like that held no appeal for him.

Holding his bag close, he made his way to the long white building that was the airport. Kind of surreal that anything so industrial had made its way to such a rugged, out of the way place. The warmth of the sun beat on his back. He should take off his jacket, but with unpredictable weather forecast, he'd not been sure what to wear.

A taxi was waiting, and Monty went to the window. 'Hello, I'm Monty MacNeil.'

'That's right,' the taxi driver said. 'In you get. You're heading to An Grianan, am I right?'

'Yes, please.' Presumably the taxi driver had correctly pronounced the name of the farmhouse where he'd booked to stay. Monty had anglicised it in his mind but repeated it inside his head as the driver had said. *Un GREE-uh-nun*, with the emphasis on 'gree'. He would try and remember that, so he didn't sound ignorant. Memories of a trip to Ireland in his younger years surfaced. He'd made some embarrassing gaffs with pronunciations there and was determined not to do it again.

The driver got out and Monty put his luggage in the boot, still holding tightly to the small black backpack which contained the urn.

'That bag can go in too,' the driver said.

'I'd prefer if it didn't.' Monty ran his hand around his lightly stubbled jaw. 'This is rather precious.'

'Right you are.'

Monty got into the passenger seat and strapped himself in. Once he was ready, the driver took off down the winding island road. The sea sprawled to his left, looking almost tropical in the bright sunlight. To his right were hills of scraggy rocks and tufty grass. Pink and white wildflowers danced in the light breeze along the roadside. No wonder his father had raved about this place. Monty opened the window and got a lungful of clear, fresh air.

'Are you here on business?' the driver asked.

Maybe dressing in a shirt had made him look more like he was going to work than on holiday, but he wasn't good at dressing down. In fact, he tended to wear a similar style of outfit wherever he went – shirts and trousers or smart jeans. If he wore trainers with it, that was him being casual.

'No. I'm having a break here, but I have got a job to do – not work, you understand? Just something I have to do.'

'Oh aye?'

'My late father's last request was that his ashes were scattered at Kisimul Castle.'

'Ah.' Realisation dawned on the driver's face. 'Is that what's in the bag?'

'Yeah.' Monty held them close.

'And your surname's MacNeil, aye? That can't be a coincidence.'

'It's not. My father did extensive research on the family tree. He was quite insistent that we were related to the MacNeils of Barra and that somewhere along the line, our family was diddled out of Kisimul Castle.'

The taxi driver looked like he was battling a smirk.

'I bet you hear stories like that all the time.' Monty leaned his elbow on the windowsill and ran his fingers through his hair. His own mother had accused his father of being fanatical, and Monty wasn't stupid. He knew the likelihood of such a connection to be slim and unlikely ever to be proven one way or another.

'I do, though usually from Americans.'

Monty huffed a laugh. 'Well, I'm not saying it's true or not. That's just what my father believed and I'm carrying out his last request.' The least he could do really. Now that his father was gone, the place where he'd always been was filled with regrets. No one had seen it coming, but the gap he left was bigger than Monty could have imagined. If he could have the time over, he'd do more. He *should* have done more. Visited more often, listened closer, just been more present.

Too late now.

'Good for you, son. You've got great weather for it.'

'Yeah.' He still had to get to the castle though. That was the next big thing. Because Kisimul Castle wasn't accessible on foot. Only by boat. Perhaps his father had set this challenge from beyond the grave, knowing how tricky that would be for his land-loving son. And maybe it was exactly what Monty needed. Time to get out of his comfort zone and do something more adventurous. This trip was supposed to be about the ashes and to give Monty a chance to connect with the island his father had loved. He needed a break from work and time to regroup. Even before his father died, it had been a trying year.

Coming here felt like travelling to the edge of the world – a remote, quiet corner of Scotland where he could hide from his normal life for a while.

No one here knew him or his history. He was far from prying eyes and expectations. His ex – the very beautiful Sophie – could take a backseat in his mind, and hopefully he could be free of her cutting words and painful accusations.

Taking a deep breath, he looked out the window, watching as they headed around the west side of the island. Monty's eyes widened as views of the sea returned. Ten-foot breakers cracked on the shoreline and rolled up the beach.

'Wow,' he said. 'That's dramatic.'

The taxi driver nodded. 'Aye, it is that.'

A little further along the road, he pulled up a little track, passing a few scattered buildings. A couple of them looked like they might be inhabited, while others were more like outbuildings or animal sheds.

An Grianan farmhouse was a beautiful old stone building, painted white and surrounded by the somewhat bleak Hebridean farmland that ran seamlessly into nature. Insects hummed and wildflowers danced in the long grass at the side of the path as Monty got out of the taxi. Such a stunning place with views over the raging sea to the front and hills to the back, but something about it was forlorn, almost like it had been forgotten in the passing of time.

He paid and thanked the taxi driver, then made his way to the blue door of the farmhouse. Holding tightly to the backpack with the ashes, he knocked. As he waited, he gazed out over the sea.

'Hello.' A young woman with thin-rimmed glasses, rosy cheeks and a gentle smile opened the door, and Monty switched his focus to her. A bee buzzed past her, and she shook her long dark blonde hair, then brushed the front of her white t-shirt. 'Are you Monty?'

'Yes.'

'I'm Catriona Griffin. We've been expecting you.'

'Pleased to meet you.' Monty thrust out his hand and she shook it. When he'd seen the owner's name in the email, he'd expected someone older. This woman looked like she was in her late twenties at most.

'And you. You're in the annex for your stay, so I'll show you around. It's self-catering, like you asked for, but you're welcome to add breakfast or evening meals any time you need them.'

'Thank you. You said you had a bike I could use too. I'd like to explore a bit.' Though now he'd seen the roads, he wasn't sure cycling was a good idea.

'Yes. We've got a push-bike or a new e-bike you can use.' The roads were hilly and bumpy, and Monty was unadventurous in the extreme, though he liked running to keep fit – that was the only occasion he wore anything different from his usual attire – so an e-bike sounded very appealing.

'I'll try the e-bike, thanks.' His lack of interest in thrill-seeking activities was Sophie's issue with him and her reason for dumping him. Apparently, he was too boring and 'vanilla' for her liking. Well, maybe out here in the wilds he could learn an interesting new skill – like cycling these roads without doing himself an injury and trying to get to Kisimul Castle without getting seasick.

His mind wandered into the future. Perhaps he could send Sophie a photo of himself on 'an adventure'. It might even work as a way to win her back. That thought lifted his heavy heart. He'd always viewed Sophie as his one true love and couldn't imagine ever finding anyone he would like quite as much. Getting her back was something positive to think about.

'This is the annex.' Catriona led him around the building to a small extension on the side. 'You'll find it all quite self-explanatory, I think, but if you need help with anything, just give me a shout. I'll leave you to settle in while I go and get the bike. You've got a beautiful day for cycling, so make the most of it. The weather can turn quickly out here, but it looks like it'll stay nice for a while.'

Monty opened the annex door and smiled. Its bright interior was reminiscent of a ship's cabin, with whitewashed tongue-and-groove panelling on the wall and fresh white and blue linen on the bed. The thick windowsill had nautical instruments on it, along with what looked like part of a whalebone. A small sofa was on one side and behind a three-quarter height wall was a tiny galley-style kitchen. Behind that was a separate shower room. Monty pushed his case into the main room and placed the backpack containing the urn on the bed.

He ruffled up his hair in the small mirror. What a mess he looked. That was what lack of sleep did. Since Sophie left, he hadn't slept well and after his father died, that had made it worse. So many regrets to keep him awake. Rubbing his cheeks, he sighed. He probably should've shaved before he left that morning, but Barra was a wild place, so having a bit of stubble might help him blend in – though he didn't really think that would work. This place was gorgeous, but so far removed from what he was used to. He and Sophie had always gone on expensive foreign holidays to luxury hotels. She wouldn't be impressed with this little annex. But finding anywhere to stay at short notice on the island in the summer wasn't easy. And the room looked comfortable, which was really all Monty needed.

Catriona returned shortly after with the bike and demonstrated how it worked. Monty listened carefully, all the while thinking how much easier it would have been if he'd brought his car. But there was no chance of that. The car ferry was a four-and-a-half-hour trip from Oban, and Monty knew his limits. That length of time on a boat was sure to kill him. So, a bike it was. If Sophie could see him now!

After Catriona had gone back to the farmhouse, Monty saw no reason to delay his trip to the castle, especially with the weather this good. Maybe he could even get on a boat today. And if not, he could book one. If he found someone who would do a private trip, that would be even better. At least if he got seasick, he wouldn't disgust all the other passengers – and the chances of him getting seasick were very high. The only time he remembered going on a boat, he'd spent the whole time throwing up and never wanted to repeat the experience.

Stowing the urn carefully in his backpack, he mounted the bike and set off towards the main village of Castlebay – aptly named because of the castle in the bay. He'd seen so many pictures of it he was looking forward to seeing it for himself. The air was so clear here, and as he topped a hill and freewheeled down, his mind flew to Sophie again. So much for him not thinking about her. She had a way of hijacking his brain at every quiet moment. Despite her labelling him 'boring' and 'vanilla', he couldn't see her doing this. Even if he'd offered to go trekking in the Andes or ice-climbing in the alps, he couldn't imagine her wanting to do that either. It begged the question; what kind of excitement *did* she want? He steered his mind to the bedroom door. If she meant that kind of adventure, he wasn't sure he wanted to go there. Kinks weren't ever going to be his thing; he was sure of that. Was that what she meant? It didn't seem likely, but she'd never said. And she'd only told him she was dissatisfied when she left. The thought made Monty a little queasy. Getting over her was taking a long time – they'd been separated for almost six months, but it still felt so fresh.

He descended into the village, spotting the castle straight away. About a mile of sea separated him from his destination, though it wasn't as far out as he'd pictured it in his mind. Maybe his ancestors should have thought of putting down a drawbridge, albeit a very long one, or maybe a causeway. He left the bike close to the ferry terminal and walked along the seafront. Not far off was a bench, though the way down to it looked a little uneven. He picked his path carefully, then took off his backpack and sat down. Dad would have loved this. Monty took the urn from the bag and sat it on his knee. If only he'd made time to do this trip when Dad was alive.

He sighed, raising his eyes to the castle. 'Now I just need to get you out there.'

A few boats were dotted around the bay. Surely someone would give him a lift over. There were definitely boat trips, but he needed one that would land and give him some time alone to do this properly. Saying goodbye wouldn't be easy.

He got to his feet, taking the urn with him. A gull broke into a loud squawk, and Monty looked around for it as he made his way onto the road, his ankle turning slightly on the uneven grass and stones, but before he could remind himself to watch his steps, he tripped over something. His heart stopped as the urn slipped from his grasp. His glasses, that seriously needed adjusting, slipped. *Shit.* If the urn fell, it would either shatter or roll down the hill into the sea. Juggling the urn seemed to go on forever. His glasses hit the ground, but he had the urn. It was in his arms, safe. Thank god. Clutching it tightly, he leaned over and picked up his glasses. Thankfully they weren't broken. He rubbed them clean on his t-shirt and took a couple of steps backward, away from the offensive rock.

'Oi!' a voice yelled. A scream and a clatter followed. He spun around and rammed his glasses on to see a woman on the ground with a bike on top of her. A bag of chips had scattered across the road and seagulls descended on them, cackling and shrieking.

'Are you alright?' Monty crouched by the woman, ducking as a gull almost scalped him.

She moved slowly. Dressed only in tight black shorts and a cropped black exercise top, she'd probably grazed a lot of skin.

'What on earth were you doing?' She winced as she sat up. Her shoulder and upper arm were grey and dusty. She brushed at the mess, revealing red skin that looked chaffed and sore.

'I'm so, so sorry,' Monty said. 'I didn't look.'

'That much is obvious.'

'Can I help you at all? Call an ambulance?'

'An ambulance?' She raised an eyebrow, like she suspected him of losing his mind.

Her dark blue eyes bored into him from under her cycle helmet, and his stomach did a weird little flip. He really had an incredible knack for making an idiot of himself. If the ground would please just open up and take him away. She glowered at him and shook her head, then turned away and lifted her bike.

'Should I help you with that?' he asked.

'No thanks. Just look where you're going in future. And clear off.' She shooed the gulls as soon as she was on her feet. Monty kept his distance, not sure if it was her or the gulls he wanted to be furthest away from. 'That's all my chips gone,' she muttered.

'I'm happy to replace them.'

'It's fine.' She mounted her bike again.

'Are you definitely ok to—'

She pushed the pedals and whizzed off. 'Tourists,' she muttered before she cycled out of earshot, her long tawny brown ponytail swishing in the wind behind her with a somewhat dismissive air.

Monty closed his eyes and drew in a breath. Ok. That wasn't the best start to his holiday, but hopefully she'd be ok and he wouldn't see her again. So, no harm done.

Chapter Two

Iona

Iona McKenzie stood on the bike to pedal up the hill. *Nearly at the top.* The view over the emerald sea was glorious on hot days like this, but sweat was making her crop top and shorts stick to her back. To cap it all, the skin on her shoulder and arm smarted. Not to mention the pain in her ankle from the bike landing on her when that idiot had walked into her.

People like him were what made island life so irritating. Yeah, yeah, she knew tourists were a necessary part of the economy and her business, but some of the stuff they did was full-on mental and drove her nuts. Maybe she didn't have the right to complain. She wasn't an islander, born and bred. Still, she'd come here with a view to live and work, and amazingly for her, she'd stuck it out. Tourists who came to contribute to local businesses and respect the environment were fine. That man in the town, however? Well, maybe he was contributing somehow, just not to her sanity. He certainly looked like he had money – if that shirt was anything to go by – but would he survive five minutes here dressed like that? Maybe she shouldn't have swerved and tried to miss him. She could just have powered on and knocked him down the hill into the sea.

The idea made her smirk, though she wasn't really that mean. The scrapes and bruises were aching reminders of his lunacy, that was all. They'd soon pass. Iona didn't let pain bother her for long. She was always getting something in her line of work, but when someone else caused it, it annoyed her.

She reached An Grianan, the farm where she lodged, and swung her leg off the bike, freewheeling on one pedal to the door of the shed. Taking off her cycle helmet was a relief, and she shook her long wavy hair free from its ponytail, tossing back her head and letting the breeze whisper cool air across her hot forehead. She needed a shower, and she should probably put something on her shoulder and arm, though the pain was already subsiding, and would soon be forgotten completely. All her life, she'd been like this – quick to move from one thing to another. As a child, she'd been overactive, bouncing off walls, running everywhere, banging her head, scraping her knees and picking herself up to do it all again – pretty much driving her parents insane with worry at what damage she might do to herself next. But hey, she was still here to tell the tale.

Once her bike was safely away, she crossed the yard at the back of the farmhouse, where a few chickens pecked about, and went to the backdoor.

'Hi Iona,' a soft voice said as she entered the kitchen.

'Hi Eilidh.' Iona ruffled the little girl's head. 'What are you up to?'

Eilidh lifted a pen from the paper she was drawing on as though it was obvious. 'Drawing a butterfly.'

'Don't you want to play outside on a day like this?' Iona crossed to the cupboard and took out a glass, filling it to the brim with water.

'I got too hot.'

'Yeah, I can understand that.' Iona plonked herself down at the table. The door from the hall creaked open and Catriona Griffin, Eilidh's mum, came in with a pile of laundry.

'You're back.' Catriona dumped the laundry on an empty chair with a sigh and stroked her luscious long hair into a ponytail. Iona marvelled at Catriona, who, at twenty-six, was two years younger than her, but still seemed more mature and together. How did she do it? Perhaps it was because she'd had a child already, or maybe she just had more sense. She was always hard at work – an old head on young shoulders, who also happened to look amazing despite constantly having her nose to the grindstone. Iona herself was blessed with height, a good figure and strong bone structure, but she didn't even manage a tumbled-out-of-bed look well – she generally felt messy and not well put together.

Catriona started folding the laundry, and Iona reached out to help. 'Were you paddleboarding today?' Catriona asked.

'Earlier on, yeah. Then I took a group cycling, but they were all cooked by two o'clock, so they went back to their holiday cottage to cool down.'

'Mummy, can I have an ice lolly?' Eilidh looked up hopefully.

'It's a bit close to dinner.' Catriona looked at the clock beside the dresser. 'But ok. Since this might be the hottest day we have. Might as well use it.'

'Can I have one too?' Iona grinned at Catriona midway through folding one of Eilidh's school polo shirts. Catriona raised an eyebrow, then let out a huff of a laugh.

'Like you need my permission.'

Iona winked at Eilidh. She'd been lucky to find this place to live. At first, she wasn't sure she'd like living with a family. But Catriona had been so kind from the start. Iona had almost been jealous of her at first, but she saw what a hardworking, single mum Catriona was, so she wasn't envious at all. Catriona barely had a minute for herself – between the farm, her daughter, her mother and the guests, she was stretched very thin.

'What happened to you?' Catriona eyed Iona's shoulder as she sat back down with the homemade lolly.

'Oh, that.' She glanced at the scrape marks.

'I had a run in with a tourist who wasn't looking where he was going. I swerved to get out of his way and lost balance.'

'You should clean it up. It looks a mess.'

'Yeah, I will.'

Catriona was such a mother hen.

'And is the rest of you ok?'

'I think I turned my ankle a bit, but I'll be fine.'

Catriona gave her a stern look. 'Are you sure?'

'Yeah.'

'And how is the tourist?' Catriona flapped out a shirt before folding it. 'Was he hurt too?'

'Na. I missed him. I'll try harder next time.'

Eilidh giggled, and Iona winked at her.

'You know what the worst bit was?' Iona sucked the lolly and both Eilidh and Catriona waited with wide eyes.

'I dropped my chips. I'd just bought them too. Some huge black backs swooped in and ate them all. What a waste. I was going to sit by the sea and eat them.'

'You were cycling with chips in your hand?' Catriona pulled a face.

'I would have been fine if the numpty hadn't wandered into me.' Though she might have balanced better if she hadn't been trying to save the chips before herself.

'Oh dear. And now you're having an ice-lolly instead.' Catriona shook her head. 'As soon as you've finished it, you should go and clean that scrape, just in case.'

'Yes, Mum.'

'She's not your mum.' Eilidh pointed with her pink pen. 'She's my mummy.'

'Oops, silly me.' Iona pulled an exasperated face at her own silliness and Eilidh giggled.

Catriona lifted the laundry and left the room for a moment. When she returned, she pulled some pots out from the cupboard. 'I better put some dinner on. Do you want to join us or was that lolly your meal?'

'Na, that was just a snack. I wouldn't mind joining you, if that's ok, seeing as how I lost my chips.'

'It's fine. Alex should be back shortly, and he's wanting dinner tonight. I assume he's done the jobs properly. I don't really have time to check.' A pot clanged on the work surface as she put it down. Alex was another lodger, an ex-military man who worked on the farm. Catriona, who was generally so nice to people, didn't really seem to like him. Maybe she was wary of him because he talked so little and gave nothing away. Iona didn't really get Catriona's problem with him. He always seemed nice enough. Just quiet.

'I didn't see him.' Iona washed her lolly stick and put it on the dresser.

'He's up the hill with the sheep. Oh drat.'

'What?'

'I just remembered, there's a guest in the annex. He checked in earlier, but I forgot to put extra towels in the box. I don't think he's back yet, so I'll nip in and do it now.'

'I can do it if you want.'

'No, it's fine.' Catriona wiped her hands and turned around. 'But you'll never guess what.' She raised her eyebrows and smirked. 'He's a MacNeil.'

'Oh god.' Iona rolled her eyes. 'American, by any chance?'

'He didn't sound it, but he definitely looked like someone who was into history.'

'Great,' she muttered. 'So do we need to give him a guard of honour or something?'

'I can see him being the type to ask you all your favourite questions.'

'What questions?' Eilidh asked.

Iona rolled her eyes. 'I could write a book about the daft questions tourists have asked me about this island.' Especially the history seekers who bought into all the clan stories, then insisted their ancestors gave them special rights over the island. She didn't mind the ones who were genuine and knew of Barra's humble past. Or the ones whose families had emigrated on well-documented voyages, usually to Canada. But the ones who claimed they were descended from clan chiefs and expected service to match were the ones that drove her crazy. She'd once been asked by a group if they could hire a limo for a tour around the island. Which, of course, they could, but they'd have to bring it over on the ferry. Barra wasn't a place for hiring limos. It was wild and beautiful, and Iona got annoyed when people trampled over it with their delusions of grandeur. 'I need to have a shower before dinner.'

'I should tell Mum,' Catriona mused. 'We have MacNeils on her side of the family, though she probably won't have the energy to talk to him.'

Iona made her way upstairs, still thinking about the number of visitors they'd had who'd assumed all sorts of privileges. So many people with the surname MacNeil assumed they were descended from what they viewed as Barra royalty and often came looking for their supposed ancestors' graves. Sometimes they told stories that had so little basis in fact they may as well have been Disney adaptations. But there was no telling them. Iona had half a notion to dress up in a kilt and a bunnet with a feather in it and greet the new guest the following morning, pretending she was his Scots girl Friday for the day and lead him to the home of his ancestors – wherever he imagined that might be.

She turned on the shower, and the pipes clanked into action. Maybe there was money to be made in that scenario. She already had a boat that she'd taken some paying punters out on, though it wasn't made for going too far. A costume might add interest, and she could do the short trip out to the castle – that would be enough. She already took groups of paddleboarders and kayakers out to it. She could see tourists lapping up a boat trip with a wee Scot's lassie dressed in tartan to take them to the castle – even if it would completely do her head in. *Stick to surfing and kayaking! Leave the dressing up to someone else.*

And really, she was trying to limit her contact with that kind of history tourist. The ones who came for the waves and hills were much more up her street. Give her a vanload of twenty-somethings ready for a day on the surf over a carload of whisky-drinking, golf-playing fifty-somethings searching for the grave of old Tam-o-Shanter MacNeil any day.

As she towelled herself dry – wincing a little at the scraped skin on her shoulder – she pushed open the window in her little bedroom at the back of the house. Voices carried up from below, but with the way the annex jutted out, it was impossible to see who was there. Catriona's voice, with its gentle island lilt, was recognisable, but not the man. It wasn't Alex anyway. He had a very distinct low, gravely tone. Maybe it was the guest in the annex? Iona leaned her right ear out, straining to catch what he was saying. Something about a bike, maybe? She frowned. The voice sounded vaguely familiar, but she couldn't quite place it.

Ah well. She let out a sigh, dropped the towel on the floor, and sat down. Her fingertips skimmed the now clean skin on her shoulder and upper arm. It was mostly just a surface scrape apart from one small place where blood seeped out. She held her finger to it. It reminded her so much of times when she'd skinned her knees and her mum had tried to stop her running off long enough to put a plaster on it.

But no one could ever stop her from running off. That was what she did. When the going got tough, she ran. It was the reason she was here, organising paddleboarding lessons and renting a bedroom in a farmhouse on a Hebridean island, and not in a nameless city anywhere in the world, working in the civil service, with a sensible pencil-pushing and besuited boyfriend.

Those days were long gone, and she wasn't going back, not to the city, not to a desk, and not to a career man who had as much excitement about him as a lecture on tax codes.

Chapter Three

Monty

Monty leant on the doorway of the annex, enjoying the cool evening breeze, so welcome after the heat of the day. Some chickens pecked around the yard behind Catriona, perhaps hopeful she was dishing up something tasty.

He frowned. 'So, the boat trips to the castle aren't running anymore?'

Catriona brushed a strand of hair out of her face. 'The castle's closed for restoration work at the moment. None of the tour boats stop there anymore; they just circle around it. You get a better view from the outside though.'

Monty's insides fell. No way did he want to hang over the edge of a tour boat to scatter the ashes. Jeez, even the thought made him queasy. The chances of his throwing up were already high, but if he had to stand up and move – nope, he wasn't doing that. No way. Seasickness aside, his father had requested to be scattered at the castle, not in the sea. 'That's unfortunate.' He let out a sigh. 'It's just... Well, it's really important that I get there.'

Catriona watched him for a moment through her large, thin-framed glasses, and he had a strange sensation that she was sizing him up. 'Well...' She tapped her fingertips together. 'My brother has a boat, but he's away just now. If you can wait until next week, he would take you. Or there's Iona, our lodger. She has a little boat, and she's taken it out to the castle before. She might be able to help you, but I wouldn't like to speak for her. She's pretty busy with her water sports business at the moment.' Her eyes strayed upward towards an upstairs window. 'I think she's already gone up to her room, but why don't you come in for breakfast tomorrow morning? You can meet her and see if she can take you.'

Monty straightened up and smiled. 'That's great. Thank you so much. I'll do that.'

'You're welcome.' Catriona gave him a nod. 'She also takes paddle-boarders across to the castle. You could always try that.'

'Oh no.' He held up his hands. 'That's definitely not for me. I like to stay dry.'

She chuckled. 'Yeah, it's not for everyone. My mum's mum was a MacNeil. If it's family trees you're interested in, she might be able to help. She knows a lot about the family history. But she doesn't keep very well, so she might not be up for too many questions.'

'That's ok. I wouldn't want to impose on anyone.'

'Well, you enjoy your evening, and I'll see you in the morning.'

'See you.' He turned the doorknob and opened the door to the annex. Inside it was pleasantly cool, with its simple furnishings. The white timber-framed bed was against the back wall under a canvas featuring a wide blue seascape.

Monty leaned over the wide windowsill and opened the little window, letting in the fresh sea air. He then collected his backpack and took out the urn containing his father's ashes, placing it on the windowsill next to the piece of whalebone.

'There you go. Back on Barra. And tomorrow I'll try to get you to the castle.' He dropped onto the sofa, listening to the distant murmur of the sea. His dad would have wanted to meet Catriona's mum and discuss his theories about the Macneils, but Monty didn't know enough to ask the right questions. And he wasn't convinced any of his dad's stories were true.

The cool breeze from the open window was soothing. It was early yet, but he didn't feel like going out. The bed looked inviting, and he could read. If now wasn't the time to read *Whisky Galore*, then when? The book was set on the island of Eriskay just a few miles north of Barra. That seemed ideal. Not that Monty would make it to that island in person. It involved a ferry ride and that was a no-no. A short boat trip to Kisimul Castle would be quite enough.

He moved to the edge of the bed, bouncing slightly to test the mattress. It wasn't overly soft, and it didn't creak, which was perfect for him. He kicked off his shoes, unbuttoned his shirt and tugged it off. Lying back, he stared at the wooden beams overhead. If he closed his eyes, he might sleep already, though he'd prefer it if he could sleep through the night instead of randomly nodding off at eight thirty, when he'd probably be awake again by ten. But such was life at the moment.

———————— ♥ ————————

The following morning, Monty made his way around the farmhouse to the main door. Hazy clouds had replaced the glorious sunshine from the day before and the breeze was stronger, rustling around the machair where the chickens pecked at some scattered seeds. A liver-coloured dog lay panting in the grass and it leapt up when it saw Monty, running over and wagging its tail.

'Hello there.' Monty gave it a quick pat as it sniffed around his ankles, then went inside and down the narrow hallway, following the sizzling scent of bacon more than the directions Catriona had given him. First door on the left. A stairway led up to the right and Monty heard someone coming down as well as voices from the room behind the door. He reached for the handle, but the door swung open before he could touch it. He stepped back quickly to avoid getting hit by the door and collided with someone behind him.

'Oh, I'm so sorry!' Monty spun around. His eyes almost popped out of his head. He was face to face with the woman from the day before – the same one he had knocked off her bike. *Oh god.* She was almost as tall as him and he was six foot one, so that was saying something. Her dark blue eyes narrowed, and she glared at him before letting out an exasperated sigh.

'You,' she muttered.

The heat in Monty's neck stung. *Great. Just great.* She was staying here too. Bit rich her moaning about him being a tourist when she was obviously one herself. 'I... Listen, I'm really sorry. Are you alright? I didn't mean to—'

'Yeah, I'm fine, thanks.' She brushed past him. Without another word, she disappeared into the breakfast room. The people who'd opened the door had come into the hallway and were eyeing Monty.

'I... um... well,' he mumbled. Why was he such an idiot sometimes? Talk about embarrassing. With a deep breath, he made his way inside the breakfast room. It was bright with a wooden floor, a large dresser and the same rustic but homely feel the annex had, though it had slightly more mellow tones of yellow and umber in the curtains and table linen, rather than the crisp white of the annex. A large table was set with racks of toast, preserves, cereals, and a pot of tea.

A couple were sitting at the far side, and Catriona placed cooked breakfasts on large plates in front of them. The woman Monty had bumped into at the door wasn't in the room. Where had she gone? There wasn't exactly anywhere in here she could hide or keep out of sight.

Maybe he'd imagined her. If only that was the case. That way, he could imagine a normal interaction had taken place – not one where he'd collided with her again.

'Morning, I hope you slept well,' Catriona said. 'Help yourself to whatever you fancy from the table, and I can cook you something too.

Just tell me what you like. We have pretty much everything, eggs, bacon, sausages, black pudding, tattie scones, kippers. I can even do salmon if you like. And I've got vegan options.'

'Thank you.' Monty blinked, taking a seat. 'Scrambled eggs on toast would be nice.'

'With smoked salmon?'

'Yes, please. That sounds good.'

She went into a backroom that was presumably the kitchen and Monty watched her, half-expecting the other woman to reappear. But why would she be in the private kitchen?

He gave the couple opposite a brief smile and they returned it before continuing their private chat as they tucked into their breakfasts.

Monty opened his phone and checked his messages. He should probably send one to his mother telling her he'd arrived, not that she'd be too bothered. She and his father had split a long time ago and she wasn't interested in where his ashes went or what Monty did with them, but she would probably want to know he'd got here safely and was settled in.

Sipping his tea, he scrolled his messages, deliberately ignoring his work email app. This was a well-earned holiday from the daily grind of the financial world. The couple across from him were still chatting quietly but didn't seem to want to include him, which was fine. He was happy with his own company for now. He pulled up the message thread with Sophie. His last message still sat there, unanswered. He sighed. Why was it so hard to accept that it was over? Only hard for *him* to accept – she didn't seem to have any difficulty with it. Every moment she was out in the world without him cut his heart, and he clung to a sliver of hope that maybe, just maybe, he could do something to win her back, though he had no idea what... or how.

He took a notebook out of his pocket and clicked a pen. Jotting down ideas helped clear his brain. Maybe he could think of some things he could do to impress her or please her... Or maybe he should just forget about her and move on. While he knew that was the sensible course of action, his heart wasn't ready to let go.

The door creaked open, and he looked up to see Catriona. Beside her was the woman he'd now bumped into twice. *Cringe.* Where to look? Catriona was frowning slightly but had the ghost of a smile. The other woman, however, had her arms folded tightly across her chest, and was pursing her lips.

Ok. Monty held his breath. She did not look happy. Was he about to get an earful?

'This is Iona McKenzie.' Catriona gestured toward the woman. 'She's the one with the boat I was telling you about yesterday. You might want to talk about the crossing to Kisimul Castle.'

Monty swallowed and his insides flipped over. She was the one with the boat? *Great, just great.* 'Oh, um, yes. Nice to meet you.'

Iona's eyes narrowed, and she nodded in response, her lips pressed into a tight, fake looking smile.

'Well, I'll leave you to it,' Catriona said. 'While I finish the breakfast.'

Monty cleared his throat, sure the couple across the table were watching and listening in. Who wouldn't? This was probably better than *Eastenders*. 'Look, about yesterday—'

'It's fine,' Iona said. 'Catriona said you needed help with a boat?'

Monty nodded, his jaw tensing. *Count to ten.* 'I need to get to Kisimul Castle.' Though he wasn't sure he wanted to go with her. She seemed rather grumpy, and he didn't imagine she'd be in the least sympathetic if he got seasick – and that was pretty much a given. 'It's important, but I wouldn't want to impose.'

Iona glanced at the door, seemingly restraining an eye roll. 'Don't tell me your ancestors are buried there?'

He frowned and shook his head. Just as well he wasn't oversensitive about his real reason for being here. Someone else might have found that remark extremely hurtful. 'No. Not that.' He fixed her in his gaze again. 'Can you or can't you take me? I'm sure I can find someone else if you're busy.'

She gave a little shrug. 'Technically, I *can* take you, but I'm not sure when. I'm pretty busy.'

'Fair enough.' Her words stung a little and his chest smarted kind of like it had done after Sophie left him, though obviously not as badly as that. 'I'll look for someone else to do it.'

'Good luck. I'm sure you'll find someone.' She turned and walked out of the room, leaving Monty sitting like a plank. He blinked and glanced across at the other couple.

'Guess I'm not popular,' he said, and they gave him a little smile. Story of his life really. Only this time he was sure he hadn't actually done anything wrong... Not on purpose anyway.

Chapter Four

Iona

I ona kicked at a loose pebble in the farmyard, watching it skitter across the dusty ground. She let out a huff, then ground her teeth. So, she probably shouldn't have been so grouchy with the guest over breakfast. Catriona would be annoyed if she found out – and Catriona had enough to be doing – but something about him got on her nerves – on principle. She wasn't even sure what, apart from the fact that he'd made her graze her arm and twist her ankle.

'Everything ok?' Catriona came out and opened a large silver bin. She scooped out some seeds and tossed them around the yard, and the chickens skittered about, pecking at it.

'Just thinking about the numpty who's now knocked into me twice. It's like he's on a mission to take me out. That's partly why I don't want to take him to the castle, in case it's third time lucky.'

'He seems really nice.' Catriona huffed out a laugh. 'I'm sure he didn't do it on purpose.'

Iona crossed her arms. 'Well, whatever he is, he's a menace. I think I should keep out of his way. For my own safety... and his.' She slapped her hands together.

'You've really got it in for him, haven't you?'

'I could say the same about you and Alex.'

'Let's not go there.' Catriona looked away. 'I wouldn't even have taken him on. My mum did it before she got too ill to run this place.'

Iona let out a slow breath. 'What's your deal with him?' She didn't get why Catriona was so irritable with Alex. 'Has he done something bad? If he's done anything horrible to you. I'll kill him.'

'Thanks.' Catriona gave her a smile. 'But it's not that. I can't explain it. He just... I don't know... Has a way of annoying me.'

Sounded exactly what that guest did to her. 'Where is Alex anyway?'

'He's driving Eilidh to school. She had some heavy books to take for a talk today and she didn't want to carry them on the minibus.'

'I see.' Except she didn't. Why did someone so helpful annoy Catriona so much? 'That was nice of him.'

'Oh yeah. He loves Eilidh, and she loves him.' Catriona walked across the yard, and Iona raised her eyebrows at Catriona's back.

'Are you jealous or something?'

Catriona turned around and sighed. 'Not really. He just likes to disagree with me for the sake of it. He never says anything, but I know he thinks I'm too young to run this place. I can tell he thinks I'm incompetent. I know we need to diversify. But whatever I suggest, he dismisses it and makes out that I'm clueless. It's not like he knows any better. He doesn't have a background in business or finance.'

'It's just men,' Iona muttered. 'Bunch of twats who talk rubbish.'

Catriona laughed. 'Yeah. That sounds about right.'

'I bet that MacNeil character is the same – a total history nerd. Imagine being stuck on a boat with him while he prattles on about his ancestors. When's Ruaridh coming back? He can take—'

Catriona coughed and her eyes widened slightly; she made a subtle motion with her hand like she was half waving, half pointing. Iona frowned.

'What?' Iona said. 'What's wrong?'

Catriona's eyes flicked behind Iona's shoulder, and she raised her eyebrows meaningfully. Iona turned around slowly, her cheeks flushing as she saw Monty standing there, adjusting his glasses and glancing around.

'Hello again,' he said with a half-smile.

Shit. Had he heard her? Maybe she didn't care if he had. Who was he to her anyway?

'Is everything ok?' Catriona asked.

'I... um... was just wondering if you knew anyone else with a boat...' He glanced at Iona. 'The person you suggested' – he returned his focus to Catriona – 'is too busy.'

Iona felt the heat in her face. *Shit. Shit. Shit.* How bad did this make her look? Why did she always do this? Opened her mouth and put her foot in it. Exactly the reason she lost her job in the civil service. Why did she never learn? Would she ever?

'It's a bit windy,' Catriona said. 'Making a landing today might be tricky. My brother Ruaridh will be back at the end of the week. He has a boat too and that might be better.'

'Oh?' Monty glanced at Iona. 'Is he a better driver?'

Iona folded her arms and narrowed her eyes. Ok, so she probably deserved that, but really? Could she let him get away with it?

'Not at all,' Catriona said. 'But Iona has a job teaching water sports.'

'Of course.' He smiled at Catriona, and she returned it. Iona sucked on her lower lip. Did they fancy each other? *Jesus Christ.* What did Catriona see in Monty? He looked like a lost academic who'd wandered into the wilderness.

'Would you like to have the bike again today?' Catriona asked him.

'Yes, please. If I can't do the boat trip, I guess the bike will do.'

'The waves are good for body boarding and surfing today, not for landing on the island.' Iona turned away from him. His eyes were distracting, bizarrely his arms were too, with those rolled-up shirtsleeves exposing nicely tanned skin with a light dusting of hair. *WTAF?* 'And that's my job, so that's what I'm doing.' As well as waffling. *What is the matter with me?* Though she had a fair idea. In fact, she'd suspected for a while now that she had ADHD. It was why her brain bounced around all over the place and she so often had difficulty focusing. But was it just that? Or was something else happening here?

'Of course.'

'Well...' Catriona looked between the two of them.

'I, uh, overheard your conversation...' Monty scraped some stray strands of hair off his face and Iona caught his eye. Heat flared inside her. *Fuck*. This wasn't good. What if he asked Catriona for a refund? Or left a bad review? *Why didn't I keep my mouth shut?* But she never could. She blinked, not wanting to see Catriona's expression. Iona had let her down. How could she hurt her friend like this?

'...about diversification,' Monty continued, giving Iona the smallest of glances.

What? Just what? Iona chewed her tongue. For all his smart clothes and the nerdy guy in glasses look, he knew how to play. If he'd heard that, he'd heard the other bit and now he was toying with her, making her squirm.

'It's part of life on an island,' Catriona said. 'We have to adapt to survive. My family's been doing it for centuries.'

Monty nodded, adjusting his glasses. 'I work in finance and corporate banking. I've worked on a few similar projects. Nothing quite as remote as this, but places with the same vibe. You know what's really popular?'

'What?' Catriona cocked her head, smiling a somewhat goofy smile, and Iona wanted to look away and retch.

'Glamping pods. They're all the rage, and you've got such a perfect spot for them.'

Iona snorted before she could stop herself.

Monty raised an eyebrow and their gazes locked. 'Why not?'

What? The depth of his hazel eyes, half hidden behind his glasses, transfixed her. Flecks of green and gold in his irises sparkled like gems. His gaze was gentle, and her heart flickered, making her breath catch. The noise of the chickens and lull of the sea nearby faded away, leaving nothing but the two of them.

Catriona coughed and waved her hand before her mouth, breaking the spell. 'Excuse me. Something caught in my throat.'

Iona glanced at her, then realised Monty was still waiting for an answer. 'Well, nothing... I didn't say anything.' But she hadn't needed to. She just didn't like the idea because he'd thought of it, not for any concrete reasons. Exactly what Catriona had been complaining about Alex doing. Honestly, she was so bad for this kind of thing, leaping in, opening her mouth before thinking. 'But you know this is a working farm?'

'I do.'

'Actually, it's not a bad idea.' Catriona tilted her head. 'It would mean more work, but I don't feel people are looking for B&Bs as much these days. They want their own space and freedom.'

Iona bit her lip. She needed to get the hell away from this guy. He was bringing out the worst in her, and she didn't even know him. Or want to. 'Yeah, well, you two can enjoy discussing it. I'm going off to find some waves.'

Monty nodded at her like he was a regency gentleman.

Catriona was still looking at him and smiling. Iona let out a groan as she headed for the house. They so obviously fancied each other.

'Hey.'

Iona jumped as she entered the kitchen. 'Alex. You gave me a fright. I didn't know you were here.'

'Sorry.' He moved across to the window, limping slightly, and peered out. Something had happened to his leg when he was in the army, though he didn't really talk about it. He was always too busy working on the farm, and Iona didn't like to pry. 'Who's the man?'

'A really irritating guest.'

'Hmm.' He didn't turn around, but stared out of the window.

'Catriona seems to like him.'

'Yeah, well, she's got weird taste.' Alex ran his fingers through his hair.

'Does she?' Iona had never known Catriona to date anyone, and she was tight-lipped about Eilidh's father.

'She must do. After all, she picked some dick who abandoned her and left her to bring up her kid alone.'

'He was a dick alright, but it wasn't her fault for picking him. How was she to know?' Iona joined him at the window, watching as Catriona chatted to Monty.

'Yeah. You're right. I was joking, but that was in poor taste.' Alex had a strong jawline accentuated by a day's worth of stubble, and his sandy blond hair was perpetually tousled, giving him a ruggedly charming look. His eyes were a striking shade of blue and Iona found them hard to look at for too long. She inhaled his freshly washed scent and frowned. Surely it should do something for her? She'd always felt like she should fancy him. And the same went for Ruaridh, Catriona's brother. Both guys were nice and handsome in their own way, but she never felt anything romantic for them – which was maybe just as well.

One time she'd been sure Ruaridh was on the verge of asking her out, but she'd changed the subject and steered well clear. Because she was most certainly *not* looking for love. Concentrating on her business was her priority, though she'd never been that great at concentrating on anything. But after being burned by a cheating man, who seemed nice in the beginning, she wasn't going to fall into that trap again. This life suited her perfectly. She was a happy single girl and if she needed male company... Well, there was never a shortage of passing tourists and the ones who came to do water sports were often single guys, more than happy to hook up. And why not? It was nothing to be ashamed of.

She checked the time. She wasn't teaching her paddleboarding class until later, which meant she had all morning to play on the waves. Just the tonic and the best way to forget whatever had been bothering her. Her eyes lingered on Catriona and Monty. *Yeah, him.* She felt a little stab in her chest and rubbed it. Was that heartburn? She went to the cupboard and took out a glass. Some cold water would help. She downed it quickly.

'See you,' she said to Alexander. 'I'm off to find a wave.' She nipped upstairs to grab a hoody from her bedroom. The window was still open, and her shoulders relaxed as she entered the cool room. She hated getting too hot and rarely shut the window except in the depths of winter. Outside, Monty was still talking to Catriona. Their voices sounded cheery. Iona rolled her eyes, crossing the small room to her dresser and pulling open the drawer to grab her hoody. These casual clothes were so comfy compared to the hideous tight suits she and killer heels she used to wear to the office. Thank god those days were done.

She leaned forward, tweaking her cheeks in the mirror and pulling her long unruly waves into a ponytail. Her face was a little red. Perhaps she'd got a bit too much sun the day before. She shook her head. No. Not that. This was because of that ridiculous exchange with Monty.

Like someone had grabbed her by the shoulders, she tensed. Memories rolled in like the waves she loved so much. But they weren't calm and soothing; they were tumultuous, making her stomach writhe. The faint nausea reminded her of that day. The day she'd given up on the old life she'd spent years at a boarding school preparing for.

One high-stakes meeting had seen to it. She'd been in charge of presenting a crucial report to senior officials. Such pressure. The room was filled with expectant eyes, all waiting for her. She had to say something. Her hands trembled uncontrollably, her voice wavered, the carefully prepared speech was gone. She blurted something out, a half-baked attempt at summarising the report, that turned into a bashing session. She hadn't meant it but there were so many injustices, and they were all she could remember. Before she'd got very far, someone else had stepped in and suggested she took her seat and let him finish. Talk about humiliating. The mansplainer of the year had 'saved' her. But only momentarily. No way could she keep going in her job after that. Especially when she'd discovered Tom, her 'reliable' boyfriend, with his neat suits and scheduled life, had been cheating on her. Well, fuck him and all of them. She had a better life now than she'd ever had.

Pulling the hoody over her head, she breathed deeply, shaking the memory out of her head. But Monty reminded her of that bastard Tom: intellectual, composed, smartly dressed, publicly a gentleman, everything she no longer trusted. She'd never trust someone like that again. No men were worth coveting. She didn't want to 'win' one only to lose him again. She'd faced enough humiliation. No one here knew about her past. She could avoid their pitying looks and pointless sympathy and be who she wanted to be.

She could surf and swim. The water sports school was something she enjoyed doing. Who cared if it didn't work in the long run? She could always do something else.

Not trying is better than failing. It was safer not to dream, not to hope. After all, dreams were for talented people, not for someone who always choked when it mattered. People couldn't count on her, and she couldn't afford to let herself believe otherwise. She was safer on her own, where she couldn't disappoint anyone or herself. If she stuck to teaching people to enjoy the water, she could take joy from that and that was important.

'Right.' She shook her head, pushing away the latest round of negative thoughts. They could get out of her mind. Waves called and she could let loose and be free. No risk to her heart or her pride, just her body, and she didn't mind that. The thrill was what it was all about, and she was here for it.

Chapter Five

Monty

Monty pedalled down the rugged path from the farm, strong gusts threatening to push him off balance. He tightened his grip on the handlebars and squeezed the brakes. The restless energy jumping around inside him matched the wildness of the day. He wanted to scatter his dad's ashes and get that job done. Then perhaps the pressure in his mind would ease a little.

He sought closure, but equally every sight here opened a new thought or idea. One day he and his dad had planned to come here together. It wasn't meant to be like this, with Monty roaming free and his dad's remains in an urn. Poor Dad. Taken too soon and so suddenly. It almost didn't seem real. Nothing did. Daily life went on, but Dad didn't, and somehow that was a hard thought to process.

One thing Dad had always enjoyed though was spirit. He admired people who were strong and had a spark about them. This island was like that – and some of its inhabitants. The landscape spread before Monty. Rocky hills and sprawling beaches were a world away from the city confines he was used to. Part of him was already enjoying the wild freedom more than he'd ever imagined possible.

What would Sophie make of it?

'Is this adventurous enough for you?' he called. No one would hear him out here, so what did it matter if he'd taken the first step to madness and started talking to himself? It was easier than the first step to adventure anyway. The bike wavered precariously. *Jesus*. He should slow down. Maybe make a stop and get some pictures.

A rocky outcrop ahead looked like a good place. He laid down the bike, pulled out his phone, and snapped a few shots and short films of the crashing waves. The sea was a churning mass of frothy white caps. Such untamed beauty. His heart raced to see nature like this, so rugged, free, and dangerous. He didn't want to get close to that raging water. He stood for a moment, just looking as the breakers rolled in, listening to their crashing melody and smelling the salt on the air.

As he continued along the main road around the western coastline, the wind picked up even more, rumbling through the dunes and sending sprays of seawater into the air. Monty paused again to photograph a cluster of seabirds taking flight. Their calls mingled with the roar of the ocean. Even in dull weather, this place was impressive. No wonder Dad had raved about it. If only Monty had made this journey while Dad was still alive, and they had seen this together.

But he hadn't. That was why if he wanted to do something about getting Sophie back, he had to do it now. Waiting for nameless dates and times caused regrets and he didn't want any more of them.

He hopped back on the bike and rode further around the island. The road wound through hillsides of grass dotted with stones and sheep – one almost indistinguishable from the other. The wind had got so strong he was finding it hard to stay upright. Maybe he should turn back and not stray too far from An Grianan. He'd seen a smaller road close to the house; he could go down that and see if it led to a beach. Battling against gusts, he made his way back and turned into the track that led to the farmhouse. Instead of going up to it, he carried on straight ahead, along the winding route. Some distance along, he saw dunes rising ahead. To the right-hand side of the track was an area heavily covered with bracken and deeper into that was what looked like a house hidden beneath bushes and tangled plants. His dad had told him stories about the abandoned villages in the Hebrides, where people had been forced off the land to make way for sheep. But that house didn't look old enough for that. Just a sad, forgotten little place. He pedalled on by, pushing forward and up to the top of the dunes. He went along the crest, doubling back a little. From up here, he could see the abandoned house a little better. Although it was almost completely covered by bracken, a garden area was just discernible. It seemed to go from the house, skirting the edge of the dune, until it opened onto a beautiful sandy beach.

Monty braked and dismounted, walking the bike to the edge of the dune to take a better look. He inhaled deeply. Waves crashed against the shore below, relentless and powerful. The tide looked to be coming in and he guessed when it was out, there was a larger expanse of sand. He took more photos, holding tight to his phone. Even up here, the spray reached him, cool droplets against his skin.

He sat on the tufty grass, letting the wind tousle his hair, and closed his eyes. Dewy rain started to fall, the kind that was like fine mist and soaked you without even trying. He dug in his backpack and pulled out a roll-up waterproof, hastily putting it on and tugging up the hood.

The waves broke and fizzed beneath him. He pulled his waterproof jacket tighter as the misty rain continued to fall. Scanning the horizon, he took in the endless expanse of grey water. Such an utterly terrifying force of nature. He didn't want to get any closer; this was enough.

His gaze locked onto something in the near distance. On the water, a lone surfer cut through the waves, gliding over the churning sea. Bloody hell. Who would have the nerve? Wasn't it freezing? He took off his glasses and tried to clear off the water drops on a dry part of his top by lifting the waterproof. When he put them back on, he watched as the surfer rode the waves with a confidence that bordered on recklessness. He gasped as the figure dropped into a swell, then carved back up again. *Please don't let them get into trouble.* No way could he rescue them.

Maybe it was time to move on. He didn't need to see any more. His cycling 'adventure' was so lame compared to this.

Oh Christ! The surfer caught a particularly large wave. They rode it all the way in, weaving back and forth, until they finally jumped off the board and into the shallow water. As they stood and shook out a long, soaked ponytail, Monty realised it was Iona.

His mouth fell open slightly. *Wow!* The sea wasn't the only untamed beauty out here today. What a display.

He watched as she dragged her board up onto the beach, the wind whipping her ponytail around her face. She didn't seem to mind the rain or the cold.

He tried to imagine himself out there, but the thought made his stomach twist. Bikes were one thing, but the sea? No chance.

As she reached the edge of the beach, she glanced up, but he stepped back, hopefully far enough to be out of sight. A jolt of something he couldn't quite place barrelled into him. He edged forward until he could see her again. Even if she saw him, she wouldn't recognise him, surely. Not in this outfit? From this distance? But *he'd* recognised *her*, so it stood to reason she could do the same. He wasn't a striking young woman however, just an average thirty-something man. Or if you listened to Sophie, a very boring thirty-something man.

He took a few steps back. He needed to get moving, keep cycling, and not linger here. Maybe he should get back in case the weather turned worse.

As he picked up his bike, he felt a slight resistance. Glancing down, he realised the front tire was flat. Seriously? This was what adventure did. It caused problems. Now what? He pulled a face and adjusted his glasses that were misty with rain. A small, sharp rock was lodged in the tyre. Great. He sighed, fumbling with the straps of a little bag attached to the frame. Presumably this would have something he could fix it with, though he wasn't sure what.

While he searched for the tools, the wind picked up, snatching his hood back and sending a chill down his spine. The drizzle had turned to steady rain, making his hands cold and slippery. How the hell did you patch a puncture? He should look it up before attempting it. His fingers were numb as he pulled out his phone. Would anything stick properly in the damp conditions? Rain dripped from his hair and into his eyes. He took off his glasses and wiped them again. When he returned them to his face, he caught movement down below.

He blinked away the raindrops clinging to his lashes and adjusted his glasses. Iona was peeling off her wetsuit. He looked away, feeling awkward, but something about her drew his eyes. The rain and wind seemed not to bother her at all.

Focus on fixing the puncture. Yes, that was what he had to do, but his eyes kept drifting back to Iona. She stood with her back to him and dragged a Dryrobe around herself, before kicking off her costume from under it.

Monty held the puncture repair kit suspended in midair as he watched her run a hand through her wet hair, squeezing out the excess water. As if sensing him, she turned around and he almost dropped the kit. Swallowing, he took a step back, but too late. She'd seen him.

Their eyes met. Monty's heart skipped a beat. So much for him thinking she might not recognise him. She most definitely had. He swallowed, hoping the rain would cool the heat rising in his cheeks. If he could sort this bloody puncture, he could hit the road and get away from her. He pulled open the bag, determined to do it. Hopefully she'd leave the beach by another route. It wasn't like this was a main path. The beach was vast and could be accessed in all number of places. If he could just work out how to get this bike going again. Maybe he should just push it. It wasn't that far.

'Enjoying the view?' a voice cut through the rain.

Monty spun around. Ok, so Iona had decided to come this way. She folded her arms and raised an eyebrow.

'Oh, um, no – I mean, yes, but – I was just fixing the bike.' He held up the repair kit like a shield, though it wouldn't do anything if she got mad. She was wildly beautiful but looked powerful too, and scary, like an ocean warrior princess.

'Do you enjoy watching people changing on the beach?'

'What? I... I didn't mean to watch. Sorry. I just need to fix this bike. If I looked... Well, my apologies.'

She cocked her head. 'Just as well the Dryrobe hides my modesty.' Her gaze dropped to the bike. 'Need some help with that?'

Monty glanced at the bike, then back at Iona. 'Actually, I haven't a clue what I'm doing.'

'I can tell.' She shook her head. 'Here, give that to me.'

He passed her the kit, his damp hand brushing against hers, and her skin was cool. She gave him a sharp look, like his touch had annoyed her. She knelt beside the bike. 'You look like you could use a lesson or two in bike repair.'

'No doubt.' Monty scratched the back of his neck. 'I didn't exactly grow up fixing bikes.'

'No kidding.' She set to work patching the tire. Monty watched, his insides rolling like the waves not far off. What was it about this woman that made his pulse rate speed up and his temperature rise? Possibly fear.

'There,' she said after a few minutes, standing up and brushing her hands on her Dryrobe. 'Good as new. Well, good enough to get you back, at least.'

'Thanks.' He ran his fingers through his hair. 'I owe you one.'

She shrugged. 'Just try not to run into me again, and we'll call it even.'

Monty gave her a small smile. 'I'll do my best.'

Iona nodded, her lips quirking at one corner. 'By the way, you've got a bit of oil or dirt or something on your face.'

'Oh, right.' Monty rubbed at his chin.

'Not there. Here.' She reached out and ran her thumb gently across his cheek. His heart stopped, and his stomach clenched as a tremor ran through him, hitting him low and deep. Her skin was so soft and delicate. More than he'd expected from someone as abrasive as her.

'Thanks.' He touched the spot she'd wiped as she moved back.

'No worries.' She narrowed her eyes a little and rolled her thumb around her fingers, perhaps rubbing away whatever she'd removed from his cheek or perhaps wondering why she'd done it. 'You should go straight back. That repair won't work on rough terrain and I'm not sure how long it'll last.'

'I'll do that.'

'Good. I need to go back and get my board and my clothes. I only came up here to see what you were up to.' She waved and headed back to the beach with a brief raise of her hand.

Monty watched her go, not entirely sure what had just happened. Had she just been nice to him?

He pedalled back to the B&B, grateful that the patch held. After he parked the bike, he headed inside, shaking off the rain like a wet dog. He wasn't sure where he'd find Catriona, but he should look around for her and tell her about the bike. Inside the breakfast room was a door marked private. Maybe he should knock. It was worth a try. He took off his shoes and made his way through the now empty room and rapped on the door.

'Come in,' Catriona's voice said.

Monty opened the door and peered around. At the kitchen table was Catriona, sitting with a laptop open in front of her.

'Is everything ok?' She smiled at him.

'Yeah.' He leaned against the doorframe. 'It's just that the bike got a flat tyre. It probably needs replaced. I should pay for it.'

'Don't worry about it.' Catriona waved away his words. 'It happens all the time around here. I'll get a new one sorted. Did you manage to fix it enough to get back, or have you walked?'

'I met Iona. She helped me fix it.'

'Did she?' Catriona raised her eyebrows. 'That was lucky; she doesn't always have the patience for that kind of thing.'

'Yeah, she was... very helpful. I saw her surfing. She's really good.'

'Aye, she is. There's a water sports festival next week. She's very involved in it. You should go and watch.'

Monty nodded. 'Sounds interesting.'

Catriona smiled, turning back to her laptop briefly before looking at Monty again. 'She's a good soul is Iona. Single too, if you're wondering.' She flicked him a little wink.

'I'm not looking for anything like that.' Monty huffed out a laugh, shaking his head. 'I'm just here for a holiday, not a holiday fling... That's not really my style.' And Iona wasn't his type. She was far too wild and terrifying. Plus, he wasn't ready for anything like that. Not after Sophie. He was still struggling with the idea they were separated.

'Of course. I was just being cheeky. Iona would murder me if she knew I was trying to set her up like that. But she's got a good heart under that tough exterior.'

'I'm sure she does.' She must do, or he would still be back there trying to fix the puncture, but it didn't make her any less intimidating. Now, it just made her harder to read. How would he know which mood he'd find her in? 'I'd better get out of these wet clothes.'

Catriona nodded. 'Remember, if you want a meal, just let me know. I have plenty in the freezer and I can heat you something up, or you're welcome to eat it in the annex.'

'Thank you, that would be great.' He headed back to the annex, and thoughts rushed into his mind like the wild breakers in the ocean and wouldn't go away. He was here for a reason, and getting sidetracked was not part of the plan. This was meant to be a time of peace and reflection. A fond farewell to his father.

Still, he couldn't help being intrigued by Iona, and that was unsettling. As he changed into dry clothes and towelled his hair, his eye landed on the urn on the windowsill. What was Dad making of this? Was he looking down and frowning? Or maybe laughing?

Hopefully once Monty had scattered the ashes, his mind would calm down and return to normal. Because right now, his brain was too all over the place to think straight. And that wasn't like him.

Chapter Six

Iona

Iona slumped down at the kitchen table with a bowl of porridge. She stifled a yawn, but there was no stopping it.

''Scuse me.' She flapped her hand in front of her face. 'I really don't do mornings.'

'It's not that early. I've already done a day's work,' Alex muttered. He finished spreading jam on a slice of toast and pushed it over to Eilidh. 'Eat it up. Crusts and all, then you'll get lovely curly hair.'

'I don't want curly hair.' Eilidh started tearing off the crusts as soon as the plate was in reach.

'Don't waste food.' Catriona gave her a cup of water. 'It's a nice day.' She glanced out the window. 'I think you should take Monty to the castle today if you have a spare hour. Poor guy looks a bit lost.'

'Lost?' Iona groaned, spoon halfway to her mouth. 'I'd say helpless, more than lost. Yesterday, I had to fix his bike tyre. He didn't have a clue what he was doing.'

Alex scoffed, not looking up from his phone. 'Probably spent most of his life behind a desk, that's why.'

Catriona folded her arms. 'Not everyone grew up fixing things, you know. I'm sure he has other skills. He seems like a nice man.'

Iona rolled her eyes. 'Nice man or not, he's a pest. When's he leaving?'

'Not until next week.'

'Next week?' Iona pulled a face. 'I don't get why people like him book trips for that long to places like this. He looks completely unprepared. He was riding the bike in jeans in the rain yesterday. God knows what it was like taking them off. They must have been stuck and I bet he had an extremely sore bum.'

Eilidh giggled into her breakfast.

Catriona checked the time. 'Eat up, Eilidh. The bus will be here in ten minutes.' She leaned over close to Iona. 'Lay off the poor man. You probably make him nervous.'

Iona snorted. 'Nervous? Me? Why would he be? I was only annoyed with him because he kept knocking into me.' And creeping into her thoughts more than she liked.

Alex looked up from his phone and smirked. 'Fancies you.'

'What?' Iona almost choked on a mouthful of porridge, and Eilidh laughed.

Catriona flashed Alex a look. 'Don't be silly, but you can be intimidating, Iona.'

'Me?' Iona blinked and furrowed her brow. Was that true? She didn't mean to be. And she always made friends easily. Surely that didn't make her intimidating.

'To someone quiet like him, I suspect you're very intimidating,' Catriona went on. 'Just be nice to him.'

'Nice? I'm planning on keeping out of his way.' And hey, she'd fixed the bike for him, hadn't she?

'I think he's sweet.' Catriona leaned against the counter. 'And polite. Not bad looking either.'

Alex rolled his eyes, like this whole conversation was ridiculous.

'No way.' Iona caught Eilidh's eye, and she giggled again. 'Well, he's not my idea of good looking.'

Catriona shrugged. 'He's got that rugged, academic thing going on. Lots of women go for that.'

Alex snorted. 'In films maybe, not real life.'

'Thanks for mansplaining your opinion. Just be nice to him. Both of you. It won't kill you to try.' Catriona looked pointedly at Iona.

'I have been.' Iona held out a hand. 'Otherwise, he'd still be sitting on the dune trying to fix a flat.'

Catriona glanced at the clock. 'Come on, Eilidh. The bus will be here any minute.' She pulled out a brush from the top drawer of the dresser. 'Let's get your hair up. And, please Iona, take the man to the castle. It's not like it's a hardship for you.'

'Just mind numbing if he goes on and on about his ancestors,' Iona muttered aside to Alex.

He gave a little shrug. 'Make up some stories and give him something to think about.'

'Push him overboard more like.' Iona gritted her teeth. 'It'll be a miracle if he's still alive when we get back.' If he started banging on about his heritage, she might have to take drastic action. Though deep down, maybe that wasn't the big issue, but it was the easiest one to blame.

Alex sniggered, but Catriona threw a warning glance across the table. When she took Eilidh out to the minibus, Iona left too. She made her way into the breakfast room, scanning about. Monty was eating his breakfast and reading something on his phone. He pushed his glasses further up his nose. Iona froze in the doorway. *Hmm.* He was surprisingly easy on the eye. Irritating really because she'd rather he was as dull and uninteresting as she'd told herself he was. But his features had an almost classical look, kind of like an old movie star, though he definitely wasn't as well-groomed. Maybe that first day, he'd got close with the shirt. Now he looked like he'd been dragged through a hedge backwards – the wind here did that fairly quickly to even the toughest people. Definitely not suited to island life. A couple of days in and he was frazzled.

Iona approached him. Still engrossed in his phone, he didn't look up as she got closer. She took a deep breath, plastering on a smile. 'Hey.'

Monty looked up and blinked. His lips quirked up, though his eyes were uncertain in their focus. 'Oh, hey.' He glanced around. 'Is everything ok?'

'Fine. The weather's ok if you still want to go to the castle today.'

'Um... With you?'

'That's the general idea. Unless you've learned how to drive a boat overnight.'

'No... I haven't. I just thought you were too busy.'

She folded her arms. 'A window has opened up.'

'Well, if you don't mind, that would be great. Thank you. I really appreciate it.'

'No need to thank me.' She waved a hand. 'I assume you're paying for it.'

Monty nodded. 'Of course I am. Thanks again.'

'Yeah, well.' Iona's shoulders twitched. Why was she so tetchy around him? Normally she was a lot more chill. He had a way of bringing out something in her – like he was raking through her, turning over furrows of unwanted thoughts and feelings. Even now, his hazel eyes held her in a tight grip, and she couldn't look away. 'It's no big deal.'

'It will be for me. I don't like boats.'

'Why do it then?'

'It's not exactly a choice.'

'Well, it's just a short trip.' She held onto her eyeroll. No doubt it was a calling from his ancestors. 'We'll head out after breakfast. Make sure you've got a jacket – it's always cooler on the water.'

'Will do.' Monty took a sip of his coffee. 'I'll be ready as soon as I'm finished here.'

Iona nodded. 'Ok, meet me outside when you're done.'

Monty gave her another little smile. She wished he wouldn't. Something about that look flipped her insides like a pancake and made her oddly giddy.

She headed back to the kitchen and filled up a pint glass of water. As she sipped it, she watched Alex and Catriona through the window. Alex looked like he was describing something to Catriona, but she wasn't making eye contact, and her expression was stony. Iona's gaze travelled back to the breakfast room, and she saw Monty packing up his things, standing up and adjusting his glasses.

'Time to get this over with,' she muttered under her breath.

———————— ♥ ————————

Twenty minutes later, Iona climbed into the driver's seat of the car, waiting as Monty settled in beside her. The engine growled to life, and they set off towards Castlebay and the marina. Should she say something? But what? It wasn't like they had a lot in common. Make that nothing. But sitting like this without talking was weird. She normally made small talk without even thinking, but nothing was coming to her today.

'So, what is it you do?' she asked, forcing out the words to what was probably the most stupid and boring question, but it was that or ask about his family and she really didn't want to listen to family history stories. They reminded her too much of her mother. She'd been obsessed with genealogy and ancestry to the point where it was more important than the present. Unfortunately, Iona hadn't lived up to their family standard. She wasn't a great doctor, a missionary, a pioneering scientist, or anything of note like everyone else on her family tree apparently was. She'd disgraced her family instead – in so many ways.

'I work in banking.' Monty leaned his elbow on the windowsill and ran his fingers through his hair. The movement disturbed the air and diffused a rather pleasant scent around the car and she didn't want to find anything about him attractive.

'Banking?' She bit back a yawn. 'Oh yeah, I remember now. You said to Catriona, didn't you? I bet that's fun.'

He huffed out a laugh. 'Well, I wouldn't say fun exactly, but it has its moments. It can get pretty intense with the current economic climate.'

Iona nodded. 'Hmm.' How dry did that sound? Pencil-pushing at its finest. So like Tom – that scumbag of an ex. Her mind wandered back to her civil service days. The endless reports, the mountains of paperwork, and the constant pressure to perform. Her failure to succeed made her cringe inwardly.

'Sometimes you have to make quick decisions that can impact a lot of people,' Monty said. 'I guess that's about as exciting as it gets.'

'Sounds... challenging.' Iona kept her eyes on the road. This was Tom all over again. He'd lived and breathed numbers... When he wasn't sleeping around and cheating, that was. This time, Iona wouldn't be getting anywhere near close enough to be burned.

'It is challenging, yes, but it can be rewarding too, knowing you're making a difference, helping people secure their futures.'

She only just resisted the urge to roll her eyes again. Helping people? Yeah right! How noble did he make it sound? But she doubted it was as fulfilling as he made it out to be. More likely, he was simply justifying the long hours and stress. She'd had enough of that kind of life. She'd learned her lesson the hard way, and she wasn't going back.

They reached the marina, and she parked the car in the uneven car park near the walkway to the jetty. Monty got out, looking around; his smile had faded. The slight pink on his cheeks had dulled to an almost grey colour. He clutched a backpack in his arms.

'Let's get going then.' She unlocked a little gate and headed along a suspended walkway that led down to the jetty. When she reached the steps, she turned back.

Monty was edging his way slowly along, his eyes pinned forward like he didn't want to look at the water below him on either side. She sensed him taking deep breaths. Surely, he wouldn't get seasick on a short crossing like this? Though it could get choppy even here, especially in a boat as small as hers. She carried on down the stairs and along the jetty, then hopped aboard her little boat: a small tender driven from a wheel in the middle behind a tiny cabin in the front. She gestured for Monty to follow. He hesitated, still taking deep breaths and clutching his bag tighter.

'Are you coming?'

'Yeah.' Inhaling deeply, he stepped aboard, steadying himself on the windshield at the helm.

'You need to put this on.' She handed him a buoyancy aid, then pulled on her own and clipped it up. Monty had put his bag on the floor and was looking at the buoyancy aid as if uncertain which way it went. She turned it the right way. 'Like that.'

He zipped it up and frowned.

'You can sit there.' Iona pointed to a bench near the stern. 'And hold on. It's nice and calm, but there are always some waves.'

Monty nodded, his face another notch paler. He settled onto the bench, gripping the edge of the seat and clinging onto his bag. What was in there?

Iona started the engine and guided the boat out of the marina. The light waves slapped against the hull, and the boat rocked with the impact. She glanced back at Monty, who was staring fixedly at a point on the horizon, his knuckles white.

'You ok?' she called over the noise of the engine and the sea.

He gave a weak nod but didn't speak. His lips were pressed together in a thin line.

'If you're going to be sick, do it over the side.' She raised her eyebrows. 'We don't want to be cleaning that up.'

Monty's eyes flicked to her, and all the humour drained from his expression, before he turned his gaze back to the horizon.

'We'll be there shortly,' Iona said. 'It's really not far.'

She could see him breathing deeply, steadying himself, and she shook her head. Honestly, was it that bad? Just in the bay? She stood at the helm, steering towards the castle. After all the buildup, he wasn't even looking. This was a photo-worthy moment, but he was missing it.

Was he really that ill? He must be. It made no sense why he was putting himself through this. His sad expression gave her a twinge in her chest. Just like she hadn't been able to leave him to fix the tyre himself, she couldn't ignore his pain now either. Something in his eyes said this was more than just seasickness, but what? Surely, he didn't think he had empathic powers and was channelling a dead ancestor from the castle? That would be too woo-woo for her.

'Here.' She rummaged in a storage compartment and pulled out a bottle of water. She handed it to him. 'Take a sip. Might help.'

He took the bottle with a shaky hand and sipped gingerly. 'Thanks.' The words barely passed his lips and was more of a breath than speech.

Iona adjusted their course, keeping an eye on him. He looked miserable, clutching his bag like a lifeline, his jaw clamped shut. She sighed. *Jeez*, she'd been so harsh. This was tough to watch. Why, oh why, was he putting himself through this?

'We're almost there,' she said. 'Just hang on a little longer.'

Monty nodded again, his eyes never leaving the horizon. The castle loomed ahead, dark and shadowy against the grey sky. Iona steered the boat towards the slipway. Thank god they were nearly there.

As they approached, she cut the engine and let the boat glide in. It bumped gently against the edge and Iona secured the ropes.

'We made it.' She offered him a hand to help him stand. He took it, his grip surprisingly strong, and stumbled to his feet.

'Thanks.' The tiniest of smiles tweaked the corner of his lips. He didn't let go of her hand as she helped him onto to dry land. The pressure sent shock waves through her, not unpleasant, but unexpected and kind of weird.

'You survived.' She raised her eyebrows and their gazes met. Heat burned deep in her core and she clutched his hand firmly. If she so much as moved a little finger and grazed over him, he might get the wrong idea... Or maybe she would. *Whatever*. She just had to make sure she didn't touch him in any way other than in friendly assistance.

He nodded slightly, his eyes never leaving her. 'Thanks.'

Iona let go of his hand. 'No problem.' She glanced around. 'So, we're here now. What do you want to do? As you can see, it's not very big and you're not allowed to go inside. You can scramble about the rocks surrounding it, but not for too long. When the tide comes in, it covers the whole base and goes right up to the castle wall.'

He unzipped his buoyancy aid and tossed it back into the boat. 'I'll try not to be too long. I, um, just need a moment,' he said, his voice barely above a whisper. 'Just to... Well, if you don't mind me being alone for a bit.'

Iona nodded. 'Sure. Just take care. If you're going around the rocks, they'll be slippery.'

'Thank you. I really appreciate this.' He walked away and Iona watched him. What was his deal? Why on earth did he want to come here when he looked anything but happy about it?

She sat on the slipway, picking a few tufts of grass from the cracks and throwing them into the air. A flurry of bizarre thoughts swooped on her mind like gulls heading for a chip wrapper. Some of them involved Monty turning into a mad axe murderer and appearing behind her with a weapon he'd hidden in that bag, but most of them were even stranger, and involved wandering into his personal life. What kind of women did he like? Was he married? Why did she care? She really shouldn't. And yet, she couldn't shove the thoughts out either.

Chapter Seven

Monty

Monty wandered away from the boat, cradling his backpack in his arms. He breathed deeply, drawing in the fresh air, hoping to settle the nausea. Was it just seasickness? He suspected not. This task was going to be painful and there was no avoiding it. Now that they'd landed, this little island was serene, and almost completely taken over by the stark fortress of Kisimul Castle. As Iona had said, it was all locked up, so he made his way around the outside, clambering over the rocky outcrops, which wasn't easy, but this would be close enough. It would have to be. He didn't fancy making this journey again.

Each step he took felt heavier than the last, as if the weight of his father's ashes was pulling him down. The funeral had been bad enough, but this had an even more final feeling to it. Once the ashes were out, there was no getting them back. Why did that seem to matter? It wasn't like he wanted them back. But he needed to do this properly, get it right, and carry out his father's last wishes.

Monty found a secluded spot by a cluster of rocks at the back of the castle wall overlooking the open sea. How calm it looked now, gently lapping at the rocks, lulling him into believing it was friendly. Sitting down, he placed his backpack beside him and lifted out the urn. The rhythmic sound of the waves was soothing but didn't ease the tightness in his chest. He gazed out to sea, running his fingers through his hair that had got a little wild on top. With the wind on this island, he didn't suppose his hair would sit nicely until he was back on the plane.

The cool breeze sent ripples dancing across the water. In the distance, the Barra mainland curved around with a few smaller islands scattered just off the shore. A long sandy beach was visible, and a few little houses dotted along the coast. Monty stared forward, not moving.

How long had he been sitting here? Minutes, hours? Time had blurred. What now? Did he just open the urn and empty it? Should he say something? Out loud? Why hadn't he thought about this before? The answer to that was simple. He'd avoided thinking about it in too much detail, but now he was here, he had to decide, and he wasn't prepared.

He prised off the lid of the urn, but the sight of the ashes made him freeze. How was he supposed to do this? But he had to. There was no one else. And really, it was the main reason for this trip.

His father's voice echoed in his mind, full of his old island stories, their family's history, and how it had all been lost. Monty hadn't paid as much attention as he should. It had never seemed that interesting or occurred to him that one day all those stories would be lost. He could kick himself now. He should have hung on every word. It had always been a mystery to him why his father was so obsessed with this place, but now, sitting here with the endless sea, and blue sky gradually emerging from behind fluffy white clouds, the connection tugged at his heart. Or if not a connection, perhaps an affinity with the wildness and beauty of the place. It was definitely somewhere to come to relax and refresh, something he'd gladly do, but he had this one job to do first. And yet, he couldn't do it.

He glanced up and saw a boat gliding smoothly through the water, cutting a path and leaving a foamy trail behind. Thank goodness he wasn't on the little boat now. That trail was already increasing the speed of the waves and they rushed on the rocks more insistently than before.

Monty sighed and picked up the urn. The sound of the boat's motor carried across the silence of the bay, and he watched it as it headed further out.

He gripped the urn. *Just do it.* He'd sat here long enough.

'Hey.' Iona's voice jolted him out of his reverie. He looked up, blinking. She stood there, hands on hips, her wind-tousled hair framing her face. 'You've been gone a while, and the tide's turning. We should get going. Is everything ok?'

'Oh, um, yeah. I didn't realise how long I'd been.' He glanced down at the urn, then back at her. 'Sorry.'

She waved a hand. 'It's fine. Just thought I'd check on you.'

He nodded. Would she sit or something? The way she was towering over him like this was intimidating. *Jeez.* He ran his fingers through his hair. She was scarier than a tigress with her fearless attitude and adventurous spirit. No doubt if she had control of the urn, she'd just whip off the lid, tip the contents into the sea and be done with it. She was the type who faced challenges head-on, while he... well, he wasn't sure what he was right now.

'I, um, just... need a moment.'

She glanced at the sea around the rocks, and he suddenly noticed how high it had got. 'Are you sure you're ok?' Her gaze softened a little. 'Are you still feeling sick, because we can't hang about much longer? You've been sitting here for forty minutes.'

'Has it been that long? Oh heck. Well, I don't feel seasick anymore.' He still felt nauseous, but it was nothing to do with the boat.

'That's good... So...' She hopped down the rocks a little and crouched close by, looking like she was playing at a trampoline park and not moving over solid boulders.

'You're quite the adventurer, aren't you?' His voice was quieter than he intended. 'You live on the edge.'

She raised an eyebrow. 'Oh sure. Life on Barra is an extreme sport.'

He huffed out a laugh. 'Still, you're...' He struggled to find the right words. 'You're out there, doing things, being exciting. I've never been like that.'

Iona shrugged, a hint of a smile playing on her lips. 'Everyone's got their own thing. Just because I like a bit of adventure doesn't mean I don't have my moments of doubt.'

Really? She seemed like the epitome of confidence. 'Listen. Thanks for checking on me. I'll, um, I'll be done soon.'

'You'll have to be, because in about twenty minutes you'll be underwater if you're not back at the boat.'

'Right.' Definitely couldn't hang about then. He took a deep breath, turning his gaze back to the rising sea, trying to find the strength to do the job he had to do.

'Can I ask...?' She moved closer. He caught her eye, then saw her gaze drop to the urn. 'Is that an—'

'Urn. Yes. It's what I'm here to do.'

Iona shuffled up beside him, still crouching, her face level with his. Her irises were very blue and easy to get lost in. Such an attractive face to go with her energy and spirit. 'To do what?'

Monty swallowed hard. 'I came here to scatter my dad's ashes.' He tapped the top of the urn. 'I thought I could do it, but... it's harder than I expected.'

Iona tilted her head so her long ponytail fell over her shoulder, then shifted onto her bottom so she was sitting alongside him. She raised her knee and leaned her arm on it. 'I'm really sorry. I didn't realise.'

'It's just...' He struggled to find the words. 'He always talked about Barra and Kisimul Castle. He loved it here. It was his wish to have his ashes scattered here. I just don't know if I can do it.'

She reached out, resting a hand lightly on his arm. His focus moved to the contact point, and he stared at her hand for a moment. 'Of course you can do it. It's hard saying goodbye, but it's ok to take your time, though we should probably move further up the rocks.'

Monty inhaled deeply and closed his eyes. 'I should have prepared myself better.'

'How can anyone prepare themselves for something like this? It's not like something you have to do often in your life. Hopefully not anyway.'

'I suppose so.' Monty glanced back at the urn.

'Don't you have other family? Are you the only one who can do this?'

He nodded. 'Yup. Just me. My mother and father are divorced. I'm an only child. There's no one else.'

'Then can I help?' she asked.

'You?' He raised an eyebrow.

'Yes, me. I didn't know your dad, but maybe you could tell me something about him.'

'You won't want to hear it. He loved the idea that he was somehow descended from the MacNeils of Barra. He told many stories about how our branch of the family were diddled out of this castle.'

He glanced at her and caught a smile.

'Well, maybe this time it's actually true. What was his name?'

'Hector.'

'Then let's release Hector MacNeil. It's time to return him to his homeland. Let his ashes fly free over Kisimul, the stronghold of his ancestors.' She smiled, and Monty couldn't stop a grin from spreading across his face. Then he let out a laugh and she joined in.

'That was quite a speech.' He got to his feet, the water getting closer than he liked. 'Let's not waste it.' He unscrewed the lid of the urn and took a deep breath. A lump rose in his throat. His hands shook slightly as he lifted the urn, and Iona smiled.

'Time to fly, Hector,' she said quietly.

Monty took a step up the rocks. The gentle breeze ruffled his hair. With a deep, shuddering breath, he scattered the ashes at the wall of the castle, watching as some of them caught the breeze and drifted out over the sea.

As the last of the ashes were released, a wave of emotion crashed over him. He closed his eyes and held it in.

'Hey.' Iona patted his back. 'It's ok. You did what he wanted. He's free now.'

Monty kept his eyes closed. The sound of the waves getting closer took over his mind, and he focused on it.

'How did he die?' Iona asked.

'He had a heart attack. Just out of the blue.'

'I'm sorry. But at least you've done what he wanted.'

'Thank you,' he whispered, turning to face her. 'I appreciate what you did there.'

Iona gave him a small smile. 'No worries. We should get back to the boat now unless you want to swim back.'

'Definitely not. But do you mind if I just sit on the boat for a bit before we go back? I'd like to watch the tide swallowing the rocks... As long as it's not too choppy.'

'Sure. It should be steady-ish if I stay alongside the slipway.'

'Thanks.' His eyes met hers and the heavy sensation in his chest flickered, changing into something different, but he wasn't sure what.

'Come on then.' She led the way back around the rocks, and Monty cursed himself for sitting there so long. The water really was too close for comfort now. The wind picked up as they walked, and Iona tossed her ponytail back. She glanced over her shoulder at Monty, presumably checking he was keeping up.

As they reached the jetty, she hopped into the boat and held out her hand. Monty took it more out of politeness than necessity. He didn't think he would fall getting into the boat, but she was likely paranoid after he'd nearly knocked her over twice.

Once he was safely in, he slouched down on the bench, looking back with a sigh at the place where they'd scattered the ashes. His mission was done. Now he could relax. But an odd sensation lingered in his chest, something niggling at him. Words seemed to play in his mind, telling him this wasn't the end, but the beginning. Only he had no idea what it could possibly be the beginning of.

Chapter Eight

Iona

'You sure you're ok?' Iona sat down beside Monty on the bench in the boat. In front of them rose the walls of Kisimul Castle and all around them was the vastness of the sea, rising on the tide. A cool sea breeze ruffled her hair, and she unthreaded some strands from her lips. The silence between her and Monty was ok, but she couldn't shake the gnawing guilt at having been so short with him. If only she'd spared a moment to consider why he was here and not rushed in all guns blazing... as she so often did. Sometimes she was her own worst enemy. How bloody insensitive was she?

Monty nodded, staring out at the water. 'Yeah, I'm fine. Just processing it all.'

'Ok. Would you like a snack? I have a secret stash of chocolate for occasions like this.'

He gave her a weak smile. 'Do you often have people scattering ashes on your boat trips?'

'Ha. No. That's a new one for me. But I don't normally do boat trips at all. I usually teach paddleboarding – that's my most popular activity – but I also do surfing, body boarding, wild swimming, and kayaking, plus cycling and hiking for the land lovers.'

'You're unreal. I don't think I've ever met anyone quite as adventurous as you.'

She got to her feet, grinning, and went to the front of the boat, opened a compartment, and pulled out a large bar of chocolate. 'Hopefully, this will make you feel better and not make you sick.'

'Let's hope.'

She broke off a piece and gave it to him.

'Thanks.'

'You know, I didn't come here just for the adventure.' She sat back beside him.

'No?' Monty turned to look at her. 'Why did you come here, then?'

'Ah, you know.' She snapped off a square of chocolate. 'Shit happens. And I got caught in a proper storm. I needed to get away from my old life. Everything was so... structured and suffocating.'

'What did you do?'

'I worked in the civil service in London, then Edinburgh. Pushing papers, dealing with endless bureaucracy. Drove me mad. It was the kind of job my family expected me to do, not what I really wanted to do.' Her family wasn't short of money, and they'd sent her to boarding school as soon as they could to 'prep' her for adult life. She was pretty sure it hadn't done that. All it had taught her was that she wasn't worth much to them, and they expected her to fend for herself. Well, she was definitely doing that now.

Monty's eyes focused on her and he adjusted his glasses. 'So, you just decided to leave your job one day?'

'Pretty much.' She flicked a bug off her arm. 'I'd had enough. So, I... Well, I lost the plot. I messed up a big speech and there was no going back, so I packed my things and left. Came here to start fresh, you know? To live on my own terms, find some freedom.'

Monty nodded. 'That was brave.'

'Maybe.' Iona shrugged. Or maybe it was just running away. 'There were other factors, I guess. All of it combined pushed me to do it.'

'More than the job?'

'Yeah, my cheating ex, for example.'

'Oh.' Monty raised an eyebrow as realisation dawned on his face.

'Yup. He was well-off and my parents worshipped him. Honestly, I think they liked him more than me. He cheated on me, but my parents were actually annoyed with me. Can you believe it? They thought I'd bailed on a great opportunity. I think they even blamed me for it.' She huffed and snapped off another couple of pieces of chocolate, handing one to Monty and nibbling the other. 'Story of my life. I'm never good enough.' She hadn't meant the last words to come out aloud and had muttered them more to herself than Monty, but he'd clearly heard.

'Sounds like a difficult relationship. Families can be tricky,' he said. 'My mother can be a bit like that too. She loved my ex-girlfriend.' He glanced away and fiddled with his wristwatch. 'But then, so did I.'

'What happened?' Iona watched him closely. Surely his girlfriend hadn't died too. Was his life that tragic? And she'd been so insensitive to him.

He gave a little shrug. 'Just stuff.'

'But... Is she... Still alive?'

He smirked and gave her a funny look. 'Oh yeah. Very much alive. I can see why you'd want to move here.' He changed the subject abruptly and Iona didn't feel she could rewind or pry any more. 'It's beautiful.'

'Yeah, I needed to find myself again and I love this island.'

'It's very easy to be calm here, even on a boat, which I never thought I'd hear myself say.'

She grinned, looking out at the waves crashing against the castle walls. 'It is. But it has its challenges at times.'

'I can understand that,' he replied. 'I've felt a bit out of place here, to be honest. Everything's so different from what I'm used to.'

'I noticed,' she said. 'You're not exactly the outdoorsy type, are you?'

'Not at all.' He shook his head. 'I've spent most of my life in offices, dealing with numbers. This' – he gestured around them – 'is a whole new world to me.'

'It's a good world. It takes some getting used to, but it's worth it.'

Monty smiled and ruffled his hair. Objectively, he *was* a good-looking guy. Catriona was right; he had an academic look with the thick-rimmed glasses, but the windswept hair and the stubble made him more rugged and altogether quite pleasant to look at, but looking was all Iona would be doing. Casual hookups were fine. Why deny she liked them? But he didn't look like a hookup type guy, especially if he still loved his ex, which was what he seemed to be saying before. Probably just as well. Iona had had enough of his type to last a lifetime.

'Listen, thanks for what you did back there.' He flexed his fingers, then linked them together. 'I really don't think I could have done it without you.'

'No worries.'

Monty glanced at her again. 'That was why I booked this trip. To scatter Dad's ashes and say my final farewell, though it doesn't feel like goodbye. I've got an odd feeling... I can't really explain it, but it's like I have something else to do while I'm here. Only I'm not sure what.'

'Well, there are lots of adventures to be had on Barra.'

His brow furrowed, and he looked down at his feet. 'I'm not very good at adventures. That's the reason my ex is my ex and not still my girlfriend.'

'Because she liked adventures, and you don't?' Iona cocked her head.

'Kind of, she thinks I'm...' He looked away and exhaled with a short puff.

'Thinks you're what?'

'Too boring.'

'Oh dear.' Iona covered her mouth, trying not to let herself laugh. She obviously didn't know him well having only met him a couple of days ago, but she could see why someone might say that. His grey clothes didn't exactly help.

'Yeah. I get it. I *am* boring.'

'I didn't say that.'

'You didn't have to. I know I am. Even though in the past few days, I've had more wild experiences than in most of my life. Travelling alone can be adventurous in itself.'

'There you go then. You've already pushed out of your comfort zone.'

'True... And I went cycling. That was good. The puncture, not so much.'

'Thing is, if you've split up with her, what does it matter? Do your own thing and who cares what she thinks.'

'Yeah.' He picked at the knee of his jeans. 'I'm finding it hard to get over her. I keep thinking that maybe if I do something different I can get her back.'

'Different how?'

'I'm not sure. Something to show her I'm not as dull as she thinks... Even if I am.'

Iona glanced away with a half laugh. 'Well, I could teach you paddleboarding if you like. Sign up for a class. And the water sport festival is on next week. You could join in.'

'Hmm. That's a bit out of my depth. I'm not keen on water.'

'Ok.' Iona shook her head. 'Do you like hiking?'

'I'm not sure I like it, but I've been trying to do a bit more of that kind of thing recently.'

'You could climb up Heaval. It's the hill behind Castlebay. Look over there.' She turned around and pointed at the nicely shaped hill behind the village. 'That's it there.'

'Looks interesting, though I can see myself getting lost.'

Monty had turned the same way as her, and she was suddenly aware of his proximity. They'd sat a good while together, and she hadn't really noticed, but with him this close behind her, her skin prickled.

Am I crazy?

'You can't really get lost.' She turned back and put a bit more distance between them. 'There's not exactly a path but you can see the obvious way up. I'd go with you, if you wanted.'

'Yeah, that would be sensible.'

'Maybe once you've done that, you'll be ready for a paddleboarding lesson.'

'I'm not sure I'll ever be ready for that.' He raked his fair hair, which was quite long and tufty at the front. He'd probably just forgotten to have it cut recently with everything going on in his life, but it almost looked trendy. 'I think I can do the hike,' he said. 'I might not have the right shoes though.'

'Hmm. We could see if Ruaridh – you know, Catriona's brother – has a pair you can borrow. He's fitness mad.'

'I have trainers, but nothing fancy.'

'They'll do. As long as you don't mind them getting messy. It can be a bit boggy in places.'

'Why does that not surprise me?' He took out his phone and snapped a picture of the hill and the village.

'Do you want to head back now?'

'Well, I don't really want the boat to move, but I don't want to sit here for the rest of my life either, so let's go.'

'Ok then.' Iona got to her feet and shoved the chocolate back into its compartment. A sudden memory hit her. Ages ago, a friend had left a set of wristbands they'd used for seasickness. They were possibly still stashed in the boat. She rummaged through the compartment. 'I think I have something that might help with your seasickness.'

'Oh? What's that?'

'Aha.' She pulled out a little box with a pair of navy wristbands that resembled the sweatbands athletes wore, only they were narrower and had a little metal button stitched into them. 'These. They're supposed to help with nausea. I don't have a clue how they work, but it's worth a try, right?'

Monty took the bands from her. 'I think I've heard of them, but I'm not sure what to do with them.'

'Here, let me read this.' Iona unfolded a little slip of paper inside the box. It had instructions and a diagram for where to place the metal button. 'So, it looks like you put it in the middle of the two tendons on your wrist, about three finger widths down from the base of your hand.' She stepped closer. 'Hold out your hand.' She took his left wrist and skimmed her fingertips over the skin. 'Make a fist and flex it up, so the tendons rise.'

He did it and Iona pressed the spot. 'I think that's where the button goes.' She glanced up and found his eyes on her, his cheeks slightly pink. Their gazes locked for a moment and Iona's breath caught. 'I, um, should let you put them on.'

'Thanks.' He took the box, still with his eyes on her, then blinked and slipped the band over his wrist, adjusting it so the pressure point was on the place her finger had been just moments ago.

Monty looked down at the bands, then up at her. 'Let's see if this works then.'

'Fingers crossed. Let's get going. The sooner we're back, the sooner you're off the boat.'

'Sounds good to me.' He strapped himself back into his buoyancy aid.

Iona put hers on too and fired up the engine. A gust of wind whipped around them, rocking the little boat. Iona kept an eye on Monty, but he looked calmer, resting his hand along the side of the boat. Perhaps his knuckles were a little white, but she couldn't expect miracles. She steered the boat back towards the village. A few choppy waves bounced them higher than on the way over and some sea spray fizzed over the side, making Monty call out.

'Are you ok?' She glanced back at him.

'Yeah. The bands seem to be helping, though I keep getting water in my face.' He took off his glasses to wipe them and Iona had to look away. What was it about this man?

She manoeuvred the boat forward. As soon as they were in the confines of the harbour, the water calmed, and she approached the marina. 'Here we are.' She leaned over the side, pulling the rope, tugging them in. 'That wasn't so bad, was it?' She took off her buoyancy aid and shoved it into a compartment.

'It was ok.' Monty handed her his buoyancy aid and she put it away.

She crossed to the side of the boat and took hold of the rope again, leaning over to check it was secure. A sharp pain stabbed her side. 'Ow. What the hell?' She pulled back, clutching her abdomen.

'Are you ok?' Monty moved closer.

'Yeah.' She checked the knot was tight, then ran her hand along the edge. 'There's a sharp nail there. I need to fix that. I never noticed it before.' Glancing down, she saw her t-shirt torn and spots of red appearing. 'Seriously? I love this shirt.'

'You're bleeding.' Monty gaped at her. 'Do you have a first aid kit?'

'In the storage compartment.' This was no worse than the grazed shoulder she'd had courtesy of Monty knocking her off the bike. It just looked bad because of the blood. 'But I'll be fine.'

'You should put something on it in case it gets infected.' He fetched the kit and opened it.

Iona lifted her ruined t-shirt to inspect the wound. It wasn't deep. 'Do you faint at the sight of blood?' she asked.

'No.' He ripped an antiseptic wipe from its packet. 'Here. Put this on.' He moved forward and reached out, but before he touched her, he frowned and his hand hovered. 'Shall I? Or would you prefer to do it yourself?'

'Oh... I can do it.' Holding her t-shirt up with one hand, she took the wipe from him and held it against the wound. 'Bloody stings, and I can't believe I've wrecked this shirt. It's one of my favourites.'

He huffed out a little laugh as he unpackaged a plaster.

'It might be better if you put it on,' she said. 'This isn't in the easiest place.'

'Sure.'

Maybe it was just her imagination, but his fingers seemed to tremble as he held out the plaster and positioned it over the cut. His fingers brushed her, and she inhaled sharply, but not because of the pain. The gentle pressure of his touch was worryingly arousing. She didn't need to feel anything like that for him.

'There.' He stepped back, and she dropped her shirt.

'Thanks.' She caught his eye, and they gazed at each other for longer than was strictly necessary, but something in his deep, dark pupils held her fast. 'Not bad for a banker.'

He gave her a little salute.

They stood for a moment longer before Iona took a step away. 'We should get off the boat.'

'Yeah... We should,' Monty agreed, but his eyes lingered on her and goosebumps erupted on her arms. What the hell was happening to her? He was not her type, and she was determined not to change her mind about that.

Chapter Nine

Monty

Monty stepped out of the annex at An Grianan into the fresh evening air. The sun was still casting its golden glow over the horizon, a glorious reminder of the long summer days in Scotland. He got out his phone and took a photo, hoping to catch the colours – no filter needed.

His father's ashes were gone, but Monty still had that uncertain, neither-here-nor-there feeling. The closure he'd hoped for hadn't really happened. If anything, he felt even more confused.

He strolled along a vaguely trodden path through the grass and the thick bracken, following the gentle crash of the waves beyond. For someone who didn't like water, it was surprising how much the sea called to him. Was this how stories about sirens luring sailors into the ocean had started? Something about the sea was magnetic. As he reached the edge of grass where it met the sand, the view opened up before him. The sparkling turquoise sea, dotted with rocky outcrops, glittered in the evening sun.

Monty took out his phone again, half certain no picture or film would do this justice. The way the light danced and twinkled was magical. He adjusted the settings, hoping to capture at least something of it. He wasn't a big user of social media, but this was something he wanted to share, maybe with a brief reference to his dad. Somewhere in the back of his mind, another thought lingered. Sophie might see it. She loved social media and posted pictures almost every day.

Monty could easily keep up with what she was doing – as could the rest of the world.

He found a raised spot on the edge of the sand and sat down, leaning back on his hands and gazing out to sea. The waves rolled in gently, like a rhythmic lullaby. He let his eyelids fall closed for a moment, soaking in the pure calm. He breathed the sea air, and his body relaxed, tension falling from his chest and shoulders.

When he opened his eyes, he scrolled through the pictures in his phone's gallery. He should have some of the castle. Maybe he should make another trip there before he left, and actually look at it this time. He'd been so taken up with the ashes that he hadn't focused on much else. Also, if those wristbands worked, he might even enjoy the trip over, get some nice photos, and not spend the whole time feeling nauseous. Not that he particularly wanted to ask Iona to take him again. He'd already caused her enough grief... though she'd been a lot nicer since she'd learned about his reasons for being here.

He selected a few photos and wrote a brief caption: *Scattered Dad's ashes at Kisimul Castle today. A beautiful place for a final goodbye. Miss him every day.*

His finger hovered for a moment before hitting the upload button. Should he share this? Did people really need to know? But it was a way of acknowledging the day's significance, and he wanted to do that. He had cousins as friends on here, along with people who'd known him for a long time; they'd be interested, and happy to know he'd done the task he set out to do. He hit *post*, put the phone flat on the grass, then lay on his side, propping his head on his hand.

After a few minutes of listening to the waves, curiosity got the better of him, and he turned on the phone without lifting it off the grass. His fingers led him directly to Sophie's page. Her profile was as busy as ever, filled with pictures of her looking glamorous. It appeared she'd used today's sunshine to meet with friends. A cocktail in hand, and a wide, red-lipsticked smile on her face told him she was out living her best life and not missing him at all.

A pang of something he couldn't quite identify struck him in the chest. Jealousy, perhaps, or a sense of being left behind? Sophie had moved on so easily. Did she ever think about him?

He took a deep breath, looking out to the sea. What were the chances of her actually wanting to get back together? Was it a fool's hope? Probably, but he could give himself a fighting chance. What if he took up Iona's offer and learned to paddleboard? Could he bear to get in the sea? His insides squirmed at the thought, but another sensation sparked at the thought of Sophie's reaction if, in a few days' time, he posted pictures of himself boarding out to sea. He huffed out a laugh. Like he'd ever manage that.

Something rustled the grass behind him and a cold, wet nose nudged his hand. He looked up to see a liver-coloured dog sniffing around him, its tail wagging.

'Hey there,' Monty murmured, giving the dog a gentle pat. 'You're Catriona's dog, aren't you?' The dog's tail wagged even harder, and it sniffed the ground around Monty's phone.

'Scamp!' a woman's voice called out. Monty turned, expecting to see Catriona, but it was Iona striding through the bracken. She had a slightly annoyed expression and froze when she saw him. 'Oh, it's you. I wondered who he'd snuck up on. I always worry when he finds someone lying on the beach.'

'Um, yeah.' Monty frowned.

'Well, it might be a dead body, or people getting down and dirty in the sand. And personally, I wouldn't like to discover either.'

'No, I imagine not.' Monty pulled himself into a sitting position and scratched the dog behind the ears. 'He's friendly.'

'Friendly, nosey, and with no sense of personal space or boundaries.' Iona sighed and plopped down on the grass beside Monty. 'Go and run.' She gave Scamp a gentle prod and shooed him onto the sand. 'God, I'm so hacked off.'

Monty raised an eyebrow. 'With me?'

'No.' She gave him a sharp look, then grinned. 'Unless you're planning on knocking me over again.'

'Definitely not.'

'Sensible.' She gave him a little nudge, then threw her head back. 'Someone cancelled a paddleboarding lesson last minute. It's the third one this week. Means I'll lose money again.'

'Sorry to hear that. Is it a common thing?'

'More common than I'd like.' She ripped up some grass and tossed it in the air. 'I get it, people have their reasons, they miss boats or whatever, but it's frustrating. I rely on those bookings.'

'Maybe you need a cancellation fee.' Monty watched as Scamp snuffled around the beach.

'Yeah, maybe.' She ran a hand through her long ponytail. 'Or more reliable clients, though boarders can be... Well... boarders.'

He chuckled. 'What do you mean?'

A small smile played on her lips. 'Ah, you know, people who go with the flow.'

He shook his head and laughed too.

She leaned back and turned her head to face him. When she caught his eye, his insides lurched. Such a beautiful smile. Her gaze dropped to the ground and Monty followed her sightline. His phone was still there, open on Sophie's social media page.

'Are they friends of yours?' Iona was focused on the photo of Sophie and her girlfriends.

'Um, no.' He gently put his fingertip on Sophie. 'That's my ex.'

Iona lifted the phone and held it in front of her. 'The ex who called you boring and you want to get back together with?'

'The very same.'

'Wow. She's beautiful.'

Monty swallowed. Yes, she was. Always had been. Her slick black hair and bright red lips made her stand out from the crowd. And she wasn't afraid to dress in revealing clothes and heels. Was he crazy thinking a woman like her would ever want him? Why had she ever done so in the first place? 'Too beautiful for me.'

Iona handed him his phone back and gave him a stern look. 'Why should she be? Being beautiful isn't that important. I hope that's not why you want to get back together with her. She's a nice person, right?'

Monty frowned at her photo. 'Yeah. She's fun to be with.' But was she? When it came down to it, had he enjoyed their time together? Wasn't there always pressure to live up to? He let out a sigh. Maybe that was true, but was it his own fault? Had his failings caused the pressure? If he could just cast off the cloak of dullness.

'Well, that's something,' Iona said. 'Where's Scamp?' She squinted along the beach. 'Ah, there he is. I better get him back.'

'How's your cut?'

'Oh, that.' Iona pulled up her t-shirt and Monty held his breath. He had a feeling she'd take the whole thing off and not care whether he was looking. She had that easy-in-her-own-skin way about her. 'I think it's fine.'

'And what about the shoulder?'

'What is it about you that makes me get injuries? Honestly, I've never had so many.' She smirked, then pulled a face.

'Talent.'

'Possibly, but actually I was fibbing. I'm always getting bumps and bruises. Goes with the territory.'

'And you're trying to sell your adventures to people?' He raised his eyebrows, and she chuckled.

'Yeah. Probably better if I keep fibbing.' She craned her neck, scanning around. 'I should go. Otherwise Scamp will leave me behind.'

'Ok.'

She caught his eye again, and he pushed his glasses further up his nose. He needed to get these adjusted; they were so annoyingly loose.

'See you around.' She got to her feet. 'And if you fancy a paddle-boarding lesson, let me know. I've got plenty of space now.'

Monty stood up, brushing the sand off his trousers and watching as Iona jogged onto the beach, calling to Scamp. The evening air was cooling, but it was still pleasant, and he was in no rush to get back. In fact, watching Iona running along the beach with Scamp seemed more than enough reason to stay a little longer.

The following day, Monty got up early and jogged the path he'd been the night before. By the time he got back to An Grianan, the burn in his legs was powerful. If Iona decided to take him up Heaval, he wanted to be ready. He slowed to a walk as he reached the gate, raking his fingers through his hair, as he spotted people.

Catriona, Iona, and a tall, muscular man he didn't recognise were in the yard. The man had a broad grin on his face and longish dark hair that he kept pushing his fingers through. Iona laughed and rolled her eyes at something he said. Was this Ruaridh, Catriona's 'fitness mad' brother? He certainly looked like he'd be good at sports.

Monty wanted to sneak by and make his way into the annex. He needed a shower and wasn't in the mood for talking, but Catriona turned around and smiled. 'Hey.' She waved at him.

'Morning.' He wiped the sweat from his brow.

'Those trainers look fine for hiking up Heaval.' Iona glanced at his feet. 'But if you need another pair, this is Ruaridh that I was telling you about.'

'Nice to meet you.' Monty extended his hand.

'Likewise.' Ruaridh shook Monty's hand with a firm grip. 'I'd go up Heaval with you. I love doing it.'

Monty held his breath as he smiled. 'Great.' He could see himself being abandoned very quickly if Ruaridh and Iona both came with him.

Iona nudged Ruaridh. 'We could run up. Do you think you can beat me?'

'Easy,' Ruaridh said with a wink.

Iona rolled her eyes, but her smile said she didn't mind his teasing. They had that easy way about them, like they'd known each other forever.

'Where were you running today?' Ruaridh asked.

'Just along the beach.'

'I'll maybe join you tomorrow.' Ruaridh pushed back his hair again. 'I can show you some great runs on the island and down on Vatersay too.'

'Um, yeah.' While the idea of seeing more places was appealing, trying to keep up with Ruaridh was not.

'And you're thinking about paddleboard lessons too?' Ruaridh grinned at Monty.

'Well, possibly.' Monty's face twitched. If this guy was involved, Monty was going to look very small, very soon. Although their physical heights weren't far off, Ruaridh was bulkier and oozed confidence.

A smile spread slowly over Iona's face. 'Well, remember I have time this week.'

Ruaridh turned to her. 'I might join too. Think you can handle me?'

'Depends on what you mean by that.' Iona raised an eyebrow.

Catriona gave them a sharp look. 'Enough nonsense. Iona, can you help me move the wardrobe in room one? Someone has got it far too close to the door. God knows why.'

'Don't you want He-Man to do that?' She jabbed her thumb in Ruaridh's direction.

A pang of something struck Monty in the chest – was it jealousy? Why should it be? He had no claim on Iona. She was just a fleeting acquaintance.

'He needs to unpack.' Catriona looked at Ruaridh, and her words sounded more of an instruction than a passing comment.

'I sure do.' Ruaridh saluted her.

Catriona and Iona made their way inside. Monty should move too. He wasn't sure he wanted to be out here with Ruaridh alone in case he suggested several other painful ways they could work out.

'She's quite something, huh?' Ruaridh eyed the two women as they walked in, but it was blatantly obvious which one had his attention.

'Iona?' Monty didn't need to ask, but he didn't know what else to say.

'Yup.' Ruaridh mussed up his hair. 'She's quite the lass.' He winked. 'Doesn't give me a look in though. Anyway...' He clapped his hands together like he hadn't really meant anyone to hear his musings. 'I better get on. Give me a shout if you want to do some training, though I'm back to work tomorrow so I might not have time.'

Monty made a face of agreement and disappointment, though his insides were dancing. Thank god for that. He'd dodged a bullet nicely there. But his head hurt a little as he made his way back to the annex. His thoughts jogged around places he didn't really want them to go. Ruaridh might think Iona wasn't interested in him, but Monty wasn't so sure. She'd looked very comfortable in his presence.

'Why do I even care?' He closed the door of the annex and pulled off his shirt. After switching on the shower, he took off the rest of his clothes and jumped under the steaming water. As the water hit him, he tried to steer his mind to something pleasant and let the heat refresh him. Why then did Iona keep nudging her way back in? And how could he get her out? Because she didn't belong there.

Chapter Ten

Iona

Iona grunted as she and Catriona heaved the wardrobe into position.

'Who the heck moved this in the first place.' Iona jostled it until it was closer to the wall.

'The last guests, I assume, though I'm not sure why.' Catriona's face was flushed with exertion; she wasn't particularly tall or robust, but she looked determined. 'Just a bit more to the left.'

Iona adjusted her grip, and they shuffled the wardrobe a few inches, finally setting it down with a thud.

'I bet they pushed it across the door when they were getting jiggy.' Iona rolled her shoulders. 'You should put locks on the doors.'

Catriona shook her head. 'It'd spoil the character of the place.'

'Maybe, but not as much as moving this wardrobe will spoil the floor.'

'True, but I also don't have time. I need a drink.' Catriona made her way out of the room and headed downstairs. Iona followed.

'Isn't it a bit early?'

'You know what I mean.' She headed straight to the kitchen and filled a glass with water. 'Is he still gassing?' She looked out the window to where Ruaridh was deep in conversation with Alexander, who was leaning against the side of the house with a look of mild irritation.

'He better not appear around here with all his washing,' Catriona muttered. 'I'm not his mother.'

'You pretty much are,' Iona said.

Catriona pulled a face. 'He's six years older than me.'

Which was a fact that always made Iona smirk. Catriona certainly looked younger, but she'd grown up fast. Her mum had chronic fatigue syndrome and lived in one of the farm cottages. She relied on Catriona and Ruaridh to do a lot for her. More often than not, Catriona seemed to be the one holding the family together. Ruaridh was a wandering spirit, and their father had left them at an early age; they rarely mentioned him.

'He's old enough to do his own washing, and Alexander has better things to do than stand around chatting.' She shook her head and marched outside.

Uh-oh. Catriona didn't often get mad, but she looked like she meant business. Iona went out behind her.

'What are we doing here?' Catriona folded her arms, smiling, but not with any warmth.

Ruaridh chuckled. 'Nothing.'

'I can see that much.'

'He was just telling me about his holiday.' Alexander met Catriona's eye and Iona held her breath. A crackle of invisible electricity zipped between them. They either hated each other or had the hots for each other – big time. But Alexander must be in his late thirties, maybe even early forties. It was a curious age gap and one Iona was sure they would both have an issue with.

'Here...' Ruaridh glanced around. 'Do you think I might've freaked out that guest earlier?'

Catriona's brow furrowed slightly. 'Why? What did you say to him?'

'Just stuff about running... I think. He just had a funny look on his face, that's all.'

'He's a nice guy,' Catriona said. 'So don't go upsetting him.'

Alexander rolled his eyes but tried to quickly even out his features. Catriona had obviously seen him though.

'Don't know what that was for.' She narrowed her eyes at him. 'He's a lot nicer than some of us around here.'

Alexander pulled a face back at her.

Iona smirked. Definitely something going on there, though she wasn't sure what.

'Monty's grown on me,' Iona said. 'But he's not as fitness mad as you, Ruaridh, so just go easy on him, ok?'

Ruaridh chuckled. 'Sure, but he was the one out running. Maybe he just needs a nudge.'

'Or a shove,' Alexander added.

Catriona shot him a look. 'He's a guest. Will you please be more welcoming?'

Alexander's jaw tightened. 'It was a joke.'

Iona tossed out her ponytail. 'Well, I'm off to catch some waves. On my own, seen as how my students cancelled.'

'I could join you,' Ruaridh said.

'Sure.'

'Just so long as you don't expect me to do your washing while you do that,' Catriona said.

Ruaridh pulled a cringing face. 'On second thoughts, looks like I have a date with the washing machine.'

'Lucky you.' Iona waggled her eyebrows.

Alexander bent down and lifted something off the ground. 'Any of you drop this?' He held out a small notebook.

'I think it's Monty's,' Iona said. 'I saw him scribbling in something like that the other day.'

'Do you want to hand it to him?' Alexander held it out.

'I suppose so.' She took the notebook from Alexander.

As she strolled around to the annex, she flipped through it, wondering if there was a name in it, in case it wasn't actually Monty's. Seemed just to be a list of places on the island. Kisimul Castle had a question mark beside it. Shouldn't it be a tick? He'd already been there. But maybe he was questioning something else about it, or marked it before he went and never got back to it.

She knocked on the annex door and waited, letting the gentle breeze ruffle her hair. No reply. Had he gone out again? The door didn't have a letterbox. Well, did it really matter. She could just prop it up on the door and leave it for him to find. Bending over, she went to place it down.

The door opened.

Iona peered up. Her eyes travelled over sturdy bare legs, a fluffy white towel, a surprisingly buff chest, and eventually came to land on a bright pair of hazel eyes that were staring back at her.

'Hello?' he said.

He didn't have his glasses on, but really that was nothing compared to the rest of him. She straightened up, not sure where to focus. She'd expected him to be weedy and a bit scrawny. There was no denying he was thin, but he was well-toned, and the light smattering of coarse hair was Viking-like.

'Iona?' He raised his eyebrows. 'Is everything ok? Do you want me for something?'

She blinked. That was an interesting question. Maybe she did... Though she shouldn't. 'I, um... We found this notebook in the yard. I think it's yours.'

Monty squinted at it. 'Yeah, it looks like mine, though I suppose anyone could have one like that.'

'It's got a list of places around the island. I looked because I was checking in case it had a name in it.'

'Oh, yeah. That's mine. It must have fallen out of my pocket.'

She handed it back to him, her skin tingling a little as their hands touched. 'I assume you don't mind getting wet in the shower.' She cringed inwardly at the words – how stupid did she sound? 'I mean, it's only seawater that bothers you.'

'Pretty much. Or any water that I can't control.' His eyes held hers and another weird tremor ran through her.

'Well, I'm going to seek some waves right now.' She scanned him over. 'Why don't you come with me? I'll give you a taster lesson. No charge.'

'You're crazy... You saw me in a boat.'

'Go on. I dare you.'

A little smirk played on his lips. 'Are you for real? There's no way.'

'Why not? The only thing stopping you... Is you. If you go in, I'll take some photos and you can post them to your ex. Why not show her what a daredevil you can be?' She folded her arms and tilted her head, daring him with her eyes.

He looked like he was chewing his tongue, and she smirked, knowing full well he'd say no. Ruaridh and maybe even Alexander would have risen to the bait, but Monty was so measured compared to them. Maybe that was what had led his ex to call him boring.

'I... um.' He ran his fingers through his damp hair.

'It's ok. You don't have to.' She tipped him a little wink and his gaze locked on hers again.

'Actually, you know what, I will.'

'Really?' Her jaw dropped.

'Yeah. Just let me get something on.'

'Ok.' She smiled, though a frown was overtaking. 'Meet me in the yard in ten.'

'See you there.' He closed the door and she shook her head. She hadn't expected that.

---❤---

Ten minutes later, Iona waited by the car, tapping her fingers on the bonnet. Monty emerged from the annex, ruffling up the front of his hair. He'd swapped the towel for a pair of running shorts and a baggy white linen shirt. Why did he hide his nice bod like that?

'So, you ready?' She opened the car door.

'As I'll ever be.' Monty climbed in. 'Where are we going to do this?'

'At the beach next to the paddleboarding school.'

'When you say school—'

'I mean it's a container where I keep the equipment. It's not actually a school.'

'And will anyone else be there?'

'There might be other people using the beach but there won't be anyone else at the school.'

He nodded and leaned his elbow on the window ledge. 'I think paddleboarding might be too advanced for me. I've never even swam in the sea. I'm not sure I can swim anymore. It's been years since I tried. Like since I was at school.'

She shook her head and laughed. 'Ok. You really are a case. Well, no water sports until we check you can swim. Let's try that today and maybe we can do some bodyboarding. It's a lot easier but still loads of fun.'

'Dare I even ask what it is?'

'Oh my god, Monty. Where have you been? Bodyboarding is like lying on a board and riding it in. It's easier than surfing and paddle-boarding.'

'Ah, right. Ok.'

It was only a short drive before she pulled into the small car park beside the container that served as her storage and office.

'Here we are.' Iona hopped out and unlocked the container. She flicked on the light, revealing rows of wetsuits hanging from hooks. 'Let's get you kitted out.'

Monty followed her in, looking around. She rifled through the wet-suits, pulling one off a hanger and holding it up against him.

'This should fit.' She handed it over. 'There's a changing room in the corner.'

Monty took the wetsuit, eyeing it over like it might bite. 'Do I just... put it on over my shorts?'

'Um, not unless you want them to get wet. I'd go commando if I were you. Unless you have swimming shorts.'

'No.' He gave a little shrug.

'Well, commando it is then.' She gave him a little wink. As soon as he was behind the curtain, she took off her top and eased down her jeans. She was already wearing her bikini and lifted her wetsuit off the hook. Monty was still shuffling around as she stepped into her suit. A flutter rippled over her at the thought of him being naked so close to her. Normally, stuff like that didn't bother her, but her skin was a little tingly as she pulled on the suit and used the long string to tug the zip up the back.

A few minutes later, Monty reappeared, struggling to pull the zipper all the way up. 'How do I do this?'

'Use the string.' Iona stepped behind him. She had an urge to touch the skin on his back, maybe roll her palms over him, glide them around him... And stop! 'Here.' She handed the string to him.

'Ah, right. That makes sense.' He flexed his arms. 'Tight, isn't it?'

'It'll loosen up once you're in the water.' Maybe he would too – his rigid pose told her he was not enjoying this so far. 'Let's catch some waves.' She threw open the door and made her way onto the sand. Sure, it was irritating that her students had cancelled, but her insides were alive and crackling with energy. She couldn't wait to get started on this. She glanced back at Monty. Maybe this was mission impossible, but she liked a challenge, and she was ready to get him in the water.

Chapter Eleven

Monty

Monty stood on the cool beach at the edge of the water, staring out at the rolling waves. Some of them looked at least eight feet high – bigger than him anyway. He'd left his glasses back at the container, but even without them, the sea looked endless. A pair of wet-shoes formed a barrier between his skin and the sand, but even with them on he wasn't sure he wanted to get into the water. That was the Atlantic Ocean, for heaven's sake. A shiver ran down his spine that had nothing to do with the cold.

'Come on.' Iona turned back and smiled. She was already ankle-deep and had walked in as routinely as she might walk into the supermarket.

Monty groaned, then inched forward. A shock of cold ran up his leg and he froze, unable to go further.

'It's bloody cold,' he muttered.

Iona took a few steps back towards him. 'Once you're in, it's fine. Your body will acclimatise fast. Come on. This bit is so shallow, it's not even as deep as a puddle.'

He huffed out a laugh. Of course, she was right, but he couldn't help being cautious. He took a deep breath and waded in. As the cold water got to his waist, it shocked his nervous system. He made it to where Iona stood, taking calming breaths. 'It's baltic.'

'You'll get used to it and you'll find it surprisingly warm.'

'Really?'

'Yes.' She grinned at him.

The ocean looked vast from here, so easy to get lost in. The further out they went, the rougher the swell got; it was sure to engulf them if they went another step. The noise was incredible, crashing and slapping as wave after wave hit.

'Are you sure this is safe?' Monty called over the tumult. 'Won't we get washed away?'

'Give me your hands.' Iona held hers out.

'Why?'

'To stop you from worrying. I'll hold on to you.'

Monty gazed at her for a moment. She was a wild adventurer, but she also looked trustworthy. He placed his hands in hers, feeling the pressure of her grip. 'Now, we're just going to go a bit further.'

'Further?'

Iona moved backwards, guiding him. The water surged around them. He held on to her, allowing her to lead him. The skin-to-skin contact anchored him and he took deep breaths. The sense of uncertainty slowly edged away. If he mastered himself, he could almost see why someone might enjoy this – if they had more skill than him.

'See, not so bad.' She raised an eyebrow.

Monty laughed, the sound surprising even himself. 'Easy for you to say.'

'Just keep your eyes on me.' Her cheeks flared a little as she said it, but Monty obeyed. He wasn't sure he wanted to look anywhere else. 'That way you won't panic about how big the sea is,' she said.

As if she needed to.

She led him further out until they were chest deep. The waves lifted them gently, and the wild swells seemed to subside somehow into a calmer motion.

'Ok.' Iona stopped, still holding his hands. 'We're going to duck.'

Monty threw her a look. 'What? I'm not putting my head under.'

'You don't have to.' Her grip on his hands tightened briefly. 'Just lower yourself down so your chin is resting on the surface. Like this.' She sank down, not letting go. Her head peered out of the water like a seal. 'Now you try.'

'Ok.' With a sharp inhale, he bent his knees, pulling himself down.

'Not bad, right?' Iona beamed at him.

'Not bad at all.' He smiled in spite of himself.

Iona let go of his hands and floated back a bit, the hair from her ponytail swirling around her. How like a mermaid was she? Or maybe a siren. Because something about her was very alluring. 'Did you ever learn to swim?' she asked.

'At school. About a hundred years ago, but it was never something I enjoyed.' That was an understatement. The days of shivering at the side of the pool waiting for his turn were etched into his mind as a particularly painful part of his school life.

She raised an eyebrow. 'Well, hopefully it'll come back to you. Do you know how to tread water?'

Monty nodded. 'Yeah, I think I can manage that.'

'Great. Like this.' She demonstrated, kicking her legs in a rhythmic motion.

Monty mimicked her movements, the water pushing against him. It was harder than it looked, and he felt a bit stupid.

'That's it.' Iona's eyes travelled over him, confirming how daft he must look. Why else would she eye him like that? 'Now, try some strokes with your arms and if you're able to push forward, then do it.'

Monty took a deep breath. He'd got this far. He was in the sea and actually it wasn't as bad as he'd thought. The initial stab of cold had fizzled out and while he wouldn't call it warm, it wasn't that cold either, just bearable enough to not want to get out and curl up in a rug next to a fire – though later on he might. He pushed forward into the water, the way he remembered, but also in a way that felt intuitive. His arms cut the path and his legs moved him forward. He was nowhere near as graceful as Iona, who was bobbing around like a seal, ducking under and then surfacing with seemingly no effort at all.

'You're doing fine.' She swam closer. 'Just try raising your shoulders a little more. It'll keep your chin out of the water.' She put her hands under him, holding his shoulders as he kicked like a frog.

'I feel like a kid at swimming lessons.'

She smiled, and he blinked. Sometimes, without his glasses, he felt more exposed than ever to external scrutiny. Her face was close and, although she was holding him in this stupid position, the moment was oddly intimate. Not something he should be thinking about. Keeping afloat was really all that should matter, but breaking eye contact was difficult. When their eyes connected, strange currents of energy bolted through him. Or maybe it was just the waves lapping over him.

'You're getting the hang of it.' Iona moved her hands, almost instantly swimming off. He couldn't keep up, but he was swimming. Actual, proper swimming in the sea. This had to count for something in the adventure stakes.

Monty's chest swelled with pride and something else he couldn't quite identify.

Iona flipped over and floated on her back. 'You're doing great for someone who didn't want to come in at all.'

'Thanks.'

'Try this, if you feel up for it. It's so relaxing.'

'I'm not sure I dare.'

'Here.' She came back to him. 'Turn around and lie back. I'll hold you, so you can get the feel of it.'

Monty hesitated, then turned his back to her. He leaned back, letting the water support him. Iona placed her hands under his shoulders, guiding him.

'Just relax,' she whispered, her breath warm against his ear, sending tingles through his cool skin. 'The water will hold you up.'

He took a deep breath, forcing calm. The gently rocking waves cradled him. Iona's hands stayed steady.

'How's that?'

Monty closed his eyes for a moment, the gentle sun on his face and the cool water all around him. 'Feels weird, but kind of nice.'

Iona laughed. 'Exactly. Shall I let go?'

'Ok.' For a moment, he kept the relaxed pose, before floundering and splashing about to regain his feet. 'Sorry,' he mumbled.

'No need to be. It takes practise.'

Monty returned to his stomach and started swimming, his strokes becoming more confident. He could do this. What would Sophie make of it? He tried to imagine her face and her reaction, but his brain kept pushing Iona into the forefront. Oh well, maybe that was common sense. He should pay attention to Iona because if she wasn't here, he'd be in trouble.

'Look at you, practically a pro now.' Iona winked.

'Hardly. But you're a good teacher. I admire your patience with a noob like me.'

She smiled at him, and he returned it. Warmth seeped into his veins. When she smiled, she was very beautiful. It definitely suited her more than the scowl she'd worn the first few times he'd met her. Clearly water made her happy. And seeing her like that filtered into him. Why shouldn't he enjoy this? Whatever he'd dreaded about it wasn't happening. His limbs were lighter and tension ebbed away from his muscles. For the first time in a long while, he felt truly alive and unfettered.

'I think we could try the body boards,' Iona said.

'Sure, why not?' Monty quirked his lip, and she raised her eyebrows.

'Loving the sense of adventure.'

Hopefully she wasn't the only one who would.

Iona headed back to the shore. Monty watched her leave the water and cross the beach like someone from *Baywatch*, though without his glasses, she was somewhat blurred. Her wetsuit fitted her well and she had a lithe figure, well-toned from all the exercise. What did people think of his body? He wasn't as scrawny as he used to be thanks to the running, but he was no bodybuilder.

He practised a bit of swimming, trying to relax into the backstroke as he waited for her to return. A few moments later, she came out carrying two boards. She waded back to him.

'You ready for this?'

'As I'll ever be.' Monty ran his fingers through his wet hair. 'What do I do?'

'Watch me first.' She handed him a board. 'You hold it like this, then get ready for a wave, by watching behind. When you see one coming, lean in and ride it in.' She waited, then in a fluid movement soared into it, lying flat on her board, letting the wave carry her ashore. She got up and lifted her board before turning back to him. 'You gonna try?'

Monty held the board and checked behind him. If this worked, it would be nothing short of a miracle. A wave passed but he wasn't quick enough. 'I haven't got the timing,' he muttered.

Iona reached him and positioned herself, looking back over her shoulder. 'Here comes another good one. Get ready, we'll go together.'

Monty glanced back, seeing the swell approaching. 'Ok.'

'Now!' Iona surged forward.

Monty threw himself onto the board, but his timing was off, and the wave crashed over him. For a second, he was blind and couldn't breathe. Cold dread and fear slapped him as he scrabbled about, flat on the board. Then something gripped his arm, and he opened his eyes, blinking water out of them. Iona came into focus, grinning as she pulled him to his feet.

'You ok?'

'What happened? I thought I was drowning.'

She shook her head with a little laugh. 'You just kind of faceplanted. Let's try again, only keep the board angled up a bit.'

'There's so much to remember. I don't think I'll manage it.' He ran his hand through his wet hair.

'Don't overthink it. Use intuition more than technical stuff. Just kind of feel the waves.'

'I'm not sure my brain works that way.'

'Try. Watch and listen to the waves. Feel the motion and the pattern.'

He did as she said, somewhat surprised he wasn't feeling seasick, as he fell into the rhythm and the movement. Natural and erratic as it was, it still had a pattern, like Iona said, and he waited until he was certain. Then he chose a wave, watched it... caught it. He clung on as it lifted him. For a moment, his breath stopped. Would he be pulled under again? But the wave carried him forward, and he glided onto the beach. Still lying clinging to the board, he heard Iona speaking not far away.

'You did it.'

He breathed and pulled himself to his feet. 'That wasn't as bad as I thought.'

'Well done.' She reached out and patted him on the arm. 'That was great. How did it feel?'

'Not bad, I guess.'

'Let's do it again.'

'Ok.'

They paddled back out. This time, it didn't seem as daunting. In fact, it was almost enjoyable. Each time he waited, feeling the rhythm, then caught another wave, an invisible hook seemed to tug him back into the water to do it again and again, either in an attempt to do better this time or something else entirely.

'You can't say you're not enjoying this now, can you?' Iona caught his eye as they waited for the next wave.

'Yeah... It's ok.'

'Ok?' She raised an eyebrow. 'Come on, Monty. Give me something more. Show me the passion, the fire.'

He chuckled. 'You're crazy.'

'Me? Watch out, you're missing one.' She leapt onto the board and glided on the wave. Her movement was so elegant, she almost looked like she didn't need the board.

Monty waited for a moment, then caught a wave, riding it all the way to the shore again.

As they waded back out again, Iona moved closer. 'I think you've really got the hang of this.'

'Which is somewhat surprising.'

Clouds had rolled over the sun and some warmth drained from the surrounding air.

'Looks like it might rain.' Iona glanced up. 'Not that it matters. We're wet anyway. But if you want to stop at any time, just say.'

'Maybe one or two more.' Monty eyed her, and she grinned.

'You've got the bug.'

They waded out again, catching more waves. The sea, so intimidating an hour ago, now felt like a playground. This was actually quite fun, but with the gathering clouds, cold was creeping in and Monty shivered a little. Maybe this was the right time to call it a day.

'Let's get dried and dressed then,' Iona said. 'I've got a kettle in the container. I can make us some tea or hot chocolate to warm up with.'

Monty followed her up the shore, across the tarred area and into the container. Getting the wetsuit off wasn't the easiest now his limbs were cooling off. He vigorously towelled himself down in the tiny changing area, and his mind wandered to Iona. Where was she changing? Was there another cubicle? Why did he even care? But his blood rushed south at the thought, and he ground his teeth.

Seriously?

It'd been a while since he'd had any bedroom action. Sophie had stopped being interested in the end of their relationship. No doubt that was due to his vanilla performance. Well, today had been far from dull. He'd made the first step to doing something a little more adventurous. He pulled on his boxer briefs, adjusting the fit as more thoughts barraged his brain. Ruaridh had suggested Iona didn't mind quick flings with guys she met through surfing. Maybe she used this container for more than just changing in. Was sex on the beach more than a cocktail for her?

All of that seemed like a fantasy to him. He'd confined his sexual activities to the bedroom so far, which pretty much confirmed his status as vanilla. And make that a double scoop. But things were changing. He'd done something way out of the zone today. What else could he do if he put his mind to it?

Chapter Twelve

Iona

Iona poured boiling water into two tin mugs, then stirred a spoon through them, blending in the hot chocolate powder. She pulled a face at the result. Never would she ever be a barista, but these would be good enough to warm them up.

She glanced at Monty as he emerged from the changing room, his hair still damp and somewhat rugged. The length on the front and the fair colouring could almost pass for surfer style. She smirked inwardly as he put on his thick-rimmed glasses, turning himself instantly back to Clarke Kent. Weird how glasses could do that to a person. One minute he was verging on hot surfer, the next he was back to sensible bank employee. *Did I just call him hot?* She gave herself a mental shake.

'Here's a hot chocolate.' She held one out.

He nodded and took the mug. 'Thanks. Smells good.'

'Yeah, well, it's not exactly Starbucks level, think more roadside diner. Even that's probably pushing it.'

'I'm sure it's fine.' His eyes met hers, as they had done often that afternoon. Something shifted inside her every time it happened. Not a bad thing, just weird. Like she quite enjoyed it, but also knew she shouldn't really. He wasn't her type at all, so finding him even slightly appealing was strange. Mainly because she couldn't pinpoint what there was to find attractive about him.

'Let's take these drinks down to the beach.' She grabbed a rug from the shelf, then led the way back out to the shore, finding a sheltered spot on the sand, in front of a dune covered in grassy tufts. She spread out the rug and sat down. 'I think the rain must have blown away. For now.' It changed so quickly around here.

Monty settled beside her, not too close. He was a gentleman, if nothing else. They both cradled their mugs, looking out at the waves. The thick clouds lingered, obscuring most of the sun's brightness, but some yellow beams glowed in the distance. Iona took a sip of her hot chocolate. 'So, how do you feel about the sea now?' She glanced at Monty.

'Better than I did this morning. Thank you.'

'You're welcome. You seemed to enjoy it once you were in.'

'Yeah, surprisingly, I did. I appreciate you teaching me, even though I'm such a...'

'A what?'

'A scaredy cat or whatever.'

She laughed into her mug. 'You're funny. You can't be a total scaredy cat though or you wouldn't have gone in at all.'

'I'm getting better. You know, at leaving the comfort of my own zone.'

She shook her head, still grinning. Something about him was undeniably cute.

They sat in silence for a moment, the only sound the roaring of the waves, increasing in tempo and fizzing as they broke over jagged rocks. As Iona listened, she heard music, like someone humming a soft, low tune. Its notes seemed at first to be part of the waves, but they got stronger and in them was a deep sense of spirit, like they were connected to the island itself and its people.

Iona tilted her head, listening. 'What's that?' She turned to Monty. 'Is that you?'

He nodded, a faint smile playing on his lips. The song stopped.

'I thought I was imagining it and it was some mysterious song coming from the sea. What's the tune?'

'I'm not actually sure. I think it's a song my dad used to sing, something about the Hebrides. Or maybe I just made it up. Either way, it seems to fit.'

'Yeah, it does.' She gave him a little frown. 'So, you're a composer and a singer as well as a banker.'

He tilted his head and threw her a look. 'When you say banker like that, it really doesn't sound nice.'

She tossed back her head and laughed. 'Sorry. I didn't mean it like that.'

'Hmm. Not this time, huh?'

'You read my mind.'

He shook his head and narrowed his eyes, but he couldn't completely rid his face of the smile, and Iona knew he wasn't angry. 'But I'm not a singer or a composer...' He raised his eyebrow as he caught her eye. 'So, yes, just a banker.'

'Well, I can't comment on your banking skills, but your music is lovely.'

'Really? I guess I enjoy it. I don't have any special talent or anything.'

'Not sure that's true.' She sipped some of her hot chocolate. 'It had a kind of haunting sound, but it seemed like it was coming out of the sea. Weird.'

'Yeah. That's why it came to me.'

'Sing it again, if you like. I enjoyed it.'

He stared forward, and she assumed he didn't want to, as he was silent. But as she took another sip of her hot chocolate, the song started again, a little melancholic but alluring. It tugged at her insides, calling to her, stirring her soul. Her eyelids dropped, and she saw inside her mind images of forgotten days, harsh times, dangerous weather, all wrapped in island spirit.

The song trailed off, and she opened her eyes to see Monty gazing at the horizon.

'You know...' He blinked and looked at his feet. 'I didn't really believe in this island until I came here. Obviously, I knew it existed, but I didn't get what the fuss was about. I wish now I'd listened more carefully to my father's stories.' He glanced at her. 'I'm aware how much you hate incomers with crazy genealogy stories, but I do genuinely feel somehow attached to this place.'

Iona turned to face him. 'I'm an incomer myself, though I've been here a couple of years now. Your story might be true. I just object to tourists who come here thinking they have some claim to the island and believing that claim gives them the right to act as they please with no respect for the people who live here. And when they insist on their ideas being fact it annoys me – especially when it's something that they're telling others about without giving the island a chance to be heard or to defend itself. I guess that all sounds crazy, but I know what I mean.'

'No, I get it.' Monty took a deep breath. 'You want the island to be known for its authenticity, not the stories people make up – especially ones with little basis in fact.'

'Yeah.' She nodded. 'Nicely put. What was your father's story?'

'I can't even fully remember. According to him, our branch of the MacNeils was descended from the illegitimate son of one of the Mac-Neils of Kisimul. He believed we were diddled out of Kisimul Castle because the chief was persuaded not to wed the woman for political reasons. So she and her child were never officially recognised. He reckoned our ancestors were the rightful heirs. It was a big point of pride and frustration for him.'

'That's quite a story.' Iona didn't like to mention she'd heard many like it before. 'I think Catriona's mum mentioned talking to a visitor about that before. Do you believe it?'

He shrugged, a half-smile on his lips. 'It's a family legend, but there's no way of knowing if it's true or not.'

'Exactly.' She glanced up at him. Had he read her mind?

'It happened too long ago, and records weren't well kept, or even wholly accurate. Evidence was easily covered up with money. My dad was always so passionate about it. He'd go on about how we should reclaim our heritage, our rightful place.'

'And now you're doing it.'

'Not really. I mean, I love what I've seen of the island already, but I'm not planning on storming Kisimul Castle or anything so ridiculous.' Monty tapped his finger on his mug. 'I wish I'd listened to what my father had told me and that we could have come here together. Maybe I should speak to Catriona's mum.'

'She sometimes has good days. You could ask Catriona. And at least you came.' Iona looked out at the sea. 'Not everyone would have. Or they might have come, scattered the ashes and gone again. You've at least given yourself time to get to know the island.'

'I suppose. My father would probably have been one of the tourists you didn't like. He'd have expected you to serve him as clan chief MacNeil.'

'Are you serious?'

Monty laughed. 'No. But he would probably have tried to make you believe his version of the truth.'

'And you're not going to do that?'

'I wouldn't dare.' Monty downed his hot chocolate, then raised an eyebrow at her.

Iona grinned, shivering a little. The wind had picked up and was gusting hard. Her hot chocolate was finished, and she wasn't in particularly warm clothes. Her thin t-shirt and jeans would have been fine if the sun had stayed, but it had vanished completely.

Monty let out a sigh, staring ahead again. Iona narrowed her eyes, trying to work him out. He seemed like a different person to the one who'd knocked her off her bike just a few days ago. Maybe she'd just got to know him a bit better. Funny how she'd got so pissed off at him being a crazy tourist, when really, he possibly had more claim to the island than her. Maybe even island blood. *She* couldn't claim that. Her reasons for being here were all to do with her incompetence. She couldn't hack city life and she didn't intend to try ever again.

But randomly, they'd both been pulled to Barra, then thrown together. Was it mere coincidence? Or one of those predestined moments the universe had in store for them? If they were meant to meet, then why? She sneaked another glance at him. Were they meant to help each other? Or was it one way? Was this his party, and she was just here to help him with the ashes?

The wind picked up, tugging at the rug, and half of it lifted, flapping over Monty.

'I'm being attacked.' He tugged at it, but the wind was persistent. It caught Iona's side too, engulfing her, and she squealed, closing her eyes as sand blew around her.

She grabbed the edge of the rug and pulled it over her head like a hood, anchoring it to shield herself from the sandstorm. Monty did the same and suddenly they were very close, wrapped tightly together. A rush of warmth surged through her, not just from the rug, but from the touch as her bare arm rubbed against his. He was radiating heat and her insides ached for it to infuse her with energy. Her tummy clenched and a lower tingle burned her deep. She glanced at him, their faces now inches apart. 'Keeps the wind off our backs, I guess.'

He turned a little and stared at her, his gaze shifting from her eyes to her lips, sending an electric current zipping through her. She returned the favour, first taking in his amber irises, glowing behind his glasses, then dropping her focus to his lips. They looked soft and had a hint of stubble around them that hadn't been there when they first met. The rugged island was having an effect on him.

'Do you enjoy sitting out on beaches in bracing winds with strange men?' Monty asked, his voice low.

'Are you a strange man?' Iona smiled. 'If you are, you said it, not me. And yeah, I quite like sitting out in any weather here. Even when it's wild, I like it. Makes me feel alive.'

'Suits you.'

'What being alive?'

He rolled his eyes. 'Being wild.'

'Am I wild?'

'As wild as I'm strange,' he said.

'Very wild then.'

He huffed out a little laugh.

A few drops of rain started to fall, splattering on the sand and the rug. Monty glanced away from Iona and peered heavenward. 'Do you think we should go?'

Iona shook her head. 'Not unless you especially want to. I actually enjoy the rain on the beach. It's kind of... soothing.'

'I guess.' He stared out to sea and started to gently hum again. Iona felt like a sleepy snake being charmed out of its basket. The rain fell around them in a gentle patter on the sand, blending with the sound of the waves, and Monty's singing. When she awoke fully, she'd strike, but not in anger. No. That wasn't what her insides were burning for. She desired to wrap herself around him and place her lips on his. Where were these thoughts coming from? She wasn't even sure. She'd had her share of hookups with guys who came to the surf school, but not guys like Monty. And even if she wanted to – which if she was honest, she probably did – she knew he wouldn't.

He wanted to get back with his ex. He'd told her so.

'What's your ex's name?' she asked.

'What?' Monty stopped singing and turned to face her.

'The woman you want to get back together with. What's her name?'

'Sophie.'

'And she's adventurous, is she?'

'She's definitely more outgoing than me.'

Iona weighed up his words with a little sway of her head. 'And did you and Sophie ever go bodyboarding or swim in the sea?'

'No. She liked beaches but only in hot places and for sunbathing on.'

Iona raised an eyebrow. 'Nothing else?'

'Meaning what?'

'Well, did she enjoy, you know...'

'On the beach? Are you serious? The kind of beaches she liked usually had several hundred other people on them. She didn't do anything like what you're thinking... And neither would I.'

Iona giggled at the indignant look on his face. 'So, you never even kissed on the beach?'

'I...' Monty frowned and rubbed his forehead. 'I don't think so. Why are you asking me stuff like this?'

'I'm curious. And you've missed out.'

'Have I?'

'Sure you have. Everyone knows kissing on a beach is very romantic...'

'Yeah, well... I'm not very romantic.'

'Yesterday, you weren't very adventurous but look at you now. Perhaps you should try kissing on a beach in the rain. That's romantic and adventurous.'

'When you say I should try it, do you mean now... As in, with you?'

'God no.' She flicked her jeans as though it was the most abhorrent idea ever. But that was a lie.

'Good. Glad we cleared that up.'

'But actually, maybe you should.'

'What?' He drew back a little and pulled a face.

'For practise – in adventure and romance. We could look at it as an extension of the bodyboard lesson.'

'What? Are you mad?'

She shook her head. 'A bit. But just trying to help.'

'I don't see how that could possibly help me. Sophie dumped me because she thinks I'm boring. What if everything I do is boring...? I'm not risking some random kiss as practise, not if there's even half a chance you'll go back and tell the world what a crap kisser that Monty is.'

'This isn't school. I wouldn't do that. If you're worried about being a crap kisser, then you should definitely kiss me, and I'll tell you what I think.'

'You really are crazy.' He picked up a piece of driftwood and tossed it across the sand.

'Yeah. I know. Sorry. I don't know what came over me.' *Fucking lust.* How cringe could she get. She'd never had to work so hard for a kiss before and this with a guy she didn't even fancy.

Did she fancy him?

No. She mustn't.

'What if I *am* really bad?' He swallowed. 'Just say I agreed, and we did... If you say it's boring, then what the hell will I do?'

'Practise?'

'Are you serious?'

'It's the only way to get better at anything.'

They looked at each other for what seemed like a very long time and she was caught in his gaze, unable to look away, even though it was burning into her.

'Well... ok, then. Let's do it.'

Now her heart was pounding a little faster than she expected. This was what she craved in some ways, but a bundle of nerves she wasn't used to were tingling around her tummy. She leaned in. Monty hesitated, then closed the gap between them. His lips pressed against her in a tentative, thoughtful kiss. His touch was gentle, almost too gentle, like he was afraid of breaking her. Her nerve ends sprang to life. This was a teaser. Nice, but not enough.

Monty pulled back before it had barely started, his eyes searching hers. 'Well, was it boring?'

'No.' Iona shook her head. 'But I can tell you're holding back.'

'Of course I'm holding back. I hardly know you.'

'Then pretend that you do. Pretend I'm Sophie...'

He shook his head. 'But you're nothing like her.'

'Use your imagination. Or close your eyes.'

'I'm not sure that'll work.'

'It will... You'll see. Be intuitive. Like you were with the waves.'

He tilted his head, his eyelids falling and Iona leaned in to meet him. When their lips met, the pressure was firmer. His hands found her waist, pulling her closer. She responded, slipping her hand around his jaw. Sparks ignited inside her and she opened her mouth, eager for more. Their tongues touched and they both let out a moan and at the same time. Monty moved like he was about to pull back, but Iona clutched his cheek, holding him close, deepening the kiss. When he returned it, Iona smiled into it, which only heightened the pleasure in her nerve ends. The raw impulses inside her were shouting; she wanted to be touched.

But Monty wasn't kissing her. He was kissing an imaginary Sophie. This was how much he wanted her back.

When they finally broke apart, Iona was breathless, her cheeks were too warm and her breasts felt heavy, almost painful.

Monty eyed her, his brow a little furrowed. 'How was that?' His voice was hoarse.

'Good... Very good... and definitely not boring.'

'Um... right... Well, that's something then.' He glanced out to sea again. 'Should we... go back?'

'Probably should, yeah.'

'Can you...' He looked at her, though his gaze was a little shifty and unfocused. 'Well, not mention that kiss to anyone.'

'Of course. My lips are sealed.' She mimed zipping them shut, but really they didn't want to be shut. They wanted to be busy elsewhere, continuing what they'd just started, but she had to be sensible. Something she'd never been very good at.

Chapter Thirteen

Monty

Monty woke up to the pale morning light filtering through the thin white curtains in the annex. He'd been sleeping fairly well since he got to the island, and it was hard to wake up. The sea air was working wonders – such a luxury not having to get up for work. The week was passing too quickly though, and his time here would end before he knew it and he'd be back doing nine till five.

Ah well, such was life.

He rubbed at the corner of his eye, then reached for his glasses and his phone on the nightstand. Still lying in bed, he started swiping through his photos from the day before. Stunning beaches, rugged hills, and a few selfies flipped past. *Damn it.* He'd forgotten to get photos of the bodyboarding. He'd been so fixated on doing it, he hadn't thought to make a record of it. Would there be another chance? Part of him hoped so, but another part wanted to say he'd done it now and be done with.

He frowned. He'd heard about a water sports festival coming up. It hadn't been something that much interested him, and he had no desire to take part, but... Well, something about it lodged in his mind. What did a water sports festival entail? He wasn't sure he really wanted to examine his thoughts on the matter, so he parked it.

What he wanted to see right now was whether or not Sophie had made any comment on his social media post about scattering his father's ashes. He opened the page and scrolled to the post. *Nope.* Not even a like. Other people had commented, sending love and condolences. He liked and replied to the comments, before heading to Sophie's page. More photos had appeared of her out at a street bar with friends, including some men. Was she dating? Of course she was at perfect liberty to do so. They'd split up after all, but his stomach twisted at the thought. Still, it was fine. Once he got back, he'd be in a better place, and she might be too. Maybe she'd discover these other guys were even more 'boring'.

Was that likely? He pulled a face, his mind supplying an answer that he didn't want to hear.

How would it be if he posted some of his own photos and at least mention the bodyboarding? Maybe that would attract her attention. He selected a few of the best beach shots and a selfie with the ocean in the background. His fingers hovered over the keyboard before typing out a comment.

Tried bodyboarding for the first time yesterday. Amazing experience.

He hit post. Would Sophie even see it? Maybe she never looked at his page or maybe she'd snoozed it from her feed. Anything was possible, but he crossed his fingers. *Please see this.* He was desperate to know what she'd make of him being adventurous. Speaking of which... His fingers tapped at the screen, putting in the name Iona McKenzie. A few results came up but only one caught his eye. A tanned beauty in a bikini with long brown wavy hair spilling over her shoulder. She leaned on a surfboard, beaming back at him. Wow, she was hot. He always saw her looking a bit thrown together in casual clothes or a wetsuit, but this. He took a long, slow breath and blew it out like a whistle before opening the page.

His fingers swiped through the pictures that were public, mostly shots of her surfing, laughing with friends, and the occasional stunning sunset, and his mind drifted back to their kiss the previous day. Why had he done it?

Research?

That was all, yes?

And practise.

When he finally got Sophie back, he'd be better equipped for romance and adventure. But the taste of Iona's lips, the spark, the way she felt in his arms, lingered much longer than he wanted. So long he forgot what he'd been looking at or thinking about before.

It was just a kiss. I was pretending she was Sophie.

But even as he thought it, he sensed a lie. The kiss had felt a bit too real, stirring something inside him he hadn't expected. Shaking his head, he locked his phone and placed it back on the nightstand. He rubbed at his face, trying to push away the mess. Would Sophie be annoyed he'd kissed Iona?

'Stop,' he muttered to himself. They'd split up. She wouldn't care. She'd moved on, which was something Monty wasn't good at. Maybe he should try harder. Even if it was just temporarily. This was the time to get new experiences. Then, when the time was right, he could try again.

After breakfast, Monty pulled on a sweater and stepped into the courtyard. The prospect of a day on his own felt a bit flat after the fun he'd had with Iona, which was totally stupid. It wasn't like they were close friends. Just random acquaintances... who'd happened to have shared a kiss. She was teaching paddleboarding today, according to Catriona, when he seen her at breakfast. Monty had also asked her about the water sports festival, and Catriona confirmed it was this Saturday and Sunday, just a couple of days away. That would be the middle of his fortnight and would mark the downward turn of his holiday. He was just getting to know the place too.

Shit. He froze halfway across the yard on the way back to the annex. Iona obviously hadn't left to teach the lessons yet. She was near an outbuilding, talking to Ruaridh. Her voice carried on the breeze. The memory of their kiss flared up, making Monty's chest hurt. Why had he agreed to something so stupid?

He needed to avoid her for now. He couldn't face the aftermath of what had happened or analyse why his body reacted strangely every time he saw her. He turned and nearly bumped into Alexander.

'Morning,' Monty said.

'Morning.' Alexander gave him a brief smile. He was a serious-looking guy, kind of moody and brooding, but he always said hello. Monty had seen him playing outside with the little girl he assumed was Catriona's daughter. From what he could gather, Alexander wasn't the father.

Scamp, the dog, leapt on Monty and tried to jump up and lick his face.

'Down,' Alexander said. 'Sorry about that.'

'It's ok.' Monty patted Scamp whose tongue lolled out.

'I hear you're a banker,' Alexander said. Monty winced at the turn of phrase. Had Iona told him to say that?

'That's one name for it. More specifically, I'm a commercial banker, which probably makes it sound even worse.'

Alexander smirked. 'I'm not meaning to be rude. Just curious. In fact, if you're a commercial banker, that's even better. Maybe you could have a chat with Catriona about her diversification plans.'

'I think I put my foot in it the other day by suggesting glamping pods.'

'No, she loved the idea. But she's not sure how to go about it all.' He glanced around. 'She's a hard worker, and she's got some good ideas, but she can't do everything. She thinks she can, and she doesn't like admitting she needs help, but sometimes she does. If you were to give her professional advice, she'd take it better from you than she would from me. She reckons I interfere too much or think she's incompetent – which I don't at all. I think it's incredible what someone so young has done here, but she can't do it all alone.'

'Well, I'll try, but only if it comes into conversation naturally. If I bring it up, it'll look rather suspicious.'

'That's true,' Alexander agreed, then lowered his voice. 'Also, between you and me, I'm not sure Iona's managing that well either. She's a bit of a flake, doesn't really know how to run a business properly. She's enthusiastic, I'll give her that, but enthusiasm only gets you so far.'

Monty glanced back towards Iona, who was still deep in conversation with Ruaridh. When Monty had seen the container yesterday, it seemed well set up, as far as he could tell anyway, but he remembered the issues she had with people cancelling. Not that it was her fault, but maybe something in the setup wasn't working. 'I'm not a business advisor as such, and I'm not sure Iona would want me butting in with unsolicited advice.'

'Yeah, you're so right.' Alexander clapped him on the shoulder. 'And you're on holiday. I shouldn't be pestering you at all. I just want things to work well for them.'

'Well, if the opportunity arises—'

'Alexander,' Catriona said from behind them. Monty spun around, a guilty heat rising in his cheeks. Seriously? Why did he feel like a naughty little schoolboy doing something he shouldn't?

'Yeah?' Alex ran his hand through his hair as he faced Catriona.

'Can you take the jeep into the village and get the supplies from the shop?'

'Yeah, sure.' He glanced back at Monty. 'I should get on. We were just chatting about the glamping pods. Monty knows a thing or two about business. You should put your heads together.' With a little smile and a wave, he left them.

Catriona folded her arms and watched him with narrowed eyes.

'I... um... wouldn't want to speak out of turn,' Monty said.

'It's fine. I'm happy to do all this stuff, but I don't have time to take long boat rides to the mainland to meet financial advisors or wait for ages on a call to be connected. My life is too busy for that.'

'Well, I'm happy to give you a few pointers. Not now, necessarily. Just when you have a minute.'

'I don't want to waste your holiday. But if you did, I'd be happy to pay you with free breakfasts or dinners.'

He smiled. 'Best deal I've ever made by the sound of it.'

'Perhaps you'd be free this evening. After I've sorted the meals and got Eilidh settled.'

'Sure. No problem. Is it still ok for me to borrow a car today?'

'Yes. I'll just get the keys.' Catriona headed inside. She'd suggested he took her car and explored the other end of the island, and that wasn't a bad idea. If he'd thought he could survive a four-and-a-half-hour ferry trip, he'd have brought his own car, but his relationship with water and boats meant that was a no-no. Now he knew the size of the island however, he realised he needed transport – and the bike still had the puncture.

Iona and Ruaridh had disappeared, presumably to go to work. Monty wasn't sure what Ruaridh did, or where he lived. He seemed to be around quite a bit though. And he definitely looked like he enjoyed Iona's company, despite what he might say.

Catriona returned with the keys and led him to a small Vauxhall. It was about fifteen years old but seemed in good shape.

'It's an easy car to drive. If you want to get in and check you can find everything.'

Monty got in. It was tiny compared to his car and a little clunky. He'd got so used to an electronic dashboard. These big chunky buttons were confusing at first, but he'd soon get the hang of it. He told himself that again as he pulled off less than smoothly. Driving on roads this narrow was something of a skill in itself, especially when he came upon a campervan.

He had to reverse, looking over his shoulder. Doing this without cameras and parking sensors felt like landing a plane blindfolded. He took the bends cautiously, the Vauxhall rattling over the uneven surfaces. The rugged beauty of the island stretched out around him, with rocks and sandy beaches off to the wild sea on one side and grassy hills on the other. He pulled into an open space, stepping out to take in the panorama. The fresh air filled his lungs.

'Barra, you are a truly beautiful place.' There was nowhere on earth quite like this.

Continuing his journey, he followed signs to a local gin distillery on the edge of Castlebay he'd read about in the guidebook Catriona had left in the annex. His mother liked gin, and this seemed something fitting to take back to her. Monty parked and headed inside. The moment he opened the door, he caught the rich scent of botanicals. He might enjoy something from here too.

'Hello,' a woman behind the counter said.

'Hi.' Monty smiled, looking around at the shelves lined with bottles of gin, each labelled with intricate designs and claiming to be the spirit of the Atlantic. A film showed the gin-making process, along with some stunning clips of the island being battered by storms and waves. A beautiful but scary place.

He perused the different gins before choosing a pink rhubarb and ginger one. His mum would like the bottle, if nothing else. The shape was curious, wide at the bottom and tapering into a very thin neck.

'Are you on holiday?' the woman asked as she put through the sale.

'Yes. This week and next.'

'And how are you enjoying it?'

'It's a beautiful island. I'm falling in love.'

The woman smiled. 'It has that effect on people. I know some people who came on holiday and then returned here to live.'

Monty thanked her. He was pretty certain he wouldn't be returning to live here. A holiday was great, but this was too far from his normal life to contemplate more.

As he left the distillery, the sun was high in the sky. He drove on over the causeway to Vatersay, stopping at a beach with a famous gate he'd seen lots of pictures of. After leaving the car and walking across a grassy strand, he found the gate and took his own picture. From there it was a short walk down a narrow gap in the dunes to a stunning beach that was almost deserted; golden sands glowed and turquoise waters glittered in the June sun. Monty walked along the shore, kicking off his shoes and letting the cool water wash over his feet. He picked up a few pebbles, tossing them into the waves. The place reminded him of the beach where he'd kissed Iona. The memory was vivid. So vivid.

And just look at me!

He was in the water, paddling. This was all Iona's doing.

He pulled out his phone and took a few photos. He could add these to his social media page, but why bother? He had a quick look. Sophie hadn't reacted to his post from earlier. Who knew if she'd even seen it?

Iona's face battled in his mind with Sophie's and he wasn't entirely sure which one he wanted to win, but always Iona rose to the surface. Maybe just because she was here, fresh in his mind and easier to picture.

Returning to the car, he checked the map on his phone. There was still plenty of the island to see, but his thoughts kept circling back to Iona's business. Of course he'd like to help her if she needed it, but he didn't want her to think he was stepping on her toes. Maybe she didn't want help. Not everyone was super organised in business. Being a 'flake', as Alexander had called her, was maybe just her way. She was undoubtedly spontaneous and full of energy. It could be the same for her business.

Monty stopped in Castlebay to get some food. His eyes frequently strayed to Kisimul Castle as he walked down the little street towards the shop. Dad's ashes were there now, flying free. Maybe he was in heaven having stern words with the clan chief MacNeil who'd cut their branch of the family out of their inheritance. The thought made Monty smile. He half wished Iona was down here with her boat today. Before his time was up, he fancied another trip to Kisimul. An odd feeling rippled across his shoulders like he had unfinished business there, though what it was, he wasn't sure.

Later in the afternoon, Monty returned to the farm and parked the Vauxhall in the small parking area to the side of the main house. It was too early for dinner, so he got his book from his bag and sat on a bench outside the annex. Reading to the gentle lilt of the sea and buzz of insects was the stuff of dreams, and Monty lost track of time completely.

Dinner was served in the same room as breakfast, and a few other guests sat around the table with Monty. One particularly chatty older woman talked to him for almost the whole meal. Her husband looked thrilled that she'd found someone to tell her stories to. Monty listened as he ate Catriona's delicious version of a cheese and lentil pie.

'This is our thirtieth year coming here,' the older woman said. 'We've seen so many changes.'

'I bet.'

Catriona took the plates away and served dessert. 'Are you still ok to chat later?' she said as she leaned in to hand Monty his bowl of rhubarb crumble.

'Sure am. What time?'

'Seven thirty.'

'I'll be there.'

It wasn't long to wait after dinner, so he spent some more time reading on the bench. Voices caught his attention, and he spotted Iona returning. A young man Monty didn't recognise got out of her car with her and they laughed as they approached the house. Monty ground his teeth and tried not to look. Was this someone she'd hooked up with after a paddleboarding lesson? He wasn't sure he wanted to know.

He thumped his book shut. Time to go find Catriona.

When he knocked on the kitchen door, Iona answered it, and Monty met her eyes. His insides froze. Stay calm. All he had to do was treat his interactions with her the way he would with a client.

'Hi.' He flexed his fingers. 'I'm here to see Catriona.'

Iona raised an eyebrow and folded her arms. 'Um, ok. What about?'

'Business. She's expecting me.'

'Is she now? She never mentioned it. Well, come in.' She opened the door. 'What business are you discussing?'

'Diversification and the like.'

'Why would she discuss that with you?'

'Because I'm a banker, remember? A commercial banker, in fact, and I know all about business.'

She smirked and took a swig of beer from a bottle on the table. 'Well, she's just putting Eilidh to bed. I expect she'll be down in a minute.'

'I'm here.' Catriona marched through the door. 'She always wants about ten extra cuddles on the nights she knows I'm busy. Come into the sunroom, we can sit in there. It's a bit nicer.'

Monty followed her out of the kitchen, certain Iona's eyes were following him closely.

He took a seat opposite Catriona in the small sunroom. It was a little old-fashioned, with its rattan furniture, but comfortable nonetheless.

Catriona opened a little bureau and took out a laptop. 'Do you want to see figures? Or what? I've got the account sheets.'

'It depends what your goal is. If you want to move into glamping pods, you need to write an action plan. Decide the location, check if planning consent is needed, look into suppliers, builders, etc. Everything should be costed out as accurately as possible. Try and get a timeframe fixed and written down. I can help you draft something just now if you want. Once you have all that, you can analyse how you intend to fund it.'

Catriona raised an eyebrow. 'Right. Ok. This is where my brain starts to overload. I'm good with the practical side of things, running this place, but the paperwork is where it gets messy.'

'I'm the exact opposite.' He gave her a little smile. 'Isn't there anyone else who can help you?'

'Not really. My mum has a good business head, and she used to do all this, but she's not well. She has chronic fatigue syndrome, and she spends most of her days in her cottage. Ruaridh and I go around every day and make sure she's ok, but she isn't up to doing anything like this.'

'I'm sorry to hear that.'

'Yeah, well. Our dad left when we were young, and the same thing happened with Eilidh's dad. I learned to fend for myself, but this kind of thing is so alien to me.'

'It can seem daunting, but that's where being organised can help. A solid plan will give you the backup you need.'

'Ok. And you can help me with that?'

'Definitely.' He nodded, taking off his glasses and wiping them on the bottom of his shirt. 'If you open a document, we can get started straight away. It doesn't have to be fancy or in any special format to start with.'

They worked on it together as the sun sank a little lower, shining brightly into the room even at this time of evening.

'I appreciate you taking the time out of your holiday to help,' Catriona said. 'This is so much clearer in my mind just seeing it like this.'

'No worries. I look forward to the free meals. You're a great cook.'

'Thanks.' She grinned. 'You've earned them.'

The door opened, and Iona strolled in, carrying her beer. 'Mind if I join you for a bit? My nose is bothering me.'

'Maybe you have hay fever,' Monty said.

'I meant metaphorically. As in, I want to know what you're up to.'

He smirked because he knew fine what she meant.

'We're nearly done,' Catriona said. 'It's nothing that would interest you. I didn't think you were sold on the idea of glamping pods.'

She gave a little shrug. 'Wasn't I?'

'I think you disliked the idea on principle,' Monty said. 'Because I suggested it.'

Iona sipped her beer, but it looked like she was trying to stop a laugh. 'Maybe.' She sat next to him, and he caught the scent of a very Iona-ish perfume. Something with sweet high notes and the undertone of sea air. It was perfect for her and sent a charge through him. He held his breath. *Do not let her affect you.* Why *did* she affect him? What was it about her?

'I just remembered,' he said. 'I was supposed to pay you for the trip to Kisimul Castle. But you never said how much.'

'I'll think about my price and let you know.' She winked at him. 'I'm sure a banker has money to toss around.'

He folded his arms. 'I'm sure I don't.'

'You know what?' Catriona said to Iona. 'You should talk to Monty about business too. I'm sure he'd have good ideas for you.'

'My business is just fine,' Iona said.

'You're always moaning about it.' Catriona closed the lid of her laptop.

'Only because people keep cancelling on me last minute.'

'Maybe you need a more robust cancellation plan,' Monty suggested.

'Maybe you need to keep your mouth shut until I ask for your help.'

Bristly Iona was back, and he wasn't surprised. This was exactly how he'd expected her to react, and she had a point. None of it was his business. He held up his hands, but the way she was eyeing him looked more inquisitive than angry.

'Iona, really!' Catriona gave her a pointed look. 'Remember that thing we talked about? Being nice to the guests and all that.'

'I doubt that works for me,' Monty said.

Iona watched him closely and his breath caught again. 'You're right. It doesn't.'

Catriona stood up and put the laptop away in the bureau. 'Well, at least try.' She shut the bureau with a sharp click. 'Thank you, Monty. I appreciated that.'

'You're welcome.' He got to his feet, not looking at Iona. 'I look forward to seeing how everything turns out. Maybe I'll come back in a few years and stay in a glamping pod.'

'Sounds right up Sophie's alley.' Iona sipped more beer, not meeting his eye.

'Indeed. Well, goodnight.' He shook Catriona's hand, and she smiled at him.

'Night. See you tomorrow.'

Before he left, he gave Iona a brief glance. She wasn't looking at him, but staring fixedly ahead. Maybe just as well. Obviously, their kiss had done nothing except return her to her previously grumpy mood. What did it matter? It wasn't like she was someone he was going to have anything to do with in just over a week's time. But try as he might, he couldn't get her out of his head. And no matter how often he reminded himself her opinion was of no consequence to him, he still felt a little nauseous. Thoughts that she was going about telling everyone what a terrible kisser he was swirled around his head so fast he felt dizzy. After sleeping so well previously, it took a long time for him to nod off that night.

Chapter Fourteen

Iona

Iona trudged up the hill behind An Grianan, Scamp bounding ahead of her. When she'd set off twenty minutes ago, the sun was peeking through light clouds, and she'd dressed in a vest and shorts, figuring it would stay nice and she could put in a quick run before getting to the piles of admin she had waiting for her. The fact that admin was partially the reason she was up here and not back at the house on her laptop was by the by. Any excuse not to do it... though sadly it didn't make the work go away. Dark clouds had gathered, and a few drops of rain splattered on her skin.

'Scamp!' she called, but the dog was already sniffing at something in the grass, oblivious to the impending downpour. She quickened her pace, hoping to make it back to the farm before the rain really set in, but it was too late. The sky opened up, and rain started battering her like someone had upended a bag of tiny pebbles over her head.

'Bloody hell,' she muttered, peeling her vest from her tummy, now plastered against her like a second, soggy skin. Scamp's ears drooped as his head poked out of the bracken.

Iona scanned the hillside and spotted a large rocky area with an overhang a little further down. Breaking into a jog, she made for the rocks,

Scamp following close behind. By the time she reached the shelter, she was soaked, water running in rivulets down her face and arms.

Under the overhang, she leaned against the cool stone, wiping water from her cheeks and forehead. Scamp shook himself vigorously, spraying her with more water. 'Thanks, Scamp. Just what I needed.'

She squinted out at the rain, falling in a relentless curtain. The farm below was barely visible through the haze. 'Typical island weather.' It would probably be sunny again in ten minutes.

Scamp settled beside her, resting his head on his paws. Iona leaned down and rubbed his ears. The rain hammered against the overhang and dripped off the edge. She kept herself tight against the rock, but a sudden gust of wind sent the rain almost horizontal. Holding up her arms to shield her face, she shivered. This was horrible. Maybe she should just make a run for it. She was soaked anyway.

She could embrace it, step out and throw her hands high, welcoming the force of nature. It would be more fun than hanging about here. Scamp suddenly perked up like he'd read her mind. He darted out into the downpour, but instead of going towards the farm, he was heading back up the hill.

'Scamp, come back! This way.' Her voice was all but drowned by the sound of the rain. Scamp was already bounding up the hill, his tail wagging furiously. Iona squinted through the sheets of rain. Someone was running down the hill, and Scamp was jumping around the figure. Was it Ruaridh? He was always out running, rain or shine. But no, he'd already left for work. It must be one of the other guests. Maybe Shaun, the bloke she'd come back with last night. He'd definitely seemed the running type. In fact, usually he'd be her type for everything, but she wasn't in the mood. He'd got a bit grumpy with her the night before when she'd refused him and she'd taken out her bad mood on Monty. Honestly, why couldn't men handle the word no?

As the runner got closer, she realised it wasn't Shaun.

It was Monty himself.

He was clad in running shorts and a t-shirt and was soaked through.

'Over here!' Iona shouted, waving at him.

Monty fought his way over, with Scamp jumping around him. He hesitated, taking off his completely rain-obscured glasses and fruitlessly wiping them on his soaked top. He put them back on and stepped under the shelter.

'What are you doing out here in this?' he asked.

'Same as you by the look of things.' She rubbed more water from her face.

He peered around the makeshift shelter. 'Interesting place you've found here.'

'I thought it would be better than trying to get all the way back, but it probably won't make any difference. My feet are utterly swimming. Feels more like I've been surfing than running.' She watched as he flapped his soaked t-shirt. His muscles moved under the fabric. Ok, that was surprising. They were more defined than she'd expected. She looked away quickly.

'Yeah, might be better to make a break for it.' He scanned around. 'I think it's easing a little.'

'It is.'

Monty leaned back against the rock and sighed, then slowly lowered his gaze to meet hers. 'Is this where you lure unsuspecting men to kiss you in the rain?'

She folded her arms and cast him a look. 'Is that supposed to be funny?'

He huffed out a laugh. 'Not really.'

Maybe it had been his attempt at a joke. Laughing at their predicament seemed better than crying about it. 'Well, if we're going to be around for a bit, maybe we could—'

Monty turned to her, his eyes meeting hers with an intensity that made her breath catch.

'No.' He shook his head. 'I don't think so.'

Iona opened her mouth to reply but stopped herself. That wasn't what she was going to say, but he'd said no and she knew to her cost how irritating it was when someone reacted badly to that word. 'I wasn't even going to say that.' She looked away. 'And I won't be kissing you again unless you beg me,' she mumbled.

'Right.'

She clenched her jaw, not sure what was making her so grumpy. There was just something about him, and it made her say gruff stuff when she actually wanted to say the opposite. When they'd been boarding together and out on the boat, it had been fine... Then she'd kissed him, and everything had got weird. She didn't seem able to think straight when she was around him.

The rain subsided, the sky lightening just enough to reveal the wet and very green landscape glistening with raindrops like gems. Iona shook out her hair and stepped out from under the rocky overhang, shivering as the cool air hit her soaked skin. Monty followed, Scamp darting ahead, his fur drenched but his energy undampened.

They started walking back down the hill, the wet grass squelching under their shoes.

'Listen, about that kiss. It was obviously a sore spot,' she said. 'I was only doing it to help you and now you're mad at me.'

'I'm not mad at you.' Monty looked at her and raised an eyebrow. 'If anyone's getting angry about it, it's you. You're the one who's been grumpy with me ever since.'

And wasn't that the truth? 'Yeah... Well...'

He sighed, running a hand through his wet hair. 'Really, we should just forget about it.'

'I already have,' she lied.

'Yeah... Me too.' He looked as unconvinced as she felt. 'Because at the end of the day, what are we to each other? Nothing.'

'Precisely.'

'So we can drop all the grumpy stuff, yeah?'

'I am *not* grumpy!' She glared at him, then let out a little laugh. 'Sorry.'

'Uh-huh.' He raised an eyebrow.

'I just... Ah, never mind.' There was no point in trying to explain or making excuses. It was frustrating enough figuring out what was going on in her head at the best of times, but recently, it had got downright impossible. She kept walking, her shoulders stiff, not sure what else to say. How could she trust herself not to put her big foot in it yet again?

'Who was the man you came back with yesterday?' he asked.

'Why do you care?'

'I don't,' he said.

'Why ask then? Are you judging me?'

'No. Just curious.'

'He was someone who joined the surf class. He happened to be staying at the B&B, so we came back together.' Maybe even this time last week she might have fancied a hookup with him, but something had changed. 'I mean, we shared a car home. That's all.' Why did she feel the need to clarify?

'I got what you meant.'

'So no need to think whatever you're thinking.'

'I wasn't.' He held up his hands. 'I was just curious. I thought maybe he was a boyfriend or something.'

'I don't do boyfriends. And do you really think I would have kissed you if I had a boyfriend?'

'No, I suppose not. Sorry.'

'Yeah. You should be.'

They walked in silence a bit more, the only sound their squelching footsteps, the distant call of seabirds and Iona's teeth grinding.

Scamp ran ahead and was almost back at the farm.

'Listen, I hope we can be ok,' Monty said.

'Well, sure. Because like you said, what are we at the end of the day anyway?'

'Indeed.'

As they reached the farm, a wave of cold and nausea churned inside her. She glanced at Monty, who gave her a brief nod before heading towards the annex. Scamp bounded after him, leaving Iona standing alone.

She hurried inside, shivering as the warmth of the farmhouse hit her. In her room, she peeled off her soaked clothes and wrapped herself in a towel, ready for a hot shower. She knew so little about Monty, and yet here she was, acting like an idiot around him. Why did he get under her skin so much?

———————❤———————

'Iona, you look like a drowned rat.' Catriona came into the kitchen a little while later as Iona was boiling the kettle. 'You haven't been surfing, have you?'

'I got caught in the rain,' Iona muttered. 'It was nothing.'

'Well, get yourself dry and warm. You've got a lot to do still for the water sports festival. I met Mark in the village, and he said you hadn't replied to his emails for ages.'

'I know, I know,' Iona snapped, then cringed. 'Sorry, I'm just... not in the best mood.'

'What's up?'

'Nothing. I'm fine. Just need to get on with stuff.' She went into the sunroom and got out her laptop. She hated this bit. Procrastination followed her around like a puppy whenever she needed to do admin. And she had so much to do – organising the water sports competition, finalising schedules, coordinating with vendors – but her ADHD brain was refusing to cooperate as it so often did.

She stared at the laptop, the cursor blinking back at her like it had a nervous tick. A to-do list was stuck on a post-it on the keyboard. Should she prioritise that stuff? And what did Mark want? *Oh shit.* He was supplying food for the barbecue, and she hadn't got back to him. This was turning into another Iona shitshow. She also needed to send out reminder emails, arrange the logistics for the surf gear, and touch base with the sponsors. But instead, she found herself scrolling through social media. *Fuck's sake.*

'Get it together,' she muttered to herself, rubbing her temples. The frustration was building, but she couldn't seem to channel it into productivity. Her mind kept wanting to return to Monty and when it did, she cringed, replaying their conversations and wanting to rewind them and start again. She must look like a total idiot.

With a heavy sigh, she threw back her head, trying to push Monty out of her thoughts. A knock at the door made her jump.

Catriona poked her head around. 'Are you sure you're ok? You don't seem yourself.' Catriona sat down opposite her. 'Do you need a hand with anything?'

'Maybe, but I'm fine. I've got a lot on my mind with the festival, that's all.' Iona avoided eye contact.

'What can I do to help?'

'Maybe help me reply to some of these emails. I could log you in on the other laptop.'

'Ok. I can do that.' Catriona raised an eyebrow as she got up to fetch her laptop. 'Is it just the festival that's bothering you, or is it something – or someone – else?'

'What do you mean?' Iona directed her focus back to the screen.

'I thought the guy who checked in yesterday was being a bit annoying.'

'Oh, yeah... He was a bit, but I sent him off.'

'I know you did, and that kind of surprises me too. He seemed right up your street.'

'I'm just not in the mood.'

'No?' Catriona's sharp eyes were boring into her. 'I thought maybe our guest in the annex had caught your attention.'

'What? No. Absolutely not.' Iona hammered the mouse to open her emails. 'That's ridiculous. Why on earth would you think that?'

Catriona put her laptop on the table. 'No reason. But why not? He's a nice guy.'

Iona opened her mouth to argue, but shut it again. She didn't want to protest and make herself look even more guilty. 'So what if he is? He's just another guest. Nothing special.' And she had to make herself believe that, though she'd probably take a lot more convincing than Catriona.

Catriona shrugged. 'If you say so. Now, help me get into the emails.'

Iona pulled her laptop over and logged in. As always, when someone else was there to 'hold her hand' she worked a lot better, but Catriona was already so busy, and guilt mites nibbled Iona's tummy at stealing her away just because she couldn't focus. Catriona's questions had also stirred more confusion inside her. What exactly did she feel about Monty? Because he *was* just another guest... Not that it would be the first time she'd hooked up with a guest, but she didn't want to hook up with him. Not really. Somehow, that didn't seem right. She shook her head, trying to push the thoughts away. There was no time for this. She had work to do.

But as she stared down at her laptop, she couldn't help but wonder: what was it about Monty that had got under her skin? And why did she care so much?

Chapter Fifteen

Monty

Monty made his way from the annex to the farmhouse, picking a path over the soaked yard in his boots; big puddles had collected in the uneven ground. His skin chafed a bit as he hadn't bothered to put on socks after showering. He knocked on the door and waited, ignoring the discomfort on the soles of his feet. So much for a nice early morning run. What had it achieved? If it was helping him to stay fit, then that was about the only positive, because as well as getting soaked, he now had sore feet, and he'd upset Iona. Again. He really had a bad habit of doing that – but she had a very annoying habit of getting grumpy with him. And he didn't really get why. What had he done wrong? Or did he just have a face that annoyed her?

He'd been on many holidays in his life and normally didn't meet local people other than those who served him in shops or restaurants, but the folk here had really got under his skin. Especially Iona. Her being cross bothered him... In fact, everything about her bothered him more than it should.

'Hi.' Catriona opened the door and gave him a quizzical look. No doubt he looked a fright. He hadn't dried his hair after the shower and had just thrown on a t-shirt and sweatpants. 'Are you ok?'

'Not exactly.' He mussed up his wet hair. 'I can't seem to get the radiator in the annex working. I need to dry out my trainers and running shorts. I've been fiddling about with the controls, but nothing is happening. Am I missing something?'

'Maybe the main power isn't switched on. Sometimes guests switch it off if they can't work out how to turn off the radiators. I usually check, but I can't remember if I did this time,' Catriona said, leading the way. 'It's not the easiest system to work out. We tend to leave them on all winter and turn them off in the summer but obviously on a day like this, you need to dry stuff, and warm up.'

'Yeah. I might need my trainers again soon.'

'Absolutely.'

'Um... Have you seen Iona recently?'

'Yeah, she's in the house, working. I was just with her. Why?'

'I hope I didn't upset her this morning.' Monty opened the door to the annex.

Catriona gave him a sideways glance. 'Why would you have?'

'I don't know. I just seem to have a way of doing that, even though I don't mean to.'

'Don't worry about it. She's just got a lot on her plate right now with the festival and she's easily stressed.' Catriona shook her head. 'I think doing office work is a trigger for her. It reminds her of her old job that she hated. She ends up procrastinating and leaving everything to the last minute. Then she gets angry. Don't take it personally.'

Monty nodded; Catriona was such a sensible soul for someone so young. 'Ok.' If it wasn't personal, then good, but still, why had he asked her about the man she'd come back with? That was a stupid move if ever there was one. Why did he even care? But he did, and he hadn't been able to stop himself from asking. Why? Oh, why? She'd got well and truly lodged under his skin and he couldn't get her out.

Catriona opened a little box on the wall and pressed some buttons. 'That should do it. The radiators should start to come on straight away.'

'Thanks, I appreciate that.' Monty placed his trainers by the radiator.

'No problem.' Catriona headed for the door. 'If it's not warm enough in here for you, feel free to come into the main house. The breakfast room is free.'

'Thanks. If the weather holds, I might head out for a bit.' He peered out of the window. 'Do you think I could speak to Iona? I feel bad, but I don't want to disturb her.'

He did want to ask her something though. Something that had been growing on him more and more. He really wanted to go back to Kisimul Castle at least once before his time was up.

'Well, it might be best not to disturb her, but I can ask her if you like.'

'Yes, please. I'll come over with you and if she says no, I'll go away.'

'Ok, fair enough.' Catriona marched back to the farmhouse. 'Poor Iona. She's a free spirit who doesn't like being tied to a desk. Normally, she's off chasing waves, riding her bike, or having fun... in other ways.'

'Hmm. Yeah.' Monty cleared his throat, not sure exactly what Catriona meant. Did she mean having flings?

'Right. If you just wait two minutes, I'll ask her if she can spare you a sec.'

Monty thrust his hands into his pockets and looked at the paintings along the wall of the hallway depicting island scenes, all turquoise waves and white beaches. His mind wandered along a beach much like one of them, landing him back to the other evening when he'd kissed Iona. Why had he done that? That was when her bad mood had restarted. What a stupid thing to do. Maybe he was playing with fire now in even wanting to speak to her again.

Catriona poked her head around the door. 'You can go through. She says she can give you one minute.'

'Thanks.' Monty went through the breakfast room, and then a little hallway next to a staircase that he assumed went to the private bedrooms. At the back was the sunroom, where he and Catriona had worked on her business plan. Iona sat at the desk, leaning her forehead in her hand, her long ponytail hanging to one side. She raised her eyes as he came in.

'What is it that you want?'

'Can I ask you something?'

'No.'

'Ok.' He huffed out a laugh. 'That was the world's shortest conversation then.'

'Look, I'm really busy.'

'I can see that. Maybe I could help you out, as I still haven't paid for the boat trip. I'm good at' – he gave a little shrug – 'you know, boring stuff.'

She straightened up and tossed her ponytail over her bare shoulder. She had on a strappy top and Monty noticed for the first time she had a tattoo on the back of her shoulder. 'Why would you want to help me?'

'Because I'm trying to be nice.'

She raised an eyebrow.

'And I have a favour to ask you.'

'Oh, yeah? What kind of favour?'

'I know this is not the time, and it probably won't be a good time until you're finished, but I'd really like to go back to Kisimul Castle.'

Iona leaned her chin on the back of her hand. 'Why?'

'I just feel like it. It's important. This might be my only trip here, and I want to have good memories of the castle. I wasn't feeling great, and I was a little emotional the last time, and I don't want that as my only memory.' Monty leaned against the doorframe, watching Iona.

'Ok, fine.' She checked her phone. 'I suppose if I get all this done by the afternoon, maybe we could go to the castle at dinner time and have a picnic or something.'

'Sounds great. And do you want me to help you? Or would you rather I bugger off?'

She raised an eyebrow and smirked. 'You can stay for a trial period and I'll see how you get on.'

'Fair.' He held out his hands. 'Just tell me what you want me to do. I'll be your servant for the day.'

'Yeah?' She gestured to the mess of papers and the laptop in front of her. 'Ok, fine. But don't blame me if you end up regretting it.'

Monty pulled a chair next to hers and sat down. Their thighs brushed, sending a jolt of energy through him. He glanced at her, but she was already pointing at the screen.

'These are the emails I need to respond to,' she said. 'And here are the vendor contracts I need to finalise.'

Monty nodded, focusing on the screen. 'Well, let's get going then.'

'What do you think I'm doing?' She started typing, her fingers moving swiftly over the keys.

Monty watched her, saying nothing, but heavily aware of the closeness of her shoulder and her legs. Maybe he shouldn't have chosen to sit this close, but he needed to see the screen. Scratch that. He *wanted* to be this close. Something about her pulled him and he didn't have the power to resist.

He watched her long slender fingers skimming the keyboard. What was he actually doing here? She didn't seem to need his help at all. She was getting on just fine.

Turning to him, she smiled.

'I'm not really doing anything, am I?'

'You're holding me to account. That's all I need really.'

'Well, that's easy enough.' He leaned into her a little. 'And you've got a spelling mistake. He pointed to the screen where a red line had appeared under a word.

'Obviously I would have gone back and fixed it before I sent it.' She rolled her eyes, then gave him a little nudge.

'Of course you would.'

She grinned as she carried on typing. 'Ok, that's the last email.' She leaned back with a sigh. 'I got them done really quickly.'

'What's next?' Monty took off his glasses and cleaned them on the edge of his t-shirt. When he looked back, she was eyeing him.

'Um... We need to send reminders to the vendors.' She picked up a stack of papers. 'Can you read through them and check if anyone has questions or issues in the "other information" box while I sort out the logistics for the surf gear?'

'Sure.' Monty took the papers from her.

They worked quietly, only occasionally exchanging comments or questions. The close proximity seemed to contain a pulse of energy. It built around them, intensifying with every little look, every brief touch, every word exchanged.

'Amazing. I think we're done.' Iona shut her laptop and looked at Monty, her eyes bright, but her pupils very dark and wide. 'Thanks for your help. Appreciated.' She patted him on the knee, and he inhaled but didn't let the air out. 'Shall we make a picnic and head to the castle then?'

Monty nodded. 'Yeah. Let's.'

---❤---

An hour later, Monty and Iona returned to the marina. The raised walkway from the land to where the boat was moored still gave him a queasy sensation – the fact that it felt flimsy and was open enough to see the water below didn't make it easy. But he trusted that it was a lot stronger than it looked, took a deep breath and went for it, marching along behind Iona, who was going at her usual hundred-miles-an-hour pace.

The wind picked up and tugged at his jacket as he made his way down the metal steps. Fluffy white clouds raced across the bright blue sky.

Iona uncovered the boat and jumped on. She went straight to the little compartment at the front and pulled out the buoyancy aids and the wristbands as he climbed aboard. 'Here you go.'

'Thanks.' Monty strapped himself into the buoyancy aid and slipped on the bands. Hopefully they'd work as well as the last time. 'Is this going to be bumpy?'

'Probably.' Iona untied the boat and started the engine. She reversed out of the space, then pulled away from the shore, the boat bouncing on the waves. Monty gripped the sides, trying to keep his balance. Iona stood at the front, steering, not looking too bothered by the waves. He forced himself to breathe and not watch the swell on either side. Water lapped up almost high enough to come over.

Iona glanced at him. 'You alright?'

'Yeah, I'm fine.' The bands seemed to be helping keep the nausea away, which meant he could look about him this time and not panic about being sick. But he wasn't used to boats or being out on the open water, and every little jolt felt like he was being walloped by a mallet.

When the boat hit a particularly large wave, a spray of seawater spattered over them. Iona laughed, but Monty clung on tight. *Just let's get there soon.* He sent up a silent prayer, not sure he would ever get used to this or properly enjoy it.

As they approached the castle, he steadied himself and took out his phone. He needed some photos of this, maybe even a film. The ancient stone walls of Kisimul rose up from the sea and Monty took some pictures, trying not to lose his balance or drop his phone overboard. Iona guided the boat to the slipway, cutting the engine.

'Ok, we can either find a spot on the rocks for the picnic or eat on the boat.'

'I think I'd prefer it if we were off the boat.' He removed the buoyancy aid.

'Ok, cool. I have this.' She tossed a folded-up rug to him and grabbed a bag full of food she'd raided from Catriona's fridge and cupboards.

They climbed ashore, the wind still swirling around, but in the lee of the castle it wasn't so bad. Monty scrambled over around the castle, until they found a large flat rock with a view of the sea, the waves crashing all around them.

'This looks great.' Monty unfolded the blanket and spread it out. The edges flapped, and they sat down quickly in case a fierce gust swept it away.

Iona opened the bag. 'So, I've got rolls, cheese and stuff we can chuck together. Hope that's ok.'

'Sure.' This was a picnic Iona-style. Very DIY. Sophie wouldn't have approved of this, but right now, who cared? Who even was Sophie? If Monty got together with her again sometime in the future, he could look back on this as a wild moment in his life. Maybe he should go the whole hog and have a holiday fling. With Iona?

He watched her hacking at some cheese with a blunt knife. Would she want that? She'd been the one who suggested the kiss. But who was he kidding? He was Monty MacNeil, a respectable Edinburgh banker, and he didn't do holiday flings.

He lifted a roll and pulled it open.

'Thanks for helping me earlier,' Iona said. 'I don't know why I work better with someone there. I guess it stops me running away and doing something else.'

'Have you always had trouble concentrating?' He spread some butter on his roll.

'Yup. I suspect I have ADHD, but I've never been tested or anything. I've read a lot about it, and I seem to fit.'

'You do indeed.' Monty smiled, and she returned it. For a moment, they looked at each other, eyes unwavering. A deep jolt caught him low, and he really wanted to bend in and kiss her on those beautiful, full lips again.

She leaned back on the blanket, her eyes drifting to the horizon. 'I'm so glad I don't have to do it anymore.'

Monty frowned. 'Do what?'

She sighed, fiddling with a loose pebble. 'Put up with the daily grind. I told you about my cock-up when I worked for the civil service.'

'Yeah.'

'Even before that, it was bad. I went to a boarding school and always resented being sent away. Expectations were always sky high. My family is full of high achievers, and I was supposed to be one of them. But it's not really me.'

'I can see that. This is you. Wild seas, the wind in your hair.'

She nodded. 'Yeah, that's me. My family... well, they didn't really get over me splitting with my ex. They worshipped him. He's the golden boy, the one who never did anything wrong. Oh, apart from cheat on me, which they seem to think was justified.'

'Really?'

'Oh yeah. I've kind of withdrawn from them since then. But it's hard, you know? They still talk about him like he's some kind of hero.'

Monty nodded. 'I get it. My mum loved Sophie. She would be over the moon if we got back together. She's always comparing me to other people, wondering why I can't be more like them.'

Iona looked at him and grinned. 'Listen to us, would you?'

'I know.' Monty took a bite of his roll and chewed it. 'We're not defined by what other people think of us, but it's hard to deal with when it's family.'

'Exactly.'

They sat in silence for a moment; the waves crashed against the rocks below, filling the gap with their soothing beat.

Iona broke the silence by opening a bottle of Fanta, then whipping it out of the way to stop it bubbling all over the rug. 'I guess that got a bit churned up on the way over.' She wiped her hands on the rug, then took a sip. 'So, what do you want to do here? Do you want me to disappear back to the boat and give you some time alone?'

'I don't mind you staying. And I don't have any plans. I just want to be here, existing in this place.'

'We could collect some loose pebbles and build a little tower if you like. A memorial to your dad.'

'Won't it get washed away?'

'It certainly will, but that's ok. It's transient art. The joy comes from making it, not keeping it. Process not product.'

Monty huffed out a laugh. 'Ok, let's do that then.'

They finished their food, packed away the blanket and made their way down to the edge of the rocks, looking for loose stones and pebbles, the crash of the waves growing louder as they approached. Monty crouched down, lifting a couple of flat stones, then returning to the picnic rock with them. He attempted to stack them, but each time he added another stone, his tower wobbled precariously and eventually toppled over.

'You're hopeless.' Iona winked. She was also making one. It was perfectly balanced and looked in no danger of falling down. 'Here, let me show you.'

She reached over and their fingers brushed together as she handed him a perfectly flat stone. The touch sent a small jolt through him, and he glanced at her, noticing the way the sunlight caught glints in her thick golden-brown hair. Her hand lingered for a moment longer than necessary before she pulled back.

When he made to put on another stone, she placed her hand on his, steadying it. This time the spark was unmistakable. Both pulled back, not wanting to meet the other's eye.

'I'm not very good at this kind of thing. Let me take a picture of yours. It can be the memorial cairn.'

'It's not that good.' She shuffled back so he could get a clear shot.

'I can post it on social media. I've been doing that a bit more recently.'

'Have you? You don't strike me as a social media lover.'

He scrolled through his phone to the site and uploaded the photo. 'I'm not really. Hmm...' He frowned. 'I don't think there's any reception here.'

'Do you get a lot of people looking at your photos?'

'A few. Friends and some cousins.' He let out a breath and stared into the distance. 'I only started posting again to try and get Sophie's attention. I thought the post about bodyboarding might have got her notice, but I don't think she even looked at it.'

Iona looked at him and pulled a pout. 'Why do you want to get back with her? Is it for yourself or for your family?'

'Good question.' He sighed. 'And I don't know the answer. I feel like I've got something to prove after she called me boring.'

'But that's crazy. You've proved you're not boring.'

He picked at a thread on his jeans. 'I'm not sure I have. So often I wonder if she was right. Maybe I am boring. Not just in my hobbies, but in everything.' He pulled a face. 'She said I was too vanilla. You know what that means?'

Iona laughed and covered her mouth. 'Of course I know what it means. But what the hell was she into that she called you that? Did she have a kink you didn't like?'

'I don't know. Maybe that was the problem. But she didn't tell me and... I didn't think to mix it up.'

'Well, I kissed you, and it seemed fine. After you loosened up.'

'Yeah, well...' He swallowed and sat down on a large, flat rock. 'That's something.'

Iona sat next to him, blinking slowly, and he gave her a little smile. She looked like she was sizing him up.

'Have you ever hooked up with anyone? Like casually?'

His cheeks and his neck burned. 'Um... no.'

'You should do that. Then it doesn't really matter what happens. It's not like you'll have to see them again.'

'I'm not sure I want to do that.'

'How do you know unless you try? In fact...' She glanced around as if checking for other people, which made Monty grin, because who on earth would be out here with them? 'This is exactly the right time for you to do it.'

'What do you mean?'

'You're on holiday. Have a fling. People do it all the time.'

'You want me just to walk into the pub in the village and pick up a random stranger?'

She chuckled and shook her head. 'You could do that, but you might end up with old Billy and I wouldn't advise that.'

'Not funny.'

She gave him a little nudge. 'I'll do it. I volunteer.'

He raised an eyebrow. 'Are you having a laugh?'

'No. It's not like you'll be my first.'

'Oh great. That makes it sound so much better.'

'Stop it.' She laughed again. 'Relax. Enjoy yourself. Life's too short. If you want to have a holiday fling, I'm your girl.' She gave him a wink. 'But if you don't, then fine. The offer's on the table. You decide what you want to do with it.'

'What would you get out of it?'

She glanced at him and frowned. 'Whatever you have to offer.'

'What if that's boring vanilla?'

'Who cares?' She threw out her hands. 'It's not like I'm wanting to marry you. And I'll tell you what I like, show you if you want. It could be for your benefit in the future.'

Monty stared at her, not sure he was still awake or even really here. Had he maybe fainted on the boat and this was all a very bizarre dream? Was she propositioning him? He'd never had that before. But maybe she was right. This *was* the chance to do something different. Once he left, in just over a week, he was unlikely ever to return – not for a long time anyway. So why not?

'Well, ok... But not out here... I'm not that adventurous.'

'Neither am I.' She smiled. 'Not when so many boats pass by, but how about just one kiss to start us off?'

He cocked his head. 'Only if you promise not to get grumpy this time.'

'What do you mean?'

'The last time I kissed you, you were grouchy with me for ages after that.' Even though it couldn't have been that long, not in real terms, but it felt like it.

'Ok. I'll be a good girl and no grouching.' She ran her palm over his stubbly cheek. He leaned into it, taking a long, slow breath. 'You're going to enjoy this, and so am I.' She straddled him, took his face in her hands, and their eyes met. 'You can even pretend I'm Sophie if you like.' Iona gave him a wink.

Monty's lungs felt thick, and he couldn't get enough air. Sophie? Who was that? All he saw was Iona. He couldn't remember what Sophie looked like.

'Anything you'd like to try with her, you can practise with me. Within reason. Nothing too kinky.'

'No need to worry about that.' His voice was hoarse and distant. He placed his hands on her hips and closed his eyes, leaning in. The moment their lips touched, heat flooded through him, and he groaned, letting himself go. He tugged her closer, deepening the kiss. No holding back this time.

Chapter Sixteen

Iona

Monty's grip on Iona's hips was firm. She clutched his cheeks, drinking in the taste of his lips, enjoying the prickle of his stubble. The wind picked up around them, whipping her hair into her face, but she barely noticed. All her focus was on the heat and urgency of their kiss, and the way Monty's touch sent shivers through her.

He definitely wasn't holding back this time. Was this how he kissed Sophie? If so, the woman was an idiot. This was far from boring. Intense passion filled it. Iona moaned. 'Monty,' she murmured against his lips, her breath hitching.

'What?' he said with a sharp exhale. 'Is something wrong?'

'No.' She shook her head, smiling, her lips swollen and tender. 'Why don't we take these off?' She tugged the leg of his glasses.

'Oh, sure.' He took them off and blinked.

'I'd like to kiss Superman, not Clark Kent.'

He quirked a little smile and tilted his head. Leaning in, she met his lips again. He slipped his hands from her hips, up her back, and pulled her close, so she was wrapped in his embrace. The heat was glorious, and the raging wind wasn't biting anymore. Their tongues met and Monty tensed under her. Iona ground against him, loving the friction and how into this he was. How much he wanted her... Or Sophie. Sure, he was pretending she was Sophie, but she'd take it, because while she enjoyed hooking up and the physical release that came with it, she missed the emotional connection. She had no faith in lasting relationships, but to experience something close to love was precious. If Monty loved Sophie, then Iona would take this moment and enjoy the love.

'Remember,' she panted in between kisses, linking her arms behind his neck. 'How much you love Sophie. Show her. Don't hold back.'

He made a funny little noise in his throat, almost like he was scoffing at the idea of loving Sophie, then he pulled her even closer, devouring her lips, until she thought she might pass out. She was on the verge of suggesting they threw caution – and their clothes – to the wind, when good sense kicked in. The only remaining piece in her love-drugged brain. This beach might be out of the way, but boats passed here, and she didn't fancy getting caught indecently by a whole boatload of people.

He pulled back slightly, his breath short. 'It's getting a bit stormy. Maybe we should head back.' He ran his fingertips around her forehead and down her cheek, whisking away several strands of hair that had broken free from her ponytail. 'Not that I want to stop this, or let you go.' His grip on her increased a little, and his cold fingertips lingered near her earlobe, the pad of his thumb gently caressing her cheek.

Iona melted from his touch. And his words. Had anyone ever said anything quite so romantic to her? She didn't think so. *He doesn't want to let me go.* And really, she didn't want him to let her go either. This was far too nice.

'Quite enjoying your fling now, aren't you?' She smirked at him.

'I am, but I don't like how windy it is out here.'

'Yeah, we should go.' She glanced at the sky, now darkening with heavy clouds. 'Before we get caught in the rain again.'

'But you like kissing in the rain, don't you?' He gave her a little smile.

She didn't mind what she kissed him in – or on – at this moment. Rain, sun, whatever, wherever. She just didn't want it to stop.

'I do, but probably not so much on a tiny tidal island in a storm.'

'Yeah, let's get back.' He shifted, and she climbed off him, scrambling to her feet. She grabbed the picnic bag, and he lifted the folded rug. They hurried back towards the slipway. Aggressive waves were tossing the little boat up and down. This would be a wild ride back, by the look of things. Thankfully, it was just across the harbour. She wouldn't risk the open sea in wind like this.

'Have you still got the wristbands on?' Iona turned to Monty as they ran down the slipway.

He waggled his arm, showing her his wrist.

'Cool. In we get.' She hopped onboard, thrusting out her hand and helping Monty on. Instead of sitting at the back, he followed her to the front as he did up his buoyancy aid.

She started the engine. 'This looks insane.'

'I trust you... But should I be worried?' His eyes met hers and so many unspoken thoughts passed between them.

'We'll be fine.' She steered forward, her hands steady despite the twist in her stomach. Nothing to do with the weather – everything to do with Monty.

The sea was rough, the boat tossed by the waves, but Iona held the course. Monty clung on, his knuckles white but his eyes determined.

'Hey. We're good.' She flashed him a quick smile. 'I've done this a million times.' Well, slight exaggeration, but as they approached the marina, the waves had already calmed.

'I can see that. But you know me by now... Adventure isn't my thing.'

'We'll see.' She winked. 'I think there's more to you than meets the eye.'

They reached the jetty, and Iona brought the boat home. She tied it up, checking there were no sharp nails this time, and saw Monty taking off the bands and flexing his wrists.

'They leave quite a dent, these things.' He showed her the indents.

'Well, at least they stopped you going green and throwing up.' She took them from him and shoved them back into their little box. After chucking the box and the buoyancy aids into one of the compartments, she turned back to Monty and slung her arms around his neck. He tugged her close, pinning her hips to his. With no words needed, they resumed their kiss from the castle.

'Mmmm,' Iona moaned. 'Let's take this back to the farm, shall we?'

'Yes.' He stroked her hair back. 'Let's do that.'

'Your place or mine?'

'Mine probably.' His eyes hadn't left her, and his gaze was so intense, it was like he was examining her. 'I don't want to get caught going in or out of your room. The annex is more hidden.'

Iona smirked. It wouldn't be the first time Catriona had caught someone entering or leaving her room, but she understood. And Monty, of all people. Catriona probably wouldn't believe it. Not straight-laced Monty. But Iona was gearing up to expose all his hidden depths. Sometimes she went for guys purely on looks and was disappointed. Monty was attractive in a weird kind of way, a handsome nerd-type. But he had a good body from the glimpses she'd caught. And he smelt nice. Maybe that was bizarre, but it meant he had good personal hygiene and that was important. Above all that, he was a good guy. He passed the quality control with flying colours, and she couldn't wait to extend this kiss into something a lot hotter.

But twenty minutes later, when Iona and Monty pulled up to An Grianan in the car, her heart sank.

'What's going on?' Monty frowned.

A large group of people were milling around the courtyard.

'It's people arriving for the festival. They must have got off the plane this afternoon.'

'Catriona looks a bit stressed.'

'I hope she hasn't double booked anyone. She's letting a few people camp in the field, but these people don't look like they have tents.' Iona popped her seatbelt. Catriona was frowning and pointing. Although she was always good with guests, she occasionally lost it with Ruaridh or Alex when she got mad, and steam looked to be coming out of her ears.

'Iona!' Catriona waved her over as soon as she got out of the car. 'Can you come over here?'

Iona glanced at Monty, giving him a helpless look. 'I need to go.'

Monty adjusted his glasses, his expression neutral. 'It's fine. Go help Catriona. I'll see you some other time when things are quieter.'

Scamp came charging up to them, his tail racing. He jumped around Monty for a few moments. With a vague smile, Monty patted him until Iona took his collar and tugged him back.

'Settle down,' she said. Scamp instantly dropped onto his belly. 'Come on, this way.' She shooed him back to the group and headed towards Catriona, a chill through her veins. Why had Monty said he would see her *some other time?* What did that mean? How airy fairy was that? Had he had a mini wake-up call, and this was the end of the fling?

Ah hell. This was so irritating.

Catriona excused herself from a group of people and marched up to Iona, taking her by the arm. 'People are asking questions I don't have answers to. Where have you been?'

'I was taking Monty back to the castle.'

'Couldn't that have waited until after the festival? You need to talk to all these people. They want to know everything about wave conditions and god knows what else.'

'Fine.' From the corner of her eye, Iona spied Monty making his way towards the annex, keeping his head down. *Bugger.* She wanted to be in there with him. Images of all sorts of decadent and naughty ideas paraded across her mind. Most of them involved her being naked and sprawled on a bed, her hair spread across the pillows. An equally naked Monty was kissing her, touching her... His tongue was on her lips, her nipples, her lady parts. She was writhing and gripping the sheets. His head was between her legs. Then he was on top of her, inside her... And she was on top of him, bucking her hips, moving faster—

'Iona.' Catriona waved her hand in front of her face. 'Where are you?'

'What?' *Fuck's sake.* She'd been lost in a very hot daydream.

'Please talk to the guests about schedules, equipment, rules – everything.' Catriona tossed up her hands. 'I can't handle it on my own. You're one of the main organisers. You should be here.'

'Ok, ok. It doesn't officially start until tomorrow afternoon, so I didn't expect to be needed for this, did I?' She marched up to the group. 'Hey, everyone. I'm Iona, one of the surf instructors on the island. If you have questions about the festival, I'm your person.'

People started talking to her and asking her stuff. Normally this would be right up her street, but she so desperately craved to walk away and go after Monty. It quickly became obvious that wouldn't be happening anytime soon. Even getting a minute's peace from these people was going to be impossible.

Ruaridh came over after his shift had finished, and he and Iona walked to the beach with the guests and Scamp. They talked to them about conditions and the best places. Iona kept looking behind, hoping to see Monty following them down, but he didn't appear. Scamp sniffed around the long grass in the dunes, his head popping up every now and then at something unseen.

Iona didn't dare go to the annex with all these people about, and with Catriona in such a mood. It wasn't nice to see her like that, and it only really happened if she got stressed.

So that evening, Iona headed up to bed alone, lying in the cool bedroom with the window open. The annex roof was outside her window and for a while she entertained thoughts of climbing out Romeo and Juliet style, then lowering herself down to the ground. But that was insane. And Monty might not appreciate that. If she'd just got his number, she could message him.

She dragged her quilt over her and huddled in, trying to restart the daydream she'd had earlier, but even that wouldn't come. Her messy mind was all over the place, jumping from this to that, never catching the wave, or riding it home, always just missing that one thing she wanted.

Chapter Seventeen

Monty

Monty wandered down to the beach, the warm afternoon sun making him squint; he shaded his eyes, soaking it all in. The deserted island from the previous days seemed a distant memory. People wandered about everywhere, dressed in surf gear or wetsuits, carrying boards, and chatting. Groups had set up camps on the sand with picnic rugs and changing tents. Monty had put on a pair of running shorts and a t-shirt, not quite surf gear, but the closest he had.

He hadn't seen Iona since their kiss. That kiss. *Wow.* It kept him awake for hours at night. Something had taken hold of him inside, like a hidden lion clawing to get out. A hungry lion. Was this what Sophie had wanted? Passion? Desire? And why had it found its way to the forefront with Iona? She seemed to invite it, encourage it. She'd told him not to hold back, and he hadn't – such a freeing and hot-blooded experience. The memory kept playing in his mind. The kiss had stopped too soon, but maybe that was for the best. Should they even have done it at all? Maybe it was a mistake.

He'd never had a fling in his life before.

Tinny music played nearby from someone's phone and Monty headed for a spot away from the crowd, near the dunes, and settled down. He spread out the rug he'd borrowed from the farm and sat with his bare legs stretched onto the warm sand. Opening his bag, he took out a packet of crisps and a beer, cracking it open with a soft hiss. Some surfers were out in the ocean, their boards slicing through the waves. His bodyboarding success was nothing next to this. These folks were fearless... And mental.

A tannoy crackled into action, and a man introduced some of the surfers. Monty wondered who the man was. A friend of Iona probably. *And who am I?* No one. He'd pass through her life like grains of sand through his fingers while these other friends remained.

He scanned the water, looking for her. Was she out there? It was hard to tell from this distance. His gaze landed on an easily recognisable figure. Ruaridh, looking like the Hulk on a board, muscles bulging as he paddled out. Monty still hadn't found out what Ruaridh's job was, but he obviously liked pumping iron. Monty had been trying to work out more and he was a lot more toned than he had been, but he wouldn't ever rival Ruaridh in the muscle department.

'Show-off,' Monty muttered to himself, watching Ruaridh catch a wave and ride it. He took a swig of his beer, feeling the cool liquid slide down his throat. Coming to the festival wasn't something he'd planned to do, but now he was here, he may as well make the most of it. It was almost at odds with the wild nature of the place to have so much manufactured energy. Perhaps that was why the waves crashed, and the wind pounded relentlessly, as if to drown the tannoy, the happy chatter of the people, and the low beat of music, and reassert themselves as the island superpowers.

Monty sighed, breathed it all in and scanned the beach again. Was Iona even here? Maybe she'd got caught behind the scenes somewhere, organising something. That wouldn't please her. What she'd want would be to ride these waves all day long, free as a bird, wind in her hair. He reached for another crisp, still on the lookout. The breeze picked up, flapping the edges of his blanket. At the sound of cheers, he turned to see what the commotion was.

Iona was running down the beach dressed in a tight wetsuit, carrying a board and something that looked like a parachute. The tannoy crackled to life again.

'Ladies and gentlemen, please welcome Iona McKenzie, one of the founders of our festival, who's about to give a demo of kitesurfing!'

Of what? He wrestled in his bag until he found his binoculars. He focused them on Iona, who'd reached the water's edge. She grinned as she set up her bright red kite, then clipped on some straps.

Monty lifted his phone, opening the camera app and hitting the red button to record. The surrounding crowd buzzed, eyes glued to Iona as she launched her kite and took to the waves.

She skimmed across the water, her kite soaring high, catching the wind perfectly. *Holy shit.* Monty's heart almost jumped into his mouth. Those moves must take some skill, but she looked like a natural, and so fearless. Monty couldn't tear his eyes away, but his insides crumpled at every new move. No way could he keep up with a woman like her. If he wasn't exciting enough for Sophie, he'd never be good enough for someone like Iona. She carved through the waves, catching the air and performing flips that made the crowd gasp. Monty held his breath.

'Bloody hell!' someone nearby shouted.

Monty zoomed in with his phone. Her power and grace left him gobsmacked. She was shining in a whole new light. How could he ever look at her the same again? He knew she was a daredevil, but this was incredible. *She* was incredible. Bold. Uninhibited. Everything he felt he wasn't.

She rode the waves like she was born to do it, every movement fluid and commanding. As she neared the shore, she executed a final jump, her kite lifting her high in the air before the board landed back on the water. The crowd erupted into applause, and Monty clapped along too. *Wow, just bloody wow.*

As she walked back up the beach, carrying her board and kite, the tannoy crackled again. 'Let's hear it one more time for Iona McKenzie!'

The cheers grew louder, and Monty watched people crowd around her to chat. He'd leave them to it. If there was one person whose absence she wouldn't even notice, it was him.

'Next up, it's happy hour!' the announcer said over the tannoy. 'Anyone who wants to join in, get some tips from the pros, or just have a go, now's your chance!'

Iona was chatting with a group of surfers and festival-goers, laughing and exchanging high-fives. After a moment, she glanced Monty's way and smiled. *Uh-oh...* Why did he just know this meant trouble? That smirk on her face was a bit of a giveaway. Excusing herself, she jogged over to where he was sitting.

'Hey.' She stood in front of him, shielding her eyes. 'Did you enjoy the show?'

'You were amazing. Incredible. I'm speechless.'

She grinned. 'Thanks. I love doing it.' Her eyes travelled over him, and he was pretty sure she was alluding to something other than kite-surfing too. 'Do you fancy having a go yourself?'

Monty's eyes widened. 'Me? No, no. On that kite thing? No way.'

'Na, not that. Just on a board.'

'I'm not dressed for it.'

Iona waved a dismissive hand. 'That's not a problem. I've got spare wetsuits in the container, remember? You can borrow one.'

'I don't know, Iona. I'm not really—'

'Come on.' She folded her arms. 'It'll be fun! You said you wanted to try new things, right? This is your chance. Plus, you'll have me as your personal instructor.' She gave him a wink and dropped to her knees beside him. Leaning in, she whispered in his ear. 'Call this a bit of foreplay. I haven't forgotten about our other deal.'

Monty looked away, letting out a dry laugh. She was something else. She really was... And also, totally irresistible.

'And' – she leaned even closer, so her words were almost like a kiss, setting his insides alight – 'you're at a water sports festival. When in Rome, right? Just give it a shot. Go on.'

'Ok.' He turned so the end of his nose touched hers. How satisfying would it be to kiss her, here and now? Would anyone notice or care? She sat back on her heels and pulled out the top of her wetsuit, then put her hand inside it. 'What are you doing?'

It looked like she was fishing for something. Monty's imagination leapt up, along with another part of his body that really had no business doing so. But how could he help it as he imagined it was his hands in there? Hell, he had to stop.

She pulled out a key on a string. 'Had to hide it in here. I'm scared I lose it.'

'Couldn't you have given it to someone to look after?'

'Ah, maybe. Anyway. Take that and go get a wetsuit from the container. I'd come with you, but I better not. I'm supposed to be helping people.' She pulled a face. 'I'd rather get locked in the container with you and carry on... you know what.' She winked and jumped to her feet. 'Don't be long. See you in a bit.'

Monty packed up his stuff and took it to the container. Once inside, he sighed and checked the wetsuits for one that was his size. This week was just one crazy moment after another.

Once dressed, he emerged from the container, wiggling his shoulders in the tight wetsuit, trying to make it feel comfier. How ridiculous did he look? But then, who here would even notice or care? Most of the people here were dressed like this. He made his way to the water's edge, squinting against the glare of the sun. The sea stretched out before him, a glittering expanse of blue and white foam. Surfers dotted the waves further out and some beginners played at the water's edge.

Iona was finishing up with a couple of them, showing them the basics of paddling the board. She glanced over and caught sight of Monty. With a quick smile, she excused herself and jogged over to him.

'Looking good.' She gave him a once-over. 'Ready to become a surf god?'

'As ready as I'll ever be,' he muttered, handing back the key chain.

'Come on then.' She hooked the key around her neck, grabbed a board, took his hand and led him into the water. The coolness was a shock at first, but he adjusted quicker this time than he had before. She placed the board in the water. 'Ok, let's start with the basics. First, you need to lie on the board in the correct position.'

Monty lay on the board, trying to find a comfortable spot. 'Like this?'

'Almost,' she said, lying on her own board. 'Like this, so the nose of the board is just above the water, and your nose is level with the line on the board. Perfect. Now, keep your legs together and your feet on the board, otherwise you'll fall off.'

'The bodyboarding was easier. This looks impossible.' He eyed the people around him. Most of them were barely managing a wobble on the board before falling off.

'You can do more of that in a bit. Just give this a try.'

'Ok.' Monty clung to the sides, sure every bob of the water was going to knock him off. 'Shouldn't I try this on dry land first?'

Iona laughed. 'Yeah, but I've not got long, so let's just get you in the water. Now, use your arms to paddle out. Try it, just paddle with your arms at your sides. Freestyle. Push your way through the water.'

Monty dipped his arms in and started to paddle. It felt awkward at first, but he gradually got the hang of it, moving the board forward through the waves.

'Good job.' Iona paddled alongside him. 'Keep your strokes even and steady. You're doing great.'

They paddled out a bit further, the water getting deeper. Monty's arms were starting to ache, but he was determined to keep going. After a while, they stopped.

'Ok, now that you've got the hang of paddling, let's try to catch a small wave,' she said. 'When you see a wave coming, you need to paddle hard to match its speed, then pop up into a standing position.'

'No way, will I manage that,' Monty shouted over the waves.

'It's fine if you don't. It's quite tricky, but I'll show you, then you can have a go. Don't worry if it goes wrong. Just have fun.'

Fun, huh? She was mad. 'Well, ok... I'll give it a shot.'

'So, if you push up with your knee like this first, then move your back leg like this. Then just rise into a standing position. Keep your shoulder pointing to the nose of the board, look where you're going and keep your feet flat. Ok?'

'Is that all? Easy.' He stared at her with his eyebrows raised, and she giggled.

'The more you practise, the easier it gets. Now watch this.' She paddled around, so she was facing the beach. 'Wait for a wave.' It caught her and, in a swift fluid movement, she was on her feet, gliding in.

Without waiting for her to come back, Monty copied what she'd done, waiting for a wave. When one caught the board, he felt a rush of exhilaration and he attempted to stand in the way Iona showed him, but he immediately lost his balance and toppled into the water. He leapt up, gulping for air and shaking his head. *Bloody hell.* This was why he had no desire to do stuff like this.

Iona paddled back to him. 'Are you ok?'

'I fell off. What did you expect?'

'It's fine. Try again. I'll watch and see if I can help.'

They repeated the process and Monty fell off again. It didn't feel quite so shocking this time, and he recovered himself.

'It's all good, except you're leaning too far back. Try and keep your weight centred.' Iona patted the middle of the board.

He tried again, managing to stay upright a little longer before plunging to his doom yet again.

Iona took hold of his arm as he straightened up. He wiped water from his face.

'I'm starting to think you just wanted an excuse to watch me make a fool of myself.'

Iona grinned. 'No, I'm just helping you to be more adventurous. I think we can safely say you've accomplished that. Aren't you enjoying this even a tiny bit?'

'A little bit, but I think I've had my fill of dunkings for the day.'

She edged closer through the water that was up to their waists, placed her hands on his hips, and pulled him towards her. 'You're doing great.'

He watched her closely, his body burning to get out of this wetsuit and be free. After a quick glance around, he cupped her cheek in his hand. 'Have you any idea what you're doing to me?'

'I have an inkling.' She smirked and pulled him even closer, rubbing against him, making him thank every sea god everywhere that his bottom half was underwater.

'Then stop it. This isn't what we're supposed to be doing.'

She pulled away. 'Are you calling time on the deal? We haven't even started yet.'

'No. Just not here, with so many people about.'

'Fair enough. I should probably help some other people too. It wouldn't do for you to monopolise me.'

'I'll leave you to it. I've had enough surfing for one day.'

She caught hold of him. 'Stick around though. I'm doing some more kite-surfing later.'

'Ok. But I want to get dry first.'

'If you want. There's a bunch of spare bodyboards kicking about somewhere if you want to have some fun with them.'

'I think I'll just watch.'

'Ok.'

As he left the water, he turned back to see Iona chatting with two young guys. Why was he torturing himself with her? It would be so much better to leave her with guys like that. But there she was, dangling like the forbidden fruit. And one taste wouldn't do any harm. Just something to tick off on the bucket list – the one he didn't know he had prior to this trip.

He trudged back to the container and peeled off the wetsuit with a sigh of relief. The saltwater made him feel sticky and uncomfortable as he changed back into his shorts and t-shirt. Maybe he could nip back to the farmhouse for a quick shower. He checked the time. Still early and it wasn't far.

He strolled up the dunes and along the ridge onto the track that led past the derelict croft and back to An Grianan. The wind flattened the grass and wildflowers as it whipped across the machair, and fluffy white clouds raced across the blue sky. Although it was a warm day, the strong gusts had a bite to them and Monty decided to grab a hoody while he was back.

When he got to the farm, Catriona was in the yard wrestling a bright pink hat onto her daughter's head. Another woman stood beside them with folded arms, smiling.

'Hi.' Catriona glanced up at Monty. 'I think I forgot to say, but I'm not doing meals tonight as we're going to be at the festival. Is that ok? I should have mentioned it before.'

'It's fine. No worries. I was just there myself. Iona persuaded me to surf. I got soaked and I feel a bit yucky. I'm going to have a shower, then head back.'

'Ah, I see. This is my mum, by the way.' Catriona turned to the other woman and went on, 'This is Monty MacNeil. He thinks he might have ancestors here.'

'Oh really?' The other woman came forward and held out her hand. 'I'm Nora. My mother was a MacNeil.'

'Nice to meet you.'

Catriona smiled. 'I'll leave the two of you to chat. Maybe see you later.'

'Sure,' Monty waved.

'So where do your MacNeils fit in?' Nora asked.

'I don't really know. It was my father who was into it all.'

'And what was his name?'

'Hector. He died recently. I just scattered his ashes at Kisimul Castle.'

'Sorry for your loss.' Nora put a somewhat frail hand on his arm. For someone who didn't look much over fifty-five, she had a weariness about her.

'Thank you. My father told a story many times that he was descended from a branch of the MacNeils that were somehow cut from the main family line and diddled out of inheriting the castle.'

Nora nodded. 'I've heard that story too. No one can prove it one way or another now, but I wonder if maybe you're related to us somehow. My mother definitely talked about that legend before.'

'Really?'

'Oh yes. Also, did you know that the castle's name isn't pronounced "kissy-mull" but more like "kish-mul". Only islanders usually pronounce it correctly.'

'I didn't realise. Excuse my ignorance.'

'Don't worry about it. No one bothers about it. I just thought you might like to know for your own interest. Tourists often think its name had something to do with kissing.' She let out a little laugh and Monty forced a smile – the name might not have anything to do with that, but he and Iona had done exactly that in its grounds. 'It actually comes from the Gaelic, Caisteal Chiosmuil and means castle on the rock of the small bay. If you look it up on your internet, you'll see how to spell that.'

'Thank you. I appreciate it.'

'Well, I'll let you get on, but I'll also have a look and see if I can find out where your Hector fits into things. My mother had a big box of family tree stuff. I'll dig it out and see if I can find anything.'

'That's really kind, thank you.'

'Not at all. It's a job I can do sitting down, and it'll be fun looking through it.'

He thanked her again, then headed for the annex. The shower was soon piping hot, and he spent longer than was strictly necessary, washing away the salt and sand. His body wasn't in bad shape, but he'd never

manage muscles like Ruaridh or surf-board prowess like the guys back
at the beach. All the things he supposed Iona valued.

Why do I care about that?

He emerged feeling refreshed and threw on some clean clothes
before heading back to the festival. All the way along the track, his
thoughts tumbled about like sheets on a washing line in the Barra winds
– a mix of curiosity about his MacNeil connections and Iona, who was
always on his mind, it seemed. By the time he got to the top of the dunes
and looked down, all the thoughts were tangled and twisted, and he
couldn't make sense of them.

The festival was still in full swing, with people milling about, music
playing, and laughter filling the air. As he approached the surf area, he
spotted Iona talking to the same two young guys from earlier. Something about the sight made his hackles rise. One of the guys was getting
a bit too handsy, his arm snaking around Iona's waist. She pulled away
from him, giving him a dirty look, but he didn't back off. In fact, he
looked to be moving in again for a second try. Iona was more than a
match for him. If anyone came off worse from the situation, it would be
him, but still. She was obviously trying to maintain politeness. As one
of the leaders of the festival, she wouldn't want to cause a scene, but the
guy wasn't backing away or reading her obvious body language.

Monty made his way towards them, his feet slipping a bit in the
dry sand at the top of the beach. Iona caught his gaze and wordlessly
expressed her exasperation at the guy with a slight grimace and a flash
in her eyes. The look made him keep walking, and he strode right up to
her side. 'Ah, there you are.' He slipped his arm around her shoulder. 'I
was looking for you.'

'And you've found me.' She smiled at him.

The guy frowned, looking Monty up and down. 'Who are you?'

'Monty.' He gave a little shrug, almost bursting with a laugh at the
bemused look on the guy's face.

Iona turned to Monty and slipped her hand around his cheek. 'I missed you.' She leaned in and kissed him. He didn't resist. Sure, she was making a point to this guy, but it felt good.

'I missed you too.'

She pulled back, closing her eyes and resting her forehead on his.

The guy muttered something under his breath.

'Come on.' His friend gave him a push, and they stalked away.

Monty kept his arm around Iona, feeling the tension in her shoulders ease. 'You ok?'

'Sure, but I appreciate that. He was getting impossible to shake.'

Monty gave her a little squeeze. 'He looked like a dick, but then he's probably saying the same thing about me.'

Iona laughed and prodded him in the chest. 'Well, you're a lot nicer than him. I wanted to knee him in the balls, but I didn't think that would go down well with the other organisers.'

'I could tell, but part of me wished you'd done it. I'd like to hope the other organisers care more about you than one twat who can't keep it in his pants.'

She let out a little snigger. 'When you put it like that, I wish I'd done it too. Where did he go?'

Monty raised his gaze, not seeing the two guys anywhere, but his focus zoomed in on Ruaridh, who was standing a little way off, sipping a beer and watching them. 'I'm not sure, but probably best to let him go, now that he's disappeared.' Monty let go of Iona and stepped back, running a hand through his hair. If Ruaridh had his eye on Iona, Monty couldn't compete with him and nor did he want to. His time here would be short, and Ruaridh lived here.

'Yeah. I suppose so.' Iona waved to Ruaridh, who tipped his bottle in her direction.

Monty took another step back, and his insides roared in protest at the thought of Iona with anyone else, ever.

What on earth was wrong with him?

Chapter Eighteen

Iona

Monty ran a hand through his hair, and Iona watched him take another step back. Any further and he'd trip backwards over some people who were setting up a picnic. After his record with the urn the day they met, she wouldn't put it past him.

'Look behind you.' She nodded her head towards the people, and Monty turned.

'Oh, right. Thanks.'

What was he doing anyway? He seemed to be trying to get away from her all of a sudden, which was bizarre, as he'd just helped her get rid of the persistent surfer.

'I, um, I'll leave you to get on.'

'What?' She frowned. 'I'm just chatting to people and helping them out if I can. You're welcome to stick around.'

'I'll find somewhere to sit. So I don't get in the way.' He headed off to a spot near some tufty grass at the edge of the beach. Iona kept her eye on him. Maybe it was her imagination, but he didn't look quite as weedy as she'd thought him when they first met. But as that was only a week ago, it wasn't possible that he'd beefed out in such a short time. The clothes he was wearing just accentuated him better... Or maybe she was just looking a little closer.

While she was following his progress, a movement caught the corner of her eye, and she spotted Catriona with Eilidh. The wee girl was giggling as she ran circles around her mum, and Catriona was smiling and laughing too. She took Eilidh's hands, and they did a funny little twirl together. Iona smiled. They were so cute, and when Catriona let go like that, she looked so young. She'd been forced to grow up fast and Iona sometimes felt like the younger one when she was with her. How nice to see her having fun and able to let go of some of her responsibilities.

'Iona!' Eilidh screamed and ran towards Iona. Catriona let go of her daughter's hand as Eilidh legged it across the beach.

Iona met her and swung her up. Eilidh giggled and squealed. 'Hey! Are you ready to watch some tricks? I'm on again soon, then I'm done for the day.'

'I can't wait to see this,' Catriona said, catching up with them. 'We've brought snacks and drinks so we can have a picnic after.'

'That's amazing, thank you, so much.' Iona checked the time. 'It's later than I thought. I should probably go and get myself ready. I'll catch you two later.'

Iona waved them goodbye and went to collect her kite surfing equipment. Once she had it all, she headed for the water's edge. The two guys who'd been pestering her earlier were still hanging about, but she ignored them. If they came near her again, she'd be giving them that kick. Someone whistled and catcalled. Probably one of them, but so what? Once she was out on the water, she'd be invincible.

She adjusted her harness, feeling the tug as she clipped her lines to the kite. A crowd had gathered along the shore. She smiled to herself through a buzzing in her veins. As she walked into the water, the cool waves lapped at her legs.

She waded deeper, until the kite caught the wind, pulling taut against her harness. She let it lift; the canopy rose into the sky. With a deep breath, she swallowed the swooping sensation in her tummy as the wind tugged her forward.

Her body moved instinctively at the right moment, and she launched herself onto the board. No one could teach this. You either had it or you didn't. The people who could do it were intuitive and had a bond with the elements, wind and water working together. The kite caught the wind, propelling her forward with a surge of speed. Iona's heart raced, and she wanted to laugh. The water sprayed up around her, sparkling in the sunlight as she skimmed across the surface.

Carving through the waves, she leaned back, lifting the nose of the board and launching into the air. For a moment, she was weightless, suspended between sky and sea. The thrill of the jump coursed through her with a rush of pure adrenaline.

As she descended, the board kissed the water's surface, and she adjusted her stance, preparing for the next manoeuvre. The feeling of freedom, and the way the kite responded to her, was awesome, like dancing with nature.

She executed a series of turns and jumps. Cheers and applause came from the shore, intermittently filtering into her hearing alongside the whoosh of the wind and constant thud of the waves. The crowd's excitement fuelled her own, pushing her to go higher, faster. She looped the kite, feeling the pull increase as she soared above the waves once more.

The wind whipped through her hair, and she let out a whoop, the sound lost to the roar of the ocean.

As the demo drew to a close, she steered back towards the shore, riding the final wave with a flourish. She let the kite slowly descend, bringing herself to a gentle stop in the shallows. The crowd erupted into cheers and applause.

Iona unclipped her harness and grabbed her board, a wide grin plastered across her face. How could she help it? The feeling was incredible. She waved to the spectators, her heart still pounding. Walking up the beach, she was met with high-fives and congratulatory pats on the back. She soaked it all in, the sense of accomplishment mingling with the lingering thrill of the ride. Nothing in her career had ever rivalled this.

This was her job and her life now. These were the accolades she lived for. Why not accept them and enjoy them? Others might not think this a worthy profession, but right now, it felt better than any other lifestyle she could imagine.

Catriona appeared at her side with Eilidh jumping up and down.

'That was so cool,' Eilidh shrieked. 'You're the best.'

'Thank you.' Iona high-fived her.

'I don't know how you do it.' Catriona patted her on the arm. 'I was petrified even watching.'

Iona smiled and shook her ponytail. At the back of the crowd, she noticed Monty, sipping a beer, watching her.

Catriona's gaze drifted towards him too. 'Is everything alright with you and him?'

'What? Yeah. Why wouldn't it be?'

'No reason. Just me being nosy.'

'Nothing to see here.' Iona turned back to her friend with a bright smile. 'Anyway, I'd better put all this stuff away. I'll catch up with you later. Save me some food.'

'There's plenty.' Catriona gave her a quick hug. 'And well done for your part in organising all this. It's great.'

'Yeah, it's turned out pretty good.' Iona waved and started making her way back to the container. As she made her way up the beach, the two irritating guys were hovering about. What the hell was their problem? Before she reached them, someone said her name.

'Hey.' Monty caught up with her. 'Shall I give you a hand putting that stuff away?'

She smiled. 'Thanks. I've got it but walk up to the container with me. That might help keep those two lechers away. I'm feeling so pumped I might do some damage to their pretty faces as well as their wedding tackle if they try anything.'

'Ah, yes.' He huffed out a laugh. 'And here was me thinking it was that big butch guy who's with you who was going to scare them off.'

'Well, him too.' She winked at him.

They walked towards the container, and Monty looked over at the two guys, who seemed to be deliberately focusing the other way.

'Iona's daughter is your number one fan,' he said. 'You should have heard her screaming when you were out there.'

'She's a sweetie.'

'Kids are cute. Sophie didn't want any, but sometimes when I see moments like that, I kind of do.'

Iona smirked. 'Yeah. I wouldn't mind a kid like her. I tell you something though, if I ever had kids, they will most certainly not be going to boarding school.'

'No, I wouldn't want that either. Not that we're having them together or anything... I'm just commenting, yeah?'

Iona chuckled and shook her head. 'Yeah. I worked that out.'

'I met Catriona's mum earlier. She thinks I might be related to her.'

'Oh my god, really? So you might actually have island blood and not be just an invading tourist.'

'Exactly.' He winked at her, and she looked away, grinning.

She reached the container and pushed the door open. Monty followed her inside, grabbing the other end of the kite to help stow it away. The distant hum of the festival barely filtered into this cold, dark space.

'I can't get over how good you are on that thing.' Monty adjusted his glasses, his smile almost proud.

Such a sweet guy.

'The crowd loved it too.'

Iona shrugged. 'I told you earlier, I love doing it.'

'Well, you nailed it.'

She lifted a couple of blankets from a shelf. 'Shall we watch for a bit?'

'Yeah, why not?'

'I'll get changed out of this first. Here.' She chucked the blankets to him and used the string to pull down the zip on her wetsuit. He cleared his throat and turned away. What a gent. She stepped out of the wetsuit and hung it up. 'I've got a cossie on. You can look. I'm not completely indecent.'

'Hmm, well... It just doesn't feel right. I'm not a lecher.'

'I know that.' She lifted her Dryrobe and pulled it on. 'Come on, let's go.'

He peered around and she held out her hands, waggling her fingers. 'I'm decent.'

Raising an eyebrow, he looked sideways as if to say *I don't think so*, then laughed.

They headed back to the beach and laid out the picnic blanket in a quiet spot near the grass where Monty had been sitting before. No sooner had they sat down than the two annoying guys appeared and sat down not far off.

'Seriously?' Iona glared at them before turning to Monty.

'Do you want to move?' he asked.

She cast a glance in their direction. One of them was looking back with a smug expression that made her want to march over and slap him. 'Actually no. I have a better idea.'

Monty put his hand on her arm. 'If it involves physical violence of any kind, I would advise against it.' His tone was fake formal, like he was joking, but his eyes were serious.

'I can't deny the thought has crossed my mind, but that's not what I was thinking.' She shuffled a little closer. 'How about another lesson in how to be adventurous in love?'

'Um... yeah? And what's that?'

'How to make out on a beach.'

'With all these people watching?'

She grinned and leaned closer. 'It's a festival. Half the people here will be doing it shortly.'

He let out a huff that was partway between a laugh and a scoff. 'So, when in Rome...'

'Exactly. And it'll give those two something to stare at.'

'Ok.' He took off his glasses and placed them on the rug beside him.

Iona's pulse spiked. What the hell? But something about the movement was so deliberate. So calculated. He meant business.

She'd expected to make the first move, but he raised his hand and ran his warm fingertips over her cheek before cupping it. 'It's an honour to kiss someone like you.'

'What?' She couldn't move. Her eyes were fixed on his, his hazel irises darkened by his almost blown-out pupils.

'You're just so... So incredibly talented, spirited and buzzing with energy. So fearless. It's inspiring, and it's a privilege to get to do this with someone like you.' He leaned in and pressed his lips to hers, so soft and unassuming, just like him. She returned it, relaxing into the warmth. He ran his fingers from her cheeks into her hair, cradling her head, deepening the kiss. Their tongues touched and sharp bolts of lust shocked Iona. The sounds of the beach faded, and it was just them, the taste of salt on his lips and the warmth of his body. She reached up, sliding her fingers around his jaw, and he wrapped his arms around her, holding her close. There was no great hurry. The intensity was rich and decadent, something to be savoured. The growing urge to take this somewhere else was ever present, but not so much that Iona wanted to call a halt to this moment. She couldn't recall a kiss ever having this effect on her before.

'Well, this is educational,' Monty murmured against her lips.

'I'm not sure why you ever thought you needed practise at this. You're already bloody epic.'

'You think?'

'I know. That was some kiss.'

She glanced over his shoulder. The two guys were still flicking them a look here and there, but they seemed to be searching elsewhere too. Perhaps looking for someone to hook up with.

Well, it won't be me.

Once upon a time, she might have been open to the idea, but right now there was only one man she wanted to go home with. The one whose arms were around her.

Pulling back slightly, she smiled up at him. 'You're a quick learner.'

Monty raised an eyebrow and stroked the loose hairs from her forehead. 'I think I might have missed some of the finer points. Maybe a little more practice is needed.'

'Ah... Ok. Then try this.' She lay back, leaning on one arm, and patting the blanket behind him with the other. 'Lie down.'

'Yes, Miss.' He lay alongside her, and she shuffled right in close. For a moment, they just looked at each other. Monty stroked the hair from her face. Nothing like this had ever happened to her before. In films, people did this kind of thing after sex, but she didn't recall anything like that. This was all meant to be pretend... Practice for Monty. Why then was her heart racing so fast?

When his lips touched hers again, she closed her eyes. Warmth and a deep sense of contentment flooded her system. She was drowning in his kisses, but it wasn't scary. It was perfect.

Iona pulled back eventually. 'Catriona and Eilidh have food for me. I could go and nab some and bring it over.'

'Don't you want to sit with them? I can keep out of it.'

'Catriona won't mind. I saw her when we came out of the container with some of the school mums and Eilidh was building a sandcastle with some friends.'

'Well, if you're sure.'

'I am.' Iona headed over to Catriona and got some food. Catriona was chatting to some friends, but Iona knew she had questions – thankfully none she could currently vocalise.

Catriona's food was always delicious and once Iona had got it back to the blanket, she and Monty made short work of it.

The long summer's day meant the daylight held on until late, and Iona watched the goings on with Monty.

'Shall we go back?' she said eventually, noticing several people leaving.

'Where to?'

Iona looked him up and down. 'The annex? Together?'

Monty almost leapt to his feet, and they put away the blankets, then made their way up the track back to An Grianan.

As soon as they got back to the annex, Monty pulled her close, kissing her like there was no tomorrow. He sunk deeper into the kiss, and his tongue dipped in and out of her mouth. His hips rocked against hers in a rhythmic motion, and her blood boiled, soaring through her veins like rocket fuel – similar to the rush she got kite surfing, only this time the heat pooled between her thighs, and her body coiled with need.

He most definitely didn't feel like a gentleman now. He was all sin and wickedness.

Desperate to touch him, to run her hands over his chest, she began to lift up his shirt, but his hand gently caught her wrist, staying her.

'Not yet.' He took off his glasses, and his hazel eyes bored into hers. 'Let's not be hasty.' His gaze, hot and intense, travelled down her body, then returned to meet hers again.

'Hasty? Are you serious?'

'Very.' He smoothed her hair off her face. 'Do you ever take out the ponytail?'

'Sure.' She dragged out the elastic and shook the wild mass free. It was windswept from the day at the beach and probably looked like she'd stuck her finger in a socket, but the way he was eyeing her made her breath hitch.

'You really are beautiful.'

She quirked a little smile. 'I feel like a complete mess.' She tugged the ends of her hair and held them wide.

'It's just you. Wild and free.' He smiled. 'I have to thank you.'

'What for?'

'For letting me do this with you.'

'Monty.'

'I mean it. I really do.'

She stared at him, not sure what to make of any of this.

'Now...' He stroked her hair from her forehead. 'May I touch you? I'd like to kiss every inch of you.'

She mouthed something inaudible before finding words. 'Ok, um, sure. You go ahead. That sounds... awesome.' She sucked the inside of her lip. She hadn't expected him to say anything quite so bold.

He tilted her chin, lifting it so she was looking at him. 'You sure?'

'Of course, but remember...'

'Remember what?'

'Make it authentic. Don't hold back.'

'Ok.' His lips settled over hers again, gentle but firm, the way he always started off. Those languorous, thoughtful kisses that made her stomach clench and the ache between her thighs burn. 'I want you so badly.'

Her heart hammered. This was still an act, right? Sophie and all that. Yeah. Course it was... It bloody had to be. But she'd play along. It was too good not to. 'I want you too.'

A smile swept across his face. 'Music to my ears.' Still smiling, he unzipped her Dryrobe. She shuffled out of it, so it pooled at her feet, and she stood before him in her two-piece cossie. His eyes raked over her. 'So strong. So fit. A real athlete.'

'Not really. I just like being active.'

'You look great.' He tugged her towards him, pinning her hips against his, clear evidence of his desire pressing hard against her. 'Utterly gorgeous, in fact.' He kissed down her neck, his hands snaking over her back. She threw back her head, almost dizzy, as his soft kisses caught her exposed throat. Normally, she wouldn't let anyone kiss her there. Too intimate. And it made her too vulnerable. Still holding her, he gently backed her towards the bed, then nudged her down. She lay back, and he moved in beside her, peeling off her cossie top and discarding it. His hands reached to cup her breasts. 'Beautiful.' He dipped in to kiss her again, this time toying with her nipples. Then he shifted to suck and nibble them until she let out a moan and clutched at the duvet.

'Monty, please,' she panted. 'I can't wait. I need you.' She made a play for his shirt, but he pulled away, moving down and tugging off the bottom half of her cossie.

'Why rush?' he murmured, his breath hot against her stomach as his kisses headed south. 'Is there somewhere else you need to be?'

'Definitely not.' Gentleman Monty had officially left the building, and a hot-blooded man had taken his place. One who needed no practice. What he was doing with his hands and his mouth was perfectly acceptable... in fact, far exceeded expectations. 'Oh god.' An A-plus performance if ever there was one. Her insides tightened, and she groaned. 'Oh Monty.'

'That's my name. I can spell it out for you.'

'Oh... Bloody hell.'

His tongue did the job until she was a writhing, gasping mess. A dam of pleasure burst open, and she panted, her eyes rolling. 'You fucking hot bastard.' She lay back, trying to catch her breath. 'I think you lied. You don't need practice at all.'

He shifted up beside her and stroked her hair. 'I've never been this brave before. I told you, you're inspiring. And you told me to be authentic. This is how I want to be. Thank you... Again.'

'Thank me? Why the hell do you want to thank me? After what you just did?'

'For letting me be me.'

'That's the only you I want.'

He laughed softly. 'That's sweet.'

'Unfortunately, I have bad news for you.'

'You do?' He frowned.

'Yes, sadly, you have a major fault. You're wearing too many clothes.'

'Is that all?' He levered himself up and onto his feet. 'Let's get them off then.' He stripped off his shorts and t-shirt rather matter-of-factly before opening a bag on the window seat and pulling out a foil packet. 'I even braved buying these in the village shop.'

She laughed. 'Does it bother you that much?'

'Yeah. I normally either get them online or use the self-scan in Tesco and hope I don't get flagged for a basket check.'

'Seriously? You're so funny. But before you put that on. Come here.'

'Why?'

'Let me have a turn to play. Lie down.'

'Um... Ok.' He moved back onto the bed. Now it was her turn to drink him in.

She ran her hands over his taut pecs and the hard ridges of his stomach. 'Monty, Monty. You've been hiding the goods.'

'Really?' He clenched his jaw as her fingers brushed over his dusting of chest hair. When she leaned in and kissed her way across his pecs, he said through gritted teeth, 'Please don't. I can't hold on much longer.' He had his eyes closed and Iona smiled.

'But there's so much more to explore.' Reaching inside his boxer briefs, she ran her hand over him. 'Impressive.'

With what was almost a growl, he reached for her hand. 'Stop.' He shoved off his boxer briefs, ripped open the condom packet, and rolled it on. Then he flipped her over and kissed her. 'I need you like this.' He moved in between her thighs. 'Ready?'

'Very.'

Slowly, he sank into her.

Her breath hitched and her toes curled.

'Fuck,' he said hoarsely, his hazel eyes still dark but with an almost dreamy look. 'You feel so good.'

She swallowed. Emotion from deep within soared through her like a raging swell in the sea; she could either let it engulf her, or she could ride it out. And like the surfer she was, that was exactly what she had to do. This was just an arrangement. He'd be gone by this time next week. He began to move, bringing them higher and closer together. His eyes locked unblinkingly with hers, so intensely she couldn't look away. Her heart swelled.

'Iona.' His husky voice was thick with emotion. And it was her name, he'd said. Not Sophie. Iona...

Me. It's me.

He wasn't pretending she was someone else. The storm gathered inside her and she hung on to his gaze as the world shifted around her.

Pleasurable waves sent her flying high and her whole body shuddered with the force of her climax. With a grunt, Monty stiffened. 'Oh, Iona. Iona. Iona.' He collapsed on top of her. She held him close, and the heat of his skin warmed her to the core. Her palms stuck to the faint layer of sweat on his back and his shoulder blades.

Please don't move. Don't go. Stay with me.

But he wasn't going to do that. In a week's time, it might be Sophie lying like this, holding onto him, feeling a swell of love in her heart. Iona shut her eyes, her arms tightening around him. *Love?* Oh, good god no. It couldn't be love, could it?

Chapter Nineteen

Monty

Monty couldn't move. Or maybe it was more a case of didn't want to. Iona's nails weren't long, but she was holding him so tightly the edges of them dug into the skin on his back and shoulders. It wasn't painful, well, maybe a little, but a kind of exquisite pain that told him just how much she'd enjoyed this.

He made to move. He must be crushing her, but she clung onto him.

'Don't go,' she murmured. 'I like you there.'

'Are you not squashed?'

'I like it.' Her breath landed on his ear, tickling his supersensitive skin.

'Ok.' He tightened his grip a little, so they were locked together so rigidly no one could prise them apart.

'I love this,' Iona said. 'It's so soothing. I bought a weighted blanket when I started investigating ADHD. It calms me before I go to sleep, but you're much better.'

He smiled and nuzzled her neck. 'Monty, the human blanket.' For a moment, he lay quite still. He kept himself thinking though, because if he let go, he might fall asleep, and that would be odd. He was still buried deep inside her, which made this moment even more intimate. Did she do this with everyone she hooked up with? Why should he be special? He was just inexperienced. He'd only been with two people before Sophie and no one since, and despite her claims that he was too vanilla, she never told him what she liked or appreciated him trying anything different. Being a fairly intelligent man, he'd investigated ways he could spice things up, but she'd never seemed open to it. Well, Iona had benefited from his 'research' and she certainly hadn't complained.

When he felt a wave of drowsiness wash over him, he reluctantly pulled out and quickly ridded himself of the condom. Iona might want to go. She only did casual relationships, after all. She'd let him know that on so many occasions that he should be prepared for that eventuality, even if the thought of her going made his insides feel hollow.

'Are you asleep?' he asked, returning to her side.

'No.' Her voice was quiet. With barely any light in the room and without his glasses on, he couldn't see her properly, but he sensed she had her eyes closed. He shifted in closer and wrapped her in a hug again. She nestled her head into his chest.

Guess she's staying then.

He placed a soft kiss on her forehead and closed his eyes.

———————❤———————

When Monty woke, Iona was still in his arms. He stroked her hair and kissed her. His body was all set for round two, but she might not want that. And that was fine. She'd definitely woken something in him, but he wasn't an animal who couldn't control himself. Her happiness was worth more to him than anything else, and he'd go along with whatever she wanted. Right now, he was happy just to be here with her. It hadn't been a lie when he'd said he felt honoured to kiss her. Every moment spent with her was an honour. Monty MacNeil had no business being with someone this awesome.

She woke with a moan, her hand smoothing over his stomach, making its way lower. 'Good morning,' she said, her fingers sliding further down, curling around him.

His breath hitched.

'Morning.' He closed his eyes as she toyed with him. 'Stop.' He grabbed her hand and looked down at her. She was smiling up at him, her long dark hair spread wildly across the pillow.

'You don't like it?'

'Oh, I do. I just don't like to rush.'

She grinned. 'You're a thinker.'

'Maybe.' He frowned and ran his fingers through his hair. 'Is that my problem? Is that what makes me vanilla?'

She sat up and raised an eyebrow. 'What you did last night wasn't vanilla.' She shifted a little, and her breasts bounced in a way that caught his eye and made him want to reach out and touch her, but she jumped out of the bed. 'I need to pee.' She crossed the room, stopping abruptly at the mirror. 'Jesus Christ. I also need to wash my hair. I've seen better kept bird's nests.'

She went into the bathroom, and he lay back, staring at the ceiling. He really needed to pee too. And wash. But neither was what he actually wanted to do. The bathroom door clicked open, and Iona emerged. She picked up her Dryrobe and flung it on. *Uh-oh*. He'd been too slow. Now she was leaving.

'You... Um...' What could he say?

'I'm going to grab some clothes and my shampoo.' She winked. 'Then we can take a shower.'

'We?'

'You got me into this mess, so you can bloody well help me clean up.' She left with a little wink and a wave.

Monty blinked and let out a long, slow breath. Ok. He'd never done that before, but this was a week of learning to be more adventurous after all. Tossing back the duvet, he got up and went to the bathroom. His hair was a tousled mess too. He brushed his teeth and stared at his reflection for a moment. Still the same Monty, but he felt different. Stronger maybe, which was weird. Maybe it was a new layer of confidence breaking through. He started the shower and opened the door.

A few moments later, Iona snuck back in, still in her Dryrobe with a bag. She lifted out two golden bottles and handed them to him. He read the name of the argan oil shampoo and conditioner before he became distracted by her taking off the Dryrobe and casting it aside.

'Ready for fun?' She grinned and flicked her hair over her shoulders.

'You want me to wash your hair?'

'Among other things.' She stepped forward and slipped her hand around his cheek, pulling him in for a kiss.

He wasn't sure he could concentrate on washing her hair once they were in the shower, with steam billowing around them. Their wet bodies rubbed together, and Iona swung her head back, exposing her neck as she let the water soak her hair. Monty squeezed out some shampoo and smoothed it over her, noticing how her breasts heaved. He was as hard as a rock, burning to take her. But with a deep breath, he coated her hair in liquid, then used what was left to palm her breasts and she moaned, running her hands back from her forehead, across her scalp as she rinsed the shampoo.

Dipping in, he kissed her neck. 'So beautiful.'

'I don't normally let anyone touch my neck.'

'Do you want me to stop?'

'No. I trust you. But I once had a guy put his hands on me. It's something I hate. Choking is assault and I hate how it's romanticised.'

'I won't do anything you don't like.'

'I know.' She massaged some soapy bubbles across his chest. The energy coursing through him was unstoppable. He wasn't going to last the distance at this rate. She reached for the conditioner bottle and popped the lid. 'Hand out.'

He obliged, and she squeezed a blob into his hand. The heady and sweet scent filled the air. He combed his fingers through her hair, catching every strand. 'Turn around,' he said.

She did it, pivoting so her back was to him. Her hair ran down the line of her spine, all slicked together by the conditioner. He worked it in, hand over hand, like he was pulling in a rope.

'It needs to stay in for a few minutes before I rinse it.' She glanced around. 'So we better find something to do while we wait.'

'How about this?' Monty snaked his arms around her from behind and kissed her neck again.

'I like your thinking.'

From this position, his hands could catch her breasts and work on her womanly parts at the same time. She writhed against him as he worshipped her. This was poetry.

'Take me like this.' Her voice was hoarse. 'I need you.'

Another first. He let go, only to locate a condom and roll it on, then he returned to her, bending her slightly and slipping inside her. His hands slid around her again, resuming their play. He thrust into her steadily and repeatedly until she clenched around him, breathing fast and moaning, then she cried out. He held her tight until his own climax burst, crashing through him like an earthquake.

'Oh Iona. Iona.' She was everything. His release went on longer than he expected. A couple of small aftershocks took his breath away, and he rasped for air.

'That was so good.' Letting out a sigh, she leaned back into him. He gently turned her around to face him and began rinsing her hair, smoothing his palms around her head.

'I'm glad you think so.' He cradled her in his arms as he washed out the remaining conditioner.

'Aren't you enjoying it?'

'Are you kidding me? This has been a totally mind-blowing experience.' And probably unrepeatable. Who else would ever make him feel so wonderfully free? With Iona there were no mistakes, no judgement. They could just have fun and enjoy their time together. Leaving her behind would be painful, but at least he'd experienced these moments.

He'd stepped away from boring Monty, tried new things and maybe, just maybe, it would help him with other things in life.

———————— ♥ ————————

'I've got to get to the festival.' Iona checked the time on her phone. Monty already knew the time, and he'd probably kept her a little too long, but how could he help it? They were so hot for each other anything else seemed like a waste. 'Shit. I need to go now. Are you coming with me?'

'I've already done that several times this morning.'

'Seriously?' She pulled a face at him and smirked. 'What happened to gentleman Monty?'

'Oh, he's still here, somewhere.'

'Well, find him again for a bit and behave.' She brushed a strand of hair from his forehead.

'I'll join you later.'

'Ok.' She flung her arm around his neck and kissed him. 'Thanks for a great night... and morning.'

'Any time. I told you before, it's an honour and a pleasure.'

'You're the sweetest guy.' She prodded his chest. 'And sexy too. Catch you later. We're doing bodyboarding at eleven thirty. You can join in with that. No excuses. Just grab a wetsuit from the container.'

'Yes, Miss.'

After whirlwind Iona had left the building, Monty sat on the end of the bed and breathed very slowly and deliberately, trying to regroup and catch a sensible thought or two from the haze of post-coital bliss. Ah, screw it. He got to his feet. What was the point of being sensible? Or boring, as Sophie might have called it? He was still on holiday, and he was bloody well going to enjoy it.

Monty headed into the farmhouse for breakfast. A lot of other guests were there too, no doubt for the festival. Catriona seemed a little rushed off her feet, and Alex was helping hand out some of the cooked break-fasts. Monty saw him limp a little as he returned to the kitchen.

'My mum wants to talk to you,' Catriona said, putting a plate of cooked food in front of Monty. 'She's found something out, apparent-ly. Would you have time to nip in and see her after breakfast? I can show you her cottage. It's just two minutes away.'

'Yeah, of course. I'd love to hear what she's found.'

Curious to find out what Nora had discovered, he ate quickly, before heading for her cottage.

She took a while to answer the door, but when she did, a broad smile filled her face. 'Come in, come in. I have some good news.'

'I'm intrigued.' Monty followed her into the living area of the cot-tage. The brick wall behind the fireplace was exposed and looked very cosy and rustic, while the rest of the room had obviously been mod-ernised and was bright and clean with lots of plants on tables and the deep windowsills.

He took a seat on the sofa as Nora eased herself into an armchair. 'Well, I reckon your father is my second cousin, which makes you my second cousin once removed. And that means you are a third cousin to Ruaridh and Catriona.'

Monty blinked, trying to take it all in.

She lifted a bit of paper with some scribbles on it. 'My mother was your grandfather's cousin. My grandfather and your great-grandfather were brothers, and we share a common line back from there.' She held out the piece of paper and Monty looked at how she'd sketched it out, so it made a lot more sense than him trying to visualise it.

'Wow... So, that means I really do have island blood.'

'You do. And your ancestors would have lived here. An Grianan has been in our family for many generations.'

'Since we were diddled out of the castle?' he asked with a smile.

Nora chuckled. 'As to that, we'll never know, but it's a fun thought, isn't it?'

'It really is. Thank you for looking into this.'

'Not at all. It's my pleasure. Especially now we know you're part of the family. You can tell Catriona and Ruaridh.'

'I'll do that.' He got up and handed her back the paper. 'My father would have loved to know all this.'

She nodded. 'Sometimes we forget to make the most of our time with people while we have it.'

'That's so true.'

And Monty felt it applied as much to Iona in this situation as it did to the regrets he had about his father.

When he arrived on the beach later, it was already buzzing. The voice on the tannoy was talking about the different moves the surfers were doing and people milled about, either watching or paddling and playing in the shallows. A fast-food van had set up near the container and a queue of people lined up along the edge of the grass. Monty hadn't noticed it the day before, but at least he knew where he could get lunch today.

He set up a little camp for himself and sat down, resting his hands on his knees and glancing around. What would his dad make of this? Would he approve or think it an insult to his memory? So much for a relaxing fortnight to scatter his dad's ashes. It had turned into an adventure packed two weeks with a hot holiday fling to boot. No one would have predicted this. Who would even believe it? He couldn't imagine telling anyone back home. His mum, his golfing friends, and his colleagues would all think he'd lost his mind or was making the whole thing up.

He cracked open a can of Fanta and took a sip, his eyes searching for Iona. Beautiful, wonderful Iona. When they were together, he hadn't thought about Sophie. Not once. Sophie had never inspired this kind of burning energy in him. Nope. Everything he'd done here was only for Iona. He rubbed his chest. Maybe the bubbles had gone down the wrong way, because something was niggling him. The words *I love you* were so close to his lips it was frightening. He wanted to say them to her, even though it was downright insane. But she'd told him to be authentic and not hold back... and he hadn't. Until now. Those three little words were a step too far. How could he say them? He hardly knew her, and yet, he knew her better than anyone. Laying down his drink, he sighed. Why was this so complicated?

A simple solution would be to draw a line under it, and stay away from her for the next few days, but no way was he doing that. He would take everything this island could throw at him.

For now, that meant going to the container, changing into a wetsuit, then making his way to the water's edge. When he got there, he spotted Iona handing out bodyboards.

'Ah, there you are,' she said. 'I thought you'd forgotten.'

'As if.' He smiled at her, then became aware of Ruaridh standing a little way off, talking to some other people but clearly watching Monty and Iona in his peripheral vision.

'I just discovered that he and Catriona are my third cousins.'

'What?'

'Yeah, Nora found the information in a family tree. We share a great-great-grandfather, who probably lived at An Grianan.'

'Oh my god. That means you officially have more island blood than me.'

'I do.' Monty glanced back at Ruaridh. Nora had said to tell him and Catriona about the family connection, but Monty didn't want to butt in while he was with his friends. 'Do you think Ruaridh suspects us of something?' Monty nodded subtly in Ruaridh's direction. 'He keeps looking over.'

Iona followed his gaze, then shrugged. 'So what? Ruaridh knows the deal. I don't do dating, and I especially don't get involved with someone who lives this close.'

Monty nodded. 'Yeah. I remember you said.'

'He asked me out before and I said no. I think he took it personally. He's a nice guy, but I see him more in a brotherly kind of way. I don't find him attractive like...' She eyed Monty, then handed him a bodyboard. 'I'm crap at long-term relationships and happy with short flings. Keeps things simple.'

A pang struck Monty in the chest. So even if he was planning to stick around, he wouldn't stand a chance with her. 'Yeah.'

Iona leaned closer. 'But it's not him we have to worry about.'

'What do you mean?'

'Catriona saw us kissing on the beach last night. I told her you were just helping me ward off those creeps, but...'

Monty pulled a face and ran his fingers through his hair. He hadn't seen her much at breakfast as she'd been too busy, but obviously she'd caught Iona. 'We took it too far?'

'Pretty much what she said.'

'So, do you want to stop or have me be more discreet? I can leave you here and go do something else if this is making you uncomfortable.'

She smiled and tilted her head. 'You really are a gentleman. Catriona's used to me hooking up with guys, but... Well, you're different.'

'Am I?'

'Yeah, because of our arrangement, you know. I'll be seeing you again.' She glanced around. 'Catriona doesn't want me using you or taking advantage of you.'

He let out a little laugh. 'That's not really what happened.'

'I know that and you know that, but she's only seen gentleman Monty, and she thinks I'm leading you astray.'

'Got that right then, didn't she?'

'Ha-ha.' Iona put her hands on her hips and gave him a hard look, but her eyes sparkled with mischief. 'Catriona's such a mother hen. She makes me feel completely irresponsible sometimes.'

'Does she say that?'

'She doesn't have to. I see it in the way she looks at me.'

Monty cocked his head. 'Maybe she just wishes she had some of the freedom you have.'

'Yeah. Maybe.'

'So...' He glanced at Ruaridh again. 'Shall I back off for a bit?'

Iona pouted and rolled her lips. 'You know what?'

He shook his head.

'Who cares?' She slung her arm around his neck and pulled him in for a kiss. He responded automatically. 'We only have a short time together. Let's make the most of it.'

Monty pulled back and smiled. 'Much as I'd love to, let's do some bodyboarding, otherwise you're going to land yourself with a bad reputation.'

'Again.'

'I didn't like to say so, but maybe, yeah.'

'Ok...' She winked. 'We'll save it for later. Now, let's get you back in the water.'

Without looking at Ruaridh, Monty headed into the sea.

Chapter Twenty

Iona

Iona surveyed the beach, hands on her hips, shaking her head. Litter was strewn everywhere, broken deckchairs, discarded wet-shoes and even some perfectly serviceable looking surf boards had been abandoned. Her shoulders slumped. People were so gross and utterly disrespectful. If this was the way they treated her beautiful island, she'd think twice about inviting them back.

Where to even begin?

'Bunch of twats,' she muttered. She wasn't in the best of moods anyway, and this was going to give her a migraine about thirty seconds from now.

Monday morning had come too quickly, and the beach was deserted, apart from all the shit. Everyone else had gone back to work and guests had caught the ferry or buzzed off on day trips, including Monty. She'd woken up again with him that morning. A crackle of electricity ran through her veins at the thought. If she could let this cleanup go, she would. She'd much rather spend time with him, but this was her job, and she couldn't avoid it. Plus, he was on holiday. It wasn't fair, expecting him to hang around with her all the time.

She picked up a stray bottle, tossing it into a crate already full of rubbish.

Her brain was in a similar jumble. Since when had she let her mind dwell on a person like this and not the outdoors or sport? She enjoyed being with him so much. Which was so alien to her. Every smile from him, every touch, made her heart thud a little harder. She wasn't supposed to get attached. That wasn't the deal. But he'd got under her skin. He was like a part of her. When they were together, fireworks burst around them, but when they were apart, she felt broken and empty.

'Stop being stupid,' she muttered. How was he any different from anyone else? They'd had good sex, that was all. And surely, she could have that again. She made her way down the beach, attempting to convince herself by repeating the thoughts like a mantra. But it didn't work. Her mind wandered and very soon all she'd done was add more confusion, because she wasn't certain that sex was the only thing they had going for them. If it was, she'd have already forgotten about him – like all the others. Monty was just so easy to talk to and to be around. He didn't judge her, and he accepted her quirks and all. Instead of being put off by the headstrong things she couldn't stop herself from doing or saying, he said he was 'honoured' to be with her. That in itself was something new, and it made her smile. Such a cute thing to say. His words repeated inside her head like an affirmation – pushing out the earlier mantra without much effort.

You're just so incredibly talented, spirited and buzzing with energy. So fearless. It's inspiring, and it's a privilege to get to do this with someone like you.

What was he up to today? She'd slipped out of bed early – well, early for her – and told him she had to get to work. They'd only had a brief kiss and a promise to catch up later before she'd left. If they'd started anything else, she'd never have got here.

She slapped the heel of her hand to her forehead and rubbed it. The mess on the sand wasn't the only thing needing sorted and cleaned up. The chaos in her mind could do with an industrial strength hoover and a Marie Kondo-style tidy up.

With a sigh, she headed to her car and pulled out a roll of black bags. If she didn't start now, she never would.

A gull squawked overhead, and she glanced up, watching it swoop down to the water. That's where she wanted to be. Out there, soaring over the waves. Instead, she pulled open a bin bag and a pair of gloves and started shoving in the rubbish.

She returned to the house at lunchtime to get more bin bags and some more boxes to sort some of the recyclable stuff into. Eilidh was cycling around on her bike, enjoying the early days of the summer holidays. Those were the best days. Iona remembered them lasting for what seemed like months when she was that age. Now the summer weeks passed so quickly; if she blinked, she missed them.

'You having fun?' she asked Eilidh.

'Yeah. Alex is taking me to a quiet track to cycle after lunch. Mummy says I can go if I remember to use the brakes.'

'And are you remembering?'

'I'm doing it, look.'

Iona smiled, knowing Eilidh had a habit of scraping her feet along the ground to stop. 'Great. You keep practising. I need to see if Mummy has any bin bags I can use. If not, I might have to do a wee nip into the village.'

'Can't Ruaridh get the bins?'

'Yeah. He can help me when everything's bagged up, but I'll have to do that bit.'

'Ok.' Eilidh cycled off around the path towards the annex.

Was Monty still there? Hopefully he'd gone out and found something fun to do. Catriona wasn't in the kitchen and Iona wandered through the farmhouse, calling her.

'I'm up here changing the rooms.' Catriona peered down the stairs. 'What's up?'

'I need more bin bags. Do you have any? You should see the beach. What an utter shitshow. People are such arseholes.'

'That's a disgrace. Take photos and put them on the community social media pages. I think we should make it clear this is unacceptable and if visitors are going to treat the island like this, then we won't be inviting them.'

'Yeah, I'll do that.'

'Let me sort this duvet and I'll come down and look for some bin bags.'

Iona wandered back to the kitchen, opening the fridge and snacking on some raspberries.

Catriona came in, a harassed look on her face. 'I'm never going to get all these rooms done in time. The school holidays starting and the festival is great for business, but what a rush.'

'I would help you,' Iona said. 'But I need to do the beach. It's a disaster zone. Hopefully Ruaridh can come by later with the truck and get rid of some of the bags.'

'I'm sure he will.' Catriona rummaged through a cupboard and pulled out a roll of black bin bags. 'Here you go.'

'Thanks.' Iona let out a long sigh, her eyes drifting to the window as she caught sight of a man in the backyard. For a second, she thought it was Monty, then she realised it was Alex. He crouched down by Eilidh and pressed his fingers to her bike tyre like he was checking the pressure.

'I already did that.' Catriona's eyes narrowed as she glared at Alex. 'Does he think I'm incompetent?'

'He's just trying to help. He's nice like that.'

Catriona rolled her eyes. 'You're hardly one in a position to lecture me about men. You still haven't explained about Monty. That was quite a blatant kiss on Saturday night. And Ruaridh said you were still at it during the festival yesterday.'

'At what?' Iona felt a flush creeping up her neck.

'Kissing him.' Catriona cocked her head. 'And I'm sure the fact you haven't been in your bed for the last two nights means you've found somewhere else to sleep.'

'Well, so what? Can't I have a bit of fun? It's not a crime.'

'It's a little strange considering how you said just a few days ago that he wasn't your type.'

'He's not.' She gave a little shrug. 'But... I dunno, I like him, ok?'

Catriona came over and gave her a hug. 'That's good. But be careful. Apparently, he's a distant cousin of mine, so he told me at breakfast. He seems like such a nice guy, and he's really helped with the business plan. I wouldn't like either of you to get hurt.'

'As if.' Iona snorted, a little too defensively.

'You say that. But look what happened to me.' She gave Eilidh a wistful look. 'That was what I got from fooling about with someone who was on holiday here.'

'Yeah. I know.' Iona patted her arm. 'I won't get hurt though. Casual is fine with me.' And maybe if she said it out loud enough, she would start believing it again.

'I know you don't mind casual and that's your choice, but... Well, he doesn't seem like someone who normally does casual. Though who am I to say that? We may be distantly related, but I don't really know him at all.'

'I don't think he's normally into flings, but... well, he wants some, um, practise.'

Catriona raised an eyebrow and furrowed her brow. 'Practise at having flings?'

'Not exactly, but don't worry. It's all fine. He's not serious about me and I feel the same.'

Catriona's sceptical look didn't waver.

'I better get back. See you later.' Iona headed for the door before Catriona could ask any more questions. Once outside, she jumped in the car. She almost laughed at her own words. *I won't get hurt though.* But what if she did? Because one thing was certain. In a few days' time, Monty was leaving. He was going back to the mainland, and Iona wouldn't have him anymore.

She returned to the beach, armed with the bin bags. If only there was something to keep her focused. How could she do this? She started picking up the litter, shoving it into the black bags with more force than necessary. Each piece of rubbish felt like a personal affront.

'Utter wankers,' she muttered, shoving a discarded flip-flop into a bag.

The sun was out and, as the clouds rolled away, it heated up, making her feel sticky and irritable. She wiped her brow, glancing up and down the beach. So much still to do. This was impossible. Maybe if she had a break and hit the waves, she could do some more later. But if she stopped now, she'd never come back to it. Her tummy rumbled. Those raspberries weren't enough to fill her up. If only she'd had the sense to grab some lunch when she was back at the farmhouse, but sense was something she'd been completely lacking recently.

The waves rolled in, soothing and rhythmic, and maybe that was the only reason she kept going. Their constancy was something to work to. How long had she been at it now? Every so often a car would swish past on the road beyond, or people on bikes chatting, but everyone seemed to be avoiding the beach. Could she blame them?

Another whir of a bike came by. She couldn't quite see the road from here, but she wondered if it was maybe Alex with Eilidh. She looked up, squinting against the sun. The cyclist had stopped and dismounted. He pulled off his helmet and ran a hand through his hair. Looking around, his gaze locked onto her.

Was that Monty?

A deep warmth flooded her, almost like relief, though she knew he wasn't here to rescue her from this mess. Just seeing him filled her with so many emotions.

As he got closer, he smiled. 'This is where you've got to. I wondered where you were. I messaged you, but you didn't reply.'

'I haven't looked. I've been so busy.'

He glanced around, scanning over the rows of bin bags and recycling boxes. 'You really have.' He pushed his glasses further up his nose.

'What did you want me for?'

He smiled at her, and his eyes held hers for a moment. 'Nothing in particular. I just like seeing you.'

'I would give you a hug, but I'm a sweaty mess and I've been picking up shit all day, so I probably stink.'

He let out a laugh and ruffed up the hair at the front of his head. 'I love it how you just say it like it is.'

Iona blinked, processing his words; they'd been dangerously close to "I love you," and that was what her brain wanted to hear – which was insane, right? 'Um... Have you been somewhere nice?'

'Just cycling around, getting some photos. It's so beautiful.' His eyes had initially been on the sea, but on the word beautiful, they snapped back to her. The look suckered her and all the joy of being held in his arms rushed back. She'd like to be there right now.

'Well, you should carry on doing that. Make the most of the weather. You know how quickly it changes here.'

'I certainly do. But I'm staying here.'

'Why?'

'Because your company is one of the most special things on the island.'

A smile crept onto her lips. She couldn't stop it. All her irritation with the mess dispersed, at least for the moment. 'That's sweet. You're such a nice man. But I can't hang about and chat.'

'Obviously. That's why I'm going to help you.'

'Absolutely not. You aren't responsible for this.'

'Neither are you. If we do it together, it'll get done twice as fast, and we can have fun while we work. And if that's not enough, just think about what we can use the extra time for.'

'Monty, you are some guy.' She laughed. 'Ok, I accept your offer. Thank you.'

'Let's do it then.'

She handed him the half full bag. 'You take that one and I'll get some more.'

He took it, then leaned over. She met him midway, and their lips brushed together briefly. Despite feeling like she'd waded through a midden all morning, the concentrated touch seemed to purify her thoughts. The mess wasn't so bad anymore. They could do this.

It wouldn't exactly be her first choice of date, but it gave them time to chat. By five o'clock, they were almost done, but Iona didn't want to stop.

'How about we get a carry out and keep going until it's done?' Monty suggested.

'Good idea.' She drove him into Castlebay, and they got some chips.

Monty smirked as they headed back to the car. 'The last time I saw you with a bag of chips, I knocked you over and a seagull ate them.'

'Don't remind me. I still haven't forgiven you.'

'Oh, I think you have.' He grinned at her.

'Ok, maybe.'

They headed back to the beach and carried on tidying and lugging the bags up, piling them up at the side of the container.

'Will the binmen take all these?' Monty frowned at them and wiped his brow.

Iona smirked. 'You know Ruaridh is a binman, right? He'll take them.'

'Is he? Wow, I wondered what he did.'

'He gets a bit touchy about it sometimes because he thinks people look down their noses at him.'

'Well, I don't envy him, but I do appreciate him. Where would we be without the rubbish collectors?'

'Exactly.' Iona clapped her hands together. 'Job well done.' She high-fived Monty.

'I know what we need now.'

She raised her eyebrows. 'Yeah?'

'Let's go for a dip.'

'*You're* suggesting that to *me*?'

He gave a little shrug. 'Only if you want to.'

'Of course I do, but normally I have to drag you.'

'I must be getting a bit better then.'

'Not better. You were always enough. Now you just have more confidence.'

He tilted his head and smiled. 'Thanks for saying so.'

'Do you want to get a wetsuit?'

'When I was cycling around earlier, I stopped at the thrift shop and got myself a pair of board shorts. It's a nice evening and I'm feeling brave.'

'You are awesome.' Iona flung her arms around him, forgetting about her messy clothes, but he didn't seem to mind. He hugged her back. 'Let's get them on in the container.'

They walked up to it, and Iona stripped off her manky clothes and pulled on a bikini she'd stashed in the container. 'This will have to do. My cossie is back at the farmhouse.'

Monty put his hands on his hips, glancing down at himself in the board shorts with a screwed-up face. Iona laughed, not because he looked bad, but his expression was hilarious. When he raised his eyes to her, they widened.

'What are you trying to do to me? You think that'll "have to do"? You look incredible, whereas I look like surfer Ken.'

She took hold of the waistband and pulled him towards her. 'You're much hotter than that.'

They fell into an easy kiss before heading for the sea. Iona never took time to acclimatise. Monty, however, took it slow until she grabbed his hands and pulled him in. Splashing around was fun, and she did some swimming while he treaded water, waiting for her to come back. Every time they met, they shared a kiss. Then Iona unhooked her bikini, freeing her breasts and keeping them just out of the water.

'What if people are watching?' Monty drew her close and gently caressed her nipples.

'No one's around and they can't see anything for the sea.' She pulled him down, kissing him, loving the way he touched her so gently, yet firmly. In fact, scratch that. She loved him full stop. Parting with him would kill her. She wrapped her arms around his neck and devoured his lips, pouring everything into him. If he was leaving, she'd make damn sure he had something to remember her by.

Chapter Twenty-One

Monty

Monty lay on the beach, rolling strands of Iona's hair through his fingertips. It must be late now as the sky was almost fully dark, and that didn't happen until around eleven p.m. at this time of year. But he had no desire to move. Iona's head rested on his chest, and he gazed up at the deep, velvety cloak spreading across the sky. Even now, enough light remained to make silhouettes on the landscape. Summer nights never equalled the utter blackness of winter.

A picnic rug below them and another heavier one on top was all that sheltered them from the light breeze. But the heat from their entwined bodies was more than enough. Monty had never tried sex on the beach as a cocktail, even though Sophie loved them. She'd often ordered them with a little smirk, like she was trying to make him blush. Just as well she couldn't see him now. The real thing was so much more satisfying than any cocktail could ever be. He smiled at the deep contentment satiating his whole body.

For all Sophie's assertions about him, she'd never do this. She liked fancy hotels and expensive clothes. Making love on a deserted beach in the Hebrides as darkness fell wasn't something she'd ever consider. For Iona, however... Well, Iona was Iona. No one else would ever be Iona. Monty wouldn't have entertained even the idea of doing this just last week, but Iona had changed everything. She made him bold. Or more like she let him be free. Sure, he'd still freaked that someone walking a dog might find them, but she assured him once darkness fell, and as long as they kept a cover over them, no one would see. The beach was completely deserted, though the constant thud of the waves was like an ever-present guardian.

Iona felt heavier in his arms than she had done a few moments ago, and her breathing was deeper. He kissed her brow, then her eyelids. 'Sleep tight, beautiful Iona.' He carried on stroking her hair, still staring up into the night. 'I love you.' The words barely left his lips, so if she was still awake and listening, she probably wouldn't have heard anyway. But he'd wanted to say them every time they were together. Saying her name was almost enough. He wasn't practising for Sophie anymore. Had he ever really been? He'd been making love to Iona because she was the one he loved.

He rolled a little, adjusting his position and bringing his arm more tightly around her. Should he wake her? Maybe they should go back to the farmhouse. She might have teaching to do the next day. Would this be enough sleep? But he couldn't bring himself to do it. It was much more comfortable just to lie here, listening to the sea, watching the stars and feeling the beat of her heart against his.

———————❤———————

When his eyes opened, his shoulder was dead and his spine achy.

'Monty.' Iona prodded him gently.

His feet were cold. In fact, everything was cold. The sky was brighter than when he closed his eyes, but not bright enough to be fully morning. 'What is it?' he squinted to see her.

'It's half three in the morning and I'm getting a bit cold.'

'Let's go back then.'

They wrapped themselves in the picnic blankets and headed back to the farm. The island may as well have been abandoned. They left the blankets in the container and pulled on a minimal amount of clothes. It felt like a long way back.

Iona yawned when they arrived. 'I'm knackered, but I want to stay with you.'

'Come to the annex then.'

She leaned up and kissed him on the cheek. 'Ok.'

Once they were inside, Monty felt heat returning to his body, but not enough. He went to the bathroom, not loving the cold floor on his bare feet.

Iona went in as soon as he came out and he discarded his clothes, finding a pair of night shorts to wear, more for warmth than anything else.

'Cuddle me warm?' Iona came up behind him and placed cold hands on his back. He jumped, not sure if she meant her words to be a question, but they sounded like one.

'Of course.' He pulled back the duvet, and together they got under, snuggling into each other, resuming their positions from the beach, only this time in a warmer and comfier place. But he missed the gentle lap of the sea.

He'd meant to ask Iona if she was working, and when she needed to get up, but he must have fallen asleep almost instantly. The next thing he knew, she was rubbing against him, kissing him like she was half dreaming. Maybe he was too, but if he was, it was a very good dream. He'd had more sex in the past few days than he had done in the past year, but he wasn't complaining.

'Look at me,' Iona demanded, as she rode on top of him, her hips bucking fast. If her breasts weren't so distracting, his gaze would have been on hers anyway. He snapped it up to meet her, giving her breasts the attention of his hands instead. Almost straight away, she squealed, moving even faster, then shuddering wildly. He loved this sight, watching her come undone, knowing she'd enjoyed being with him. That knowledge was power and made him strong and fearless. He let go. Maybe it was too soon, but he couldn't wait.

'Oh Iona. Iona...' He breathed heavily, still connected to her soul through their eye contact. She beamed at him as he fell back to earth. 'Sorry. I couldn't hold on.'

'You didn't have to.' She bent over and kissed him. 'I know you like to take your time, but quickies are ok too. That was what we needed. And it was still good, wasn't it?'

'Good? That doesn't begin to describe it.'

She moved off him and sat beside him, leaning on the headboard. 'I can't hang about. I'm teaching surf classes today, but I'll see you again later, yeah?'

'Sure.' He rested on her shoulder, and she leaned her head on his.

'Maybe we could climb Heaval tomorrow afternoon. I promised you we could, but I've not had time.'

'Yeah, I'm up for that.'

'I'm doing an eleven o'clock class tomorrow, but nothing in the afternoon, so we could do it then.'

'Great.'

She ran her hand around his jaw, and he remembered he hadn't shaved in days. What had happened to corporate banker Monty? A week and a half on a Scottish island and he'd gone feral. 'I wish I could spend more time with you.'

'It's fine.' He put his hand over hers, then took hold of it and kissed her wrist. Her eyes went dreamy again, but with what looked like a concerted effort, she pulled her hand away and got out of bed.

The hours without her would be torture, but they were good practise, because in a few short days' time, he'd be leaving the island and who knew when he'd be back. If ever. His mind was clearer now. Sophie was gone, and he wasn't going to go after her again. After this week, he'd learned enough about himself to realise there was nothing wrong with him. There was nothing wrong with her either. They just wanted different things and weren't as compatible as he'd wanted to believe. On paper, they were perfect, but love didn't happen on paper. Sophie could do as she pleased. Monty wouldn't be darkening her doors again.

What exactly he was going to do was another matter. Getting Sophie back had been part of a larger life plan, one he didn't want to discard completely. He was at an age and stage where he wanted to settle, but starting from scratch was so daunting.

He lifted his phone and scrolled aimlessly through social media. Iona had messaged him pictures she'd taken of him at the festival. He actually looked like he was enjoying himself. He posted them to his page, not for Sophie's benefit this time, but for his own. A couple of friends and work colleagues had commented on his previous posts. As expected, they were mostly shocked.

I thought you hated water!

Bodyboarding? WTAF!! Who are you and what have you done with Monty?

'I'm still here,' he muttered. And this time next week, he'd be back in his office, suffocating under mountains of emails and paperwork. In a dream world, he'd pack it all in and stay with Iona, but he had a job to go back to. His life wasn't here. And Iona had told him countless times that she was a free spirit. Settling down with her wasn't the long-term option he was looking for.

This was a holiday fling, and he had to accept it as that. He'd prolong it to the last minute and enjoy every last second, but when he flew out of here on Friday, he'd have to leave it behind.

Chapter Twenty-Two

Iona

I ona tightened the laces on her hiking boots and looked up at the path ahead. Heaval wasn't a particularly long climb, but it was very steep in places, and the path was little more than a deer track with several boggy patches and places where it almost disappeared. The afternoon sun was bright, however, and the views from the top would be stunning. The sky was a clear blue, with only a few wisps of clouds drifting lazily by.

'You ok?' Monty's voice came from behind as they started up the lower slope.

Iona turned to him, smiling. 'Of course. I've climbed Heaval more times than I can count. My lace keeps coming out.' She put her foot on a rock to tie it.

Monty adjusted his backpack and gave her a nod. 'You can lead the way. I looked it up and I read that the path disappears in places.'

'It gets a bit overgrown and some of it is narrow, but don't worry, we'll get there.'

'I'm never worried when I'm with you. Intrigued as to what's coming next, yes, but not worried.'

She held out her hand. 'Shall we?'

He took it without questioning it, which she was glad about. She'd given up giving him lessons. That wasn't what she was doing anymore. She was just enjoying time with a guy she liked... far too much for her own good.

They set off together, the path winding through patches of heather and rocky outcrops. Holding his hand was like anchoring herself to something steadfast. She didn't need any physical help with a climb like this, but emotionally he was a rock. Her heart was all over the place, but the warmth of his hold kept her grounded in the here and now.

'Take care. It's a bit steep here.'

'Wow.' Monty stopped and looked around. 'What a view. Let me get some pictures.'

'Wait until we get to the top. It's even better.'

'I'd like to get some of Kisimul Castle. For posterity and all that.' He held up his phone, angling it back down towards the bay where the castle sat up proudly surrounded by glittering blue water. 'How about one of us?'

'Sure.' Iona put her arm around his back and held her face close to his stubbly cheek. Unshaven Monty was sexy. After he'd snapped a selfie, she turned her face and kissed his cheek. He snapped another, then met her lips with a hot kiss, still holding out his arm and snapping. 'Is that for posterity too?' She raised her eyebrow as he pulled back.

'No. That's for my eyes only.'

They carried on up. A large white statue came into view onto a sheer rock above them. Every time Iona came up here, she thought this thing looked totally out of place. It was covered in moss these days but depicted a woman holding a child on her shoulders.

'Ah, the statue.' Monty frowned up at it. 'I saw a picture of it. It's not quite as big as I thought it would be, but it's a bizarre thing to have so far up a hill.'

'Yeah, it is. It's called Our Lady of the Sea,' Iona said. 'I don't know much about history, but I heard that a church minister had it built in the fifties as a symbol of protection for the island.'

'I read that too. How the families had collected money for the servicepeople returning from the war and their families, but in the end, they didn't want the money, so they invested it in this.'

'It's a sweet little story, but I agree with you that it's totally bizarre.'

'We are one mind.' His tone was jovial, but Iona's heart leapt. If only they were. Sometimes it felt like that. They were so in tune with one another.

They continued their climb, the path becoming steeper and more rugged as they neared the summit. Iona's breath came faster, but she loved being up here on top of the world, or at least the island.

'Not far now.'

Finally, they reached the top. Iona stopped and put her hands on her hips. The wind was stronger up here and she braced herself against it.

'This is amazing.' Monty pulled out his phone again and snapped around.

The village sprawled below, the water in the bay shimmering under the sun. Kisimul Castle was just a tiny black silhouette now. Iona smiled as she remembered taking Monty out to scatter his dad's ashes. They'd had their first kiss there. She should have realised then how dangerous this would be. That kiss had been special.

She sat down on a rock, looking out over the view, and tucking her ponytail into the neck of her hoody to stop it from blowing across her face. 'I like coming up here to clear my head. It's as if the whole world is laid out before you, but you're separate from it, you know?'

'I get it, yeah.' Monty sat beside her and put his arm around her. 'Meeting you has been the best thing that's happened to me this week... Maybe even longer.' He kissed her forehead.

She rested her hand on his thigh and squeezed it. She, in part, agreed. But then, if she'd never met him, she wouldn't have to face losing him again.

They sat in comfortable silence for a while, the gentle breeze playing in the long grass and the distant cry of seabirds filtering up from the bay.

'Thank you for everything,' Monty said. 'I'll never forget this. Or you.'

'Neither will I.'

He pulled out his phone again. 'Let's have another selfie.'

As he clicked it, it started buzzing. A picture appeared on the screen with a name as clear as the sky above. *Sophie.*

His ex was calling him. Iona watched a puzzled expression grow on his face. 'Why...?' His word was carried away on the wind.

'You better take it,' Iona said. 'It might be important.'

Maybe his dreams would come true. Had Sophie seen his posts on social media? Maybe she liked him now he'd proved his spirit of adventure. Iona was friends with him on the socials now and she'd seen the most recent pictures he'd posted from the festival. He looked happy and chilled in the water. But she'd noticed he hadn't tagged anyone in the pictures. There was no mention of her. Which was fine, but it told her that he didn't want people to have any inkling there was anyone else involved.

He hit the accept call button and put the phone to his ear, still sitting next to her. She'd assumed he'd walk away to take it.

'Hello.'

Iona sat still, trying to focus on the view instead of Monty, but he was so close, she could hear Sophie's voice over the wind as loud as if she was here with them, squashed in the middle.

'Hi, Monty. I'm so sorry.'

'What about?'

'I met your mum,' Sophie said. 'She told me about your dad. I had no idea.'

'Thanks,' he replied.

'I wish I'd known. I would have come to the funeral. And you had to scatter the ashes alone. It's awful. If I'd known, I could have flown over and been there for moral support.'

'It's fine. I, um. I've done it.'

'I know. After I met your mum, I went on social media and saw all your pictures. You look so... Well, different.'

'Do I?'

'Yeah. So confident. The sea air must be doing you good.'

Sea air? Iona raised her eyebrow, but a sharp pain stabbed her in the chest. She kept her gaze fixed on the horizon, playing deaf.

'Yeah, must be.'

'Listen, I hope you're not doing all this because of what I said,' Sophie said. 'About you being boring. I was wrong to say that, Monty. I'm so sorry. I really am. I was in a bad place with work and all that. It was wrong for me to take it out on you.'

'It's fine.'

Iona nearly grabbed the phone and told Sophie to fuck off. Did the woman have any idea of the emotional pain she'd put him through? And he thought it was fine. Well, that told her everything.

'I'd like to talk when you get back,' Sophie carried on. 'Let's put things right between us. What do you think?'

There was a pause, and Iona couldn't look at Monty. This was what he'd been hoping for since the day she met him.

'I don't know, Sophie,' he said. 'A lot has changed.'

'Please, Monty. Just think about it. We can talk when you're back. It's all I'm asking.'

Monty let out a sigh. 'Ok. We'll talk when I get back.'

'Thank you,' Sophie said. 'I'll see you soon, then.'

'Yeah. Bye.'

Monty ended the call and lowered the phone, still sitting beside Iona. The silence between them was heavy, but Iona kept her eyes on the distant castle, the wind brushing against her skin. 'Did you hear that?'

Iona nodded, her throat tight. 'Yes. It's what you wanted, isn't it?'

'It was.' His gaze shifted away. The wind picked up, and Iona felt a chill despite the warmth of the afternoon.

'We should head down.' She got to her feet. 'It's getting chilly.'

They began the descent in silence. The wind whipped around them, making conversation difficult. But even without the wind, Iona didn't want to talk. Rant and scream maybe, but she couldn't bear it. Her heart was in agony. She'd never felt this good with anyone before. Monty had made her feel alive in a way she hadn't experienced in years. But now, it all seemed to be slipping away. She remembered the crushing feeling of inadequacy when she lost her job, and it returned with a vengeance. Monty didn't want her for real. He was still in love with Sophie. He hadn't lied or led her on. She'd known the deal from the get-go and agreed to it. No point moping about it now.

She kept her eyes on the path, watching her step. The reality of the situation pressed down on her like a solid weight. Monty should go back to Sophie. That's what all the practice had been about, hadn't it? Helping him win back the prize he'd been striving for: Sophie.

As they neared the bottom of the hill, Iona's resolve hardened. She had to let him go. He deserved his chance at real happiness, and it wouldn't be with her. That option had never been on the table. She lived on this island and wasn't planning on leaving – he lived in the city and had a good job there. He'd never at any point suggested they tried to extend their relationship any further than the two weeks he was here. And that should be fine with her because she didn't do long term.

Why then did it feel like her heart was about to crack in two?

Chapter Twenty-Three

Monty

Monty picked up the clothes that were strewn around the annex. His two weeks were nearly up. He only had tomorrow left. How the hell had it gone so quickly? His chest was heavy, and he was only packing up now because he wasn't sure what else to do with himself.

The conversation with Sophie earlier had been unsettling. His mind was clear on one thing though. He wasn't getting back together with her. But her appearance had thrown a big ugly spanner in his well-oiled holiday fling. Iona had disappeared into the farmhouse as soon as they got back, saying she had things to prepare for her surf class the following day. He knew her well enough to know she was lying. She didn't do prep work for starters.

Grumpy Iona had reappeared. He huffed out a sigh as he folded his clothes and dumped them on the bed. Maybe it was better this way. They'd have to part anyway, but falling out over nothing seemed silly.

He'd find her later and talk to her. He didn't want to leave on a low note – and he wanted to thank her for everything she'd done for him.

Rain had drifted in with the wind and Monty had arranged to have dinner in the farmhouse. Catriona was still feeding him free meals in return for his help with the business and possibly because she liked the idea of him being a distant relative. Monty couldn't deny that was pretty cool, if a little difficult to get his head around.

'Is Iona about?' he asked her as he took his seat at the dining table.

Catriona paused for a moment, rubbing her hands together. 'She is, but she didn't seem in a very good mood.'

'I need to talk to her.'

'Yeah… She, um, told me about the two of you.'

Monty nodded and put his forehead into his hand, leaning his elbow on the table. 'I'm not sure I want to know.'

'She didn't say anything bad about you. It just surprised me a little. Iona is… Well, she doesn't usually stick to the same person. Maybe my brain is warped after what happened to me with Eilidh's dad, but I'm scared for her.'

'She's a very determined person, so I suspect she doesn't listen to what you have to say.'

'Not really. But I don't mind that. She has her own life to live and her choices are her own. But she's really taken to you. So, I guess that means she likes you… Quite a lot.'

He gave her a weak smile. 'And I like her, but it's difficult. This relationship, if we can call it that, can't go on once I leave. It just wouldn't be possible with the distance. I'm just sorry if I've broken your trust.'

'How do you mean?'

'By fooling around with your friend. Your lodger.'

'You're grownups. You can do what you like. Iona *is* my friend and you're part of my family, even if I didn't know that originally. But you seemed genuine from the first day and I don't want either of you to get hurt.'

'That's why I need to talk to her. I don't want to hurt anyone. I'd like us to part as friends.'

Catriona rocked her head from side to side and sighed. 'Shame you can't stay. You've got a good business head; you could help us out.'

He gave her a weak smile. 'It's a lovely thought, especially now that I have a historical connection to the place, but my job...' He held out his hands. 'I can't leave it just like that.'

'I suppose not. And island life isn't for everyone. It's not an easy lifestyle. I grew up here so I'm used to it, but Iona gave up her job to come here. That was a brave thing to do and she's coped well.'

'Yeah. She's a strong person. And look at the talents she has. She wasn't born for an office. She belongs to the sea and the wind. I don't – no matter who my ancestors were.'

Catriona nodded. 'Well, if you ever want to come back, you know where we are.'

'I'd like to come back. There's so much more to discover. I'd love to have more time to talk to your mum and hear her stories. I feel like I've only just scratched the surface of the island.'

'It never runs out of surprises.' She opened the kitchen door. 'I'll just get your dinner, then I'll see if I can find Iona.'

'Thanks.' He rested his chin on his hands and looked out the window. Most nights, other guests were in here too, but no one had arrived yet and the room was quiet except for the ticking clock.

Catriona reappeared with his dinner and put a plate down in front of him.

'Would you like some wine with that? You're not paying for it, so I can serve it to you as a friend.'

'Sure, if it won't get you into trouble.'

'It'll be fine. But if any other guests come in and ask, just say you brought your own.'

'Ok.'

She returned with a bottle and a glass. 'Drink as much as you want.'

'Thank you. I appreciate everything you've done for me this week. You've made me feel very welcome.'

'For my third cousin... Anytime.' She grinned. 'I appreciate you helping me with the business. It's really helped clear things up in my mind.'

'I'm glad.' He ate quietly, after pouring himself a liberal amount of wine. Why not? Maybe Iona wouldn't want to talk to him, and he'd need to drown his sorrows, something he'd never done in his life before.

Catriona's meals were always delicious, and tonight's spaghetti Bolognese was no exception. He wolfed it down, adding plenty of cheese from the little bowl in the middle of the table.

The door opened and Iona came in. 'You summoned me?'

He shook his head. 'As if I have that power. You're a free spirit who answers to no one.'

'Am I?' She gave him a little shrug. 'Right now, I'm not sure I know who I am.'

'You're Iona. And there's no one quite like you.'

She sat down beside him, leaned her elbow on the table, and rested the side of her head on her fist. 'So, what did you want me for?'

'Just to talk. To thank you.'

'Thank me?'

'Yes. To thank you for letting me have so much of your time... and you.'

She glanced down at the table. 'Honestly, you don't have to thank me. It was a pleasure... Literally.' She side-eyed him with a smirk. 'Shame it went so quickly.'

'Yup. We knew this day would come, but no matter what arrangement we had, it doesn't take away how difficult it is. We had something special and now it has to stop. That's never going to be easy.'

'I guess so. I suppose I'm just...'

'Sad?'

'Yeah.'

'Me too.'

'And now that you've got the prize you were after, we have to behave.'

He frowned. 'What prize?'

'Well, Sophie. She called. I heard it all, remember?'

'Sophie isn't a prize. She's a person. I can't win or lose her. All I did was in the hope that she'd see me for who I am... who I always was deep down – not someone boring and unworthy. I hoped if that happened, we might get back together. But I don't want that now. It's irrelevant because I've discovered parts of myself that I never knew existed, and that's enough for me. I don't need her opinion or her approval.'

'That's good, but maybe she likes the new you too.'

'Maybe, but she never said anything about getting back together. She just wants to talk to me.'

'But it's pretty obvious that's what she wants to talk about.'

Monty took a large swig of wine. 'Maybe, but that's on her. I don't want to think about that right now.'

'Ok. What do you want to think about?'

'You and me.' He leaned over and lifted a spare glass from the dresser, then poured some wine into it and handed it to Iona.

'Thanks.' She almost downed it in one.

'I'd like to finish my holiday fling properly.'

'Oh yeah? How exactly is that going to work?'

'Well, it means we have to keep being nice to each other. I don't want us to fall out, be in a huff with each other, or refuse to talk.'

'I like the sound of that.' A small smile crept onto her face. 'But do you realise how many rules I've broken by seeing you for a whole week?'

'Then thank you again.' He leaned forward and tilted her chin to face him. 'I appreciate your sacrifice. And I know you're probably sick of me saying it, but I really do feel honoured that you've devoted a whole week of your life to me.'

'Monty.' She grinned and knocked his hand away. 'Stop being such a sap.'

'I mean it.' He took another sip of wine. 'I value every minute we've spent together and I want to cherish every minute we have left.'

'I want to do that too.'

He met her eyes. All the beautiful moments they'd shared seemed to play in her dark irises. She'd given him a week, which, compared to what she usually gave, was something special. 'You owe me nothing,' he said, 'But if you're willing to devote one more night to me, then I'll not only be privileged but gratified beyond belief.'

'Sometimes you really sound like the banker you are.'

He raised his eyebrow, then choked out a laugh. 'I blame my upbringing. With a father who wanted me to inherit a castle and a mother who thought I'd be Prime Minister by now, I hardly stood a chance, did I?'

'You really didn't. And I can sympathise. I definitely haven't lived up to my parents' expectations. But let me tell you something.' She leaned closer.

'Anything.'

'I'm quite sure I'll be up to the task of gratifying you in any way you please.'

He leaned his forehead on hers. 'That wasn't exactly what I meant, but how can I refuse?'

'You can't.'

———————— ♥ ————————

Later that evening, Monty sat in the annex, staring at his phone, but not really focusing on anything. His mind drifted from Sophie to returning to work, to his mother, to his father's ashes, to Iona. Always, he came back to her. He'd never known anyone quite like her and he wasn't ready to say goodbye, even though he knew he must. A soft knock on the door pulled him from his thoughts. He got up and opened it, his jaw dropping.

'Iona... Wow.' He ran his fingers through his hair, gazing at her.

She smiled, leaning her hand on the doorframe. A stunning black satin dress clung to her lithe figure, and her hair was styled in a messy updo. She wore makeup, which Monty had never seen her in before. Certainly, she didn't need it, but it accentuated her features, making her look sultry, sexy and a little dangerous. She was almost eye to eye with him and when Monty saw the height of the heels she had on, it made sense. Her shapely legs looked even longer than usual. Monty gaped.

'Good evening,' she said.

'You look incredible. I mean, there was no need to dress up. You're beautiful just the way you are.'

Iona smiled. 'I rarely get the chance to dress up, so I'm using this opportunity. Do you like it?' She spread her arms wide, fanning her fingers.

'I love it. You're absolutely stunning. You always are, but this is...' He shook his head. 'Special.'

'That's what I want.' She slipped inside and closed the door. 'To make this special.'

Monty looked down at his own clothes and pulled a face. 'Now I'm completely underdressed.'

'You look pretty hot to me.'

He smirked. No one else had ever called him that and the funny thing was, he knew she meant it. If she'd thought him boring when he arrived, she didn't think so now. She saw him for who he really was, liked him for stepping out of his comfort zone, but didn't see the need to pressure him into being someone he wasn't. She just encouraged him to try new things and didn't mind if he didn't get it right the first time or made mistakes. God knew how many times he'd fallen off that surfboard. But none of it made her judge him or think him unworthy.

'Give me a second.' He turned and rummaged through his bag, pulling out the white, smart shirt he'd worn the first day he met her. He whipped off his t-shirt and replaced it with the crisp shirt, buttoning it up as he turned around.

Iona closed the gap between them, putting her hand over his, preventing him from fastening any more buttons. 'Why bother?' She raised an eyebrow. 'When I'm about to undo them all again?'

He moved his hands to her hips and held eye contact. 'I'd love to kiss you, but I don't want to ruin your make-up.'

'Not yet.' She pulled away and took out her phone from down the front of her dress.

'Why is your phone in there?'

'This dress has no pockets.' She opened it up, flicking through screens until soft music played from it. She propped it on the windowsill and returned to Monty. Putting her left hand in his, she placed her other on his shoulder. He instinctively moved into a waltz position, and keeping their eyes firmly on each other, they revolved to the music.

Monty rubbed his palm against hers and she mimicked the action until the friction become oddly sensual. He drew her closer, inhaling her wonderful sea breeze scent. She rested her head on his shoulder.

'This has been one heck of a ride, hasn't it?' She breathed the words onto his neck.

'It really has.'

'I don't do relationships. You know that, but in a different world and under different circumstances, I would choose you.'

He let go of her hand and pulled her into a tight embrace, splaying his palms across her back. 'Thank you.' He could hardly get the words out. The soft music was a melancholic background, mourning the impossibility of their situation. Having a holiday fling had never been something he'd even deemed a possibility, and now it was happening. He hadn't expected it to have such a profound effect on him. But she was right. This was something for another world. His life was in a totally different place. Neither of them could easily uproot and even if he did, she'd made it quite clear long-term relationships weren't her thing.

What mattered now was making sure these last moments together were the best they could be. That meant holding on, not just to Iona, but to every precious second. This dance was beautiful and when he kissed her, it held so much depth and meaning. Later they'd make love, but it would be so much more than just a meeting of bodies. He would show her just how wonderfully special she was to him.

Chapter Twenty-Four

Iona

Iona pulled up the zip on her wetsuit, staring out at the waves. She could so do without having a paddle-boarding class today. Not that it would make any difference whether she was here or anywhere else. Monty was leaving later, and her brain didn't have room for thoughts about anything else. If only things were different. But they weren't. Even if she admitted how she really felt, it didn't change the reality. He had a job to go back to. Possibly a girlfriend.

With an enormous effort, she forced her mind back to the paddle-boarding class. She had to do this. If she was lax, people would leave bad reviews – or worse, they could get hurt – and she didn't want that.

'Ok, let's go over the basics again before we hit the water. Everyone remembering the key steps?'

Some general murmurings, nods and thumbs up followed.

'Ok, great.' She placed her board on the sand. 'Let's just do a few more practises of standing on the board before we get in the water.

Remember, once you get in the water, if you prefer to kneel or sit, that's absolutely fine.'

As she walked among today's students – a group of ten, mostly in their twenties – she commented and checked their posture, but still her thoughts drifted to Monty. A smile warmed her a little when she recalled his effort at the water sports festival and his attempts to catch waves on the bodyboard. How he'd grown in confidence. The idea of him leaving was like a sharp stab to the chest. How could she bear it? Tomorrow she'd wake up and be back to the way she was before he'd come on the scene. That was only two weeks ago, and she'd been happy and content enough; there had been no question of her needing anything else in her life.

But now she'd found something else, she liked it, craved it. Losing him would throw her into grief. Maybe in time she'd learn to live with it, but for now it was agonising.

'Ok, let's hit the water!' She picked up her board and led the group into the sea. She watched them paddle out, her mind still elsewhere. The students were getting the hang of it, and she tried to stay present, forcing her eyes onto them. If she watched them closely, she'd have to think about them.

'Great job!' she called out as one girl paddled around very confidently, keeping her balance. But time was crawling. Iona kept glancing at her watch, willing the minutes to pass faster. She couldn't stop Monty going, but she could at least see him before he went. A weird idea was forming in her head, words she wanted to say to him, but she wouldn't. Not unless she could be sure of his reaction. She'd never told anyone she loved them before, and saying it now, when he was about to leave, was probably a stupid idea. When they'd been together last night, she'd wanted to tell him so badly, but she'd reined it in. How could she let him know? Unless she could find a way to say it that wouldn't be committal or final... A plan started to take shape in her mind. Maybe it was crazy, but now it was there she couldn't let it go.

When the session finally ended, she gathered the group on the beach.

'Well done, everyone. You all did so well. I hope you enjoyed it.'

A lot of nods of agreement followed.

'And I see you're booked in again tomorrow... which is great.'

The word "tomorrow" almost jammed in her throat. What would her life look like tomorrow?

The students thanked her and started to head off, chatting as they made their way to the container. Iona quickly packed up her gear, waiting to hang up the wetsuits. She paced and focused on her breathing. Why were they taking so bloody long to change today?

'Thanks, Iona,' a person called out as she left with her friends.

'No worries. See you tomorrow.' Iona waved. The rest of them started filing away, and Iona took the wetsuits and hung them on a rack outside the container. It was probably more haphazard than usual, but all she wanted was to get back to the farmhouse and see if Monty was still there.

Once everything was tidied up, she rushed back to An Grianan, her heart pounding like she'd run a marathon, not walked half a mile along the track. As she approached the farmhouse, she saw Ruaridh and Catriona talking outside. She hurried up to them, barely able to catch her breath.

'Has Monty gone already?' Why did she sound so desperate? But the time for beating around the bush was gone.

Catriona shook her head. 'Not yet.'

'Good. I need to talk to him.'

'Please don't do anything rash.' Catriona gave her a pleading look. 'This will be just as difficult for him.'

'I won't, I just... I need to see him.'

Ruaridh tilted his head and gave her a tight-lipped smile, perhaps aiming for sympathy. 'I'm giving my new cousin a lift to the airport in just a few minutes.'

'You?'

'Yeah. I'm heading up that way anyway.'

'Right.' Iona frowned.

'It's ok.' Ruaridh patted her upper arm. 'I'll take good care of him. He's part of my family now.'

'And you're not upset that he and I...'

Ruaridh shook his head. 'Na. Maybe I was a bit pissed that you'd go for someone else when you could have had this.' He pulled an impressive bicep and laughed. Iona glanced away, smirking. 'But you and me were never going to be together. You're my friend, and as we're two of the only single people on the island, it seemed like it would be a good idea, but I can see how much you like him.'

'Thanks.'

'He's finishing his packing in the annex.' Ruaridh pointed to it. 'Go talk to him and tell him I'm ready when he is.'

Without another word, she turned and sprinted towards the annex. She reached the door and knocked, her hand trembling. Monty opened it almost immediately, his eyes widening in surprise. Without a word, Iona stepped in and wrapped her arms around him, holding him tightly. He hugged her back, patting her gently, but didn't speak.

'I think we should have one last practice before you go,' she said, her voice muffled against his shoulder. It was warm there, and she didn't want to move. This was like the safest, most glorious place in the world.

'I don't think we can.' He pulled back slightly to look at her. 'We don't have time... And really, I don't think I need anymore practice, do you?'

'Not exactly.' She stroked her fingers around his jawline, fixing him in her gaze. Everything about him looked so appealing now, so far from how she'd seen him when they first met. 'But there's one important thing we've not done.'

'Is it the one where we say goodbye?' He tilted his head, his eyes clouding. 'Because I'm not sure I can do that. It's too painful.'

'No. It's the one where you say you love her... and mean it.'

He frowned and shook his head. 'The one where I say I love *her*?'

Iona nodded, though it made her insides ache. This was the reality she'd been preparing for. She wanted to tell him she loved him, and this could be it... If she heard the words on his lips first, even if they weren't meant for her, she could play along.

'That won't work.' He looked away.

'Why not?' Her heart sank, but his eyes refocused on her and held her there for a long moment.

'Because I don't love *her*.' He paused, still maintaining eye contact to the point where it was almost painful. 'I love *you*.'

Her insides flipped over, and her head spun... Had he just said it? And meant it... But wait, no. This was part of the act, right? Wrong? *Oh fuck*, she was so confused, and now the moment was here, she'd forgotten all her plans – what she'd wanted to say and how. Everything was a mess again.

'Wow...' She swallowed, trying to force a coherent response. 'If you say it like that, she'll definitely believe it...'

He shook his head. 'I'm never going to say it to Sophie.' Leaning forward, he planted a lingering kiss on her forehead. 'I'm saying it to you. I'm not going back to Sophie, but I am going back to work and my real life.'

'Wait... What? You're saying you love *me*? Like for real?'

'Yes. Isn't it obvious? You're the most incredible, brave, and vibrant person I've ever met. I wish things were different, and we'd met somewhere more suitable for both our careers. But I understand the practicalities. You're a free spirit and long-term relationships aren't your thing. And that's ok, because it's part of what makes you. If you weren't such a wild soul, I wouldn't have fallen for you quite so hard. It's what I love so much about you.' He pulled her close and hugged her again. 'But I have to go. I'm sorry.'

She clung to his neck, tears pricking at the corners of her eyes and she kissed his cheek, unable to move her lips until he gently pulled away.

'It's been such a pleasure knowing you.' He kissed her softly on the lips, but it didn't last long enough. 'I can't thank you enough for how you've helped me, and I genuinely wish you every happiness.' One last brief kiss, then he picked up his bag, let out a long breath, and left.

Iona stood alone, hugging herself, barely holding back tears. The annex was silent. Empty. Cold. Very similar to how she felt. After all her intentions, she hadn't said anything. All her feelings were still tumbling about inside her. Car doors banged outside, and she went to the window. Ruaridh's car was driving off, another figure just visible in the passenger seat.

Monty had gone.

She gripped the windowsill, staring after the car as it disappeared down the road. The enormity of what he'd just said hit her like a wave crashing over her and knocking her sideways off her board.

'He loves me,' she whispered to herself, her voice breaking. Who else had ever said those words? No one she could remember. Maybe her parents once upon a time before she started to disappoint them. Never a boyfriend. And now a fling. Or someone who'd started as a fling. But really, he was so much more. And she'd let him go without any hope of ever seeing him again.

Chapter Twenty-Five

Monty

Beautiful Barra rolled past like a highlights reel of Hebridean scenery just for Monty's pleasure. Ruaridh was driving, so Monty could kick back and enjoy the sunshine, the turquoise ocean and grassy tufts dancing in the breeze. Except it all felt like a sharp reminder of what he was about to lose. The wild beauty would soon be a memory to look back on in photographs... Just like Iona. Leaving her was a horrible wrench, but he couldn't take her with him.

As they drove through Castlebay, he looked out at Kisimul Castle, pressing a fist to his heart as he did so. Hopefully his father's soul was free now, carried away by crosswinds and Atlantic waves, soaring high like Iona when she kite-surfed.

'You had a good stay?' Ruaridh asked.

'Yeah. I've enjoyed it.'

'Magical place, isn't it? I've always lived here and sometimes I get bored, you know, and moan about lack of facilities and what have you, but I always come back. I was on holiday last week with some friends. We took my boat off and did some cruising around, but something pulls me home every time. Even when I see other places, they never talk to me like this place.'

'I can understand that. It definitely has a pull, something that makes me want to come back.' In a couple of days, when he was back in his office, he'd miss it even more.

'It's in your blood. You've got a history here and no matter where you are, a part of you will always want to come back.'

'You might be right.'

'Listen, I'm sorry about the whole Iona thing,' Ruaridh went on. 'I hope I didn't get in the way. She's about the only single girl on the island, you know? So I kind of thought we'd get together at some point... Just for a hookup. She isn't up for the long term. Anyway, seemed like a good idea at the time. But we're just friends. She doesn't like me any other way and, to be honest, I don't see her like that either. I was just hopeful, but she always thought it would make things awkward, and I guess she's right.'

Monty forced a smile. Ruaridh was a chatterbox who obviously didn't mind spilling his soul to everyone and anyone – or maybe it was their newfound family connection making him feel suddenly more relaxed with Monty. 'No worries. Iona's great, but she belongs here, and I don't – no matter what my history may be. It's just a practicality.'

Ruaridh glanced over at him. 'Yeah. That's harsh.'

'I'm sure we'll get over each other.' Though his words were an empty promise. It certainly wouldn't be easy. Perhaps Iona never really liked him as much as he liked her. Was he just another tourist?

No.

Something told him that wasn't the case. She hadn't spoken her feelings aloud, but she'd shown him in so many ways.

'I never thought Iona would stick around.' Ruaridh pulled into a passing place to let a car go by. 'But she's become a part of this island.'

'Yeah, she really is that.' And it would be cruel to take her away from it. Monty wouldn't dream of asking her to leave. He didn't want to force them to be together by making her abandon her beloved home. That would change her too much, and he didn't want her to change. He loved her the way she was.

'Relationships are a funny thing, eh?' Ruaridh barked out a laugh. 'Maybe I'm just out of it living here, where the dating pool is basically non-existent. But how the heck do people find each other at the right time and place?'

'I have no idea.'

'And how do you know they feel what you feel?' Ruaridh exploded his fingers in front of his forehead like the whole concept messed with his head.

'Guesswork and hope most of the time.'

'You're so right. Just got to keep trying, huh?'

Yup.

But it was easy to make mistakes. Monty had thought he'd loved Sophie. He'd built his life around that idea for a long time. But it was a false love. Comfortable, convenient, but not real. Not like the soul encompassing love he felt for Iona. When he confessed to her, it had been real and true.

He stared out the window, watching the landscape blur by. Another cracking day, but his last one here for who knew how long. Whatever happened, he wouldn't be going back to Sophie. He couldn't. Not now. Not after Iona.

'You ok?' Ruaridh said. 'Sad to leave?'

'Yep.'

'Well, whatever happens, I hope it works out for you and come back any time. We'll be happy to have you.'

Monty smiled. 'Thank you.'

As they pulled up to the tiny airport, Monty took a deep breath. Ruaridh parked and got out, moving to the boot to grab Monty's bag.

'Thanks for the lift.' Monty stepped out, stretching his arms above his head.

'No problem.' Ruaridh handed over the bag. 'Hope you get back safe. Maybe see you around again sometime?'

'Yeah, maybe.' Monty extended his hand. 'Take care.'

They shook hands, and Ruaridh clapped Monty's upper arm. 'You too. All the best, cuz.'

Monty watched as Ruaridh got back in the car and gave a final wave before driving off. He stood there for a moment, as the car disappeared down the road, before turning around and heading into the tiny terminal building.

Once inside, he pulled out his phone. Perhaps Iona would have left a message, but there was nothing. He sighed and turned his gaze to the little plane on the beach, waiting to carry him away. Soon he'd be on it, flying back to Glasgow Airport, his little holiday at an end.

His thoughts whirred back to his initial reasons for being here. How he'd cringed at the thought of landing on a small strip of sand and clung to his dad's ashes. It seemed so long ago, but in reality, it wasn't. Two short weeks. Initially he'd wanted to spend the time walking, gathering a feel for the place, and learning about why it had been so special to his dad. Some of that had happened, but he'd also taken a journey of self-discovery. Hopefully his dad was now happily at rest, and he'd be proud of Monty, not disappointed.

He adjusted the strap of his bag. Was it bad that he'd spent most of the time conducting a holiday fling? Something he'd never done before – and would very likely never do again.

After checking in at the tiny desk, he headed outside onto the beach. Time to go. He started towards the plane, each step heavier than the last. He was leaving, but a piece of himself would always be here.

Taking one last breath of Hebridean air, he climbed the steps onto the plane. The insides were small, and he found his seat quickly. Strapping himself in, he braced for the take-off. He'd got braver since his arrival but still wasn't keen on the swoop in his gut when the plane left the ground.

The plane's engines vibrated beneath him, and Monty held onto the armrests. As the engines roared louder, Monty's grip tightened. The noise was deafening, then the plane jolted forward, gaining speed, and he felt the familiar lurch in his stomach as the wheels left the ground.

He closed his eyes for a moment, then forced them open. He had to see the island one last time.

As they climbed higher, he glanced out the window. Barra spread out below and he saw its imprint, a patchwork of green fields, rocky outcrops, and the shimmering sea. The beach where he'd landed two weeks ago looked like a sliver of white against the blue water. His gaze moved inland, and he fancied he saw Iona's car parked on a rise with a tiny figure standing beside it, looking up. He couldn't be sure, but the thought made his heart ache.

The plane continued to ascend, the island growing smaller and smaller until it was just a dot in the vast expanse of ocean. Monty leaned back in his seat, closing his eyes again, the hum of the engines filling his ears. He was heading back to the mainland, but his heart was broken; smashed against the jaggy rocks like a shipwreck on the wild island below.

Chapter Twenty-Six

Iona

Iona shielded her eyes, gazing up as the plane crossed the brilliant blue sky. Her heavy heart was ready to crack open. The wind tugged at her hair, and she tossed back her ponytail. She was too late. Too late to say the words she wanted to say to Monty's face.

His plane climbed higher, becoming a speck against the sky.

'Bye-bye. I love you.' A tear rolled down her cheek, and she pushed it away with the heel of her hand. Maybe it was better that she hadn't caught him. What good would it have done? It wasn't like he could stick around. This way, she could start the healing process without muddying the water any further.

She slumped into her car, staring forward, leaving the door open for air. Suddenly the heat was stifling. Waves crashed nearby and seabirds let out their sharp cries, some of them sounding almost as miserable as she felt. Monty was gone. She crossed her hands on the steering wheel and rested her forehead on them. Moping wasn't her style, but the weight on her shoulders was so heavy she couldn't shake it off or find the energy to move. She wasn't sure what she wanted to do, or what the purpose of life was.

For a long time she sat, head down, the heat burning into her, until eventually she looked up and took a breath. Sitting here all day would be a stupid waste of time. She started the engine and drove on autopilot to Castlebay. Her mind kicked into action again as she spied Kisimul Castle. It may not be pronounced the way it looked on paper, but she'd never be able to think about it now as anywhere other than the place where she'd first kissed Monty. It really was the castle of kisses for her now.

She carried on towards the farm, completely at a loss as to what to do. Maybe she should take Scamp for a walk or go for a run. Her head told her that would help, but her body wasn't playing along, and she couldn't coax it into doing anything, because really, it would be so much easier just to go to her room and stare at the ceiling.

The stairs up to her room were like climbing a mountain. She slumped on the edge of the bed, staring at the wall. What the hell was wrong with her? This was ridiculous. She'd never known herself to have so little energy.

A few minutes, maybe longer, had passed when there was a knock at the door. She sighed and called out, 'Come in.'

Catriona peered in. 'Hey. I just came to check you were ok.'

Iona gave a little shrug. Honestly, she wasn't, but she didn't want to let on how weak she was. Running away was always easier. When shit had hit the fan before with her old job and her ex, she'd come here. Now Monty had gone, and she was far safer staying upstairs, living in denial, than trying to change things. 'I'm fine.'

Catriona raised an eyebrow and shook her head. 'No, you're not.' She walked over and sat beside her, putting an arm around her shoulders. Iona leaned into it, letting out a shaky breath.

'It's just...' Iona began, but the words stuck in her throat.

'It's ok.' Catriona gave her shoulder a squeeze. 'You don't have to say anything right now if you don't want to.'

Iona nodded, her eyes welling up with tears. 'This is so stupid. Why am I getting upset like this?'

'Because you're not fine. I understand. I was there... With Eilidh's dad. It hurts. I get it. He was a dick, so I guess that helped me get over him, but it wasn't easy. Especially when I found out I was pregnant.'

'You were so brave.'

'Not really. What else could I do? That was when he showed his true colours and decided he didn't want anything to do with the baby. At least you know Monty wouldn't do that.'

'True.' Iona nodded. 'I'm just so confused.'

'About your feelings?'

'Yes.' And even admitting it made her feel stupid. Why was she letting a man affect her so badly?

'You fell hard, didn't you?'

'It sounds idiotic when you put it like that.'

'Why? You're allowed to have feelings.'

'Why him? Why did it have to be him? Someone I can't have?' She let out an angry huff. 'I've never felt like this about anyone.'

'I don't think it ever makes sense, like why we fall for some people and not others.'

'The thing is, even if he'd stuck around, how would I know that's what I wanted?'

'I guess it's about commitment and whether or not you're willing to try. It's also about how he feels about you. Does he like you too? I thought he did, but when you told me about his ex... Well, is he going to try and get back together with her?'

Iona shook her head. 'He said he wasn't. He told me...' The words stuck in her throat, and she tried to flap away the tears. 'Told me... He didn't love her.'

'Oh...' Catriona rubbed Iona's back, watching her with a frown. 'I guess that something.'

'He also said he loved me.'

'Did he?' Catriona's eyes widened. 'Wow. And what did you say?'

'Nothing. I was too shocked, I suppose. And it wouldn't have made any difference. He can't stay here, and I can't go back to city life. Nothing can change. I just have to live with it.'

'Maybe. But you could at least message him and tell him the truth.'

'Hello...' The door opened a crack and little Eilidh peered around. 'What's wrong?' she asked Iona.

'Eilidh, sweetheart, why don't you go and fetch Iona a drink of water? Give us a moment.'

Eilidh hesitated, her gaze shifting between Iona and her mum. 'But I want to know why she's crying.'

'It's ok, Eilidh.' Iona forced a smile and opened her arms. Eilidh rushed forward, wrapping her arms around Iona's waist. 'I'm just sad that Monty had to leave.'

'Why?' Eilidh stared up at Iona with wide eyes.

Iona's heart twisted. She stroked Eilidh's hair gently. 'It's complicated. Sometimes things happen that we don't like and have no control over.'

Catriona patted Eilidh's shoulder. 'Go on, Eilidh. Get the water like I asked, please.'

'Ok, Mummy.' She darted out of the room, leaving Iona and Catriona in silence.

Iona took a deep breath, trying to compose herself. 'I need to pull myself together.'

'Be kind to yourself.'

Iona nodded. She glanced towards the window, the bright afternoon sunlight shining through. 'I just wish...'

'Things were different?'

'Yeah,' Iona whispered, her eyes drifting shut momentarily. 'But they're not.'

'It'll be worse now, but it'll get better. You're strong.'

'I hope so,' Iona sighed.

Catriona patted her knee. 'I understand it's hard, but you need to be honest with him, even if it's painful. Don't hide away and pretend none of this ever happened. Face it.'

A noise from the door made them both look up. Alex had his hand on it and held it open, and Eilidh shuffled in with a glass of water in her small hands.

'Here, Iona.' She held out the glass.

Alex's gaze landed on Catriona. 'I wanted to make sure she didn't spill it.'

Catriona looked away. 'Right.'

'Come on, Eilidh,' he said. 'Let's give your mum and Iona some space to talk. We can go down to the beach if you like.'

'Yeah cool.' She jumped on him and he laughed.

Iona smiled, but Catriona was stony faced.

'He's so great with her,' Iona said.

'Yeah.' Catriona got to her feet. 'You have a rest, then figure out what you want to say to Monty, because I have a feeling this isn't the end yet.'

Chapter Twenty-Seven

Monty

Adjusting his tie with a sigh, Monty focused on finalising his client's financial projection report. Once it was done, he was heading out for a lunchtime catchup with his mum. She enjoyed meeting in the city and dining in one of Edinburgh's finest restaurants – she always chose an expensive one and expected Monty to pay.

'Nearly there.' He scanned the spreadsheet on his screen. Rows of figures and charts filled the monitor, detailing revenue forecasts and investment strategies. The clock on the wall ticked steadily, a gloomy sound compared to the dreamy wash of the sea he'd enjoyed last week. How different things were now. He was back to normal, but normal felt odd and like it would never be the same. After his dad died, he'd thought that might be the case anyway, but this was worse than he'd ever imagined, because now he wasn't just missing his dad, but the open skies of Barra, the smell of the sea, and Iona. Always Iona.

A knock interrupted him. 'Come in.' He straightened up in his chair.

Jenny, his assistant, peeked in with a smile. 'I'm heading for lunch. You want anything?'

Monty shook his head. 'No, thanks. I'm good. I'm meeting my mum for lunch today.'

'Ah, how's she getting on?' Jenny tilted her head. 'Is she coping without your dad?'

'Sure. They were divorced, so it's not been a big issue for her.'

'Aw. Sorry. I didn't realise that. And what about you?'

He gave a little shrug and arranged his papers into a neat stack. 'It's strange.'

'It will be for a while. I lost my dad three years ago, and it takes a while to adjust. You'll get there. It never goes away, but it gets easier.'

'Thanks.' After she left, he grabbed his suit jacket from the back of his chair and exited the office.

As he walked through the busy corridors, his mind wandered to a different track, making a beeline back to Iona – his favourite subject. He missed her so much. She'd messaged him after he left, saying she was sorry she'd let him go without telling him how she felt, though in rather typical Iona style, she didn't say exactly what that was. Reading between the lines, he guessed she meant she returned the love he'd confessed before he left, but that didn't change the stark reality of his life.

He reached the lift and sighed, pressing the button for the ground floor.

Edinburgh was a beautiful city, but his heart wasn't here anymore. He walked briskly along the street in the drizzling rain towards the restaurant where he was meeting his mother. One step inside the smart modern interior made him want to turn around and go straight back out the shiny glass doors.

His mother wasn't the only woman at the table. Sophie was there too, smiling at him in a way that didn't appease him in the slightest. Why now? It was too late.

He stood near the entrance, vaguely registering a server had approached him.

'Table for one?'

'Oh... um, no.' He frowned at his mother, who had got to her feet. 'I'm with these ladies.'

'Of course, sir.'

Monty headed over, passing the bar that was lit by spotlights – they may as well be focused on him; he felt like everyone was watching him, especially his ex-girlfriend. His mother was always immaculately turned out. Her pure white hair was neatly bobbed, and she had on a bright green Chanel jacket with a thick necklace and many rings.

'Monty, darling, thanks heavens you're back safe and sound.' She took his face in her hands, pulled him down, and kissed him.

'Why wouldn't I be? Barra isn't exactly a dangerous place.' He gave her a brief hug.

'Oh, I don't know. The flight looked terrifying, and it's so out in the sticks.'

'It is.' And life there was going on without him, which was a weird thought, but he kept circling back to the idea. Did the island still look the same when he wasn't there?

'Well, you're here now.'

'Why is she here?' he whispered, indicating Sophie with a little look.

His mother turned around and smiled at Sophie. 'Sophie is here because the two of you need to talk and I'll be here as the mediator.'

'Mediator?'

Sophie got to her feet and hugged Monty. He tried to recall a time when he'd have welcomed this, but his mind kept leaping back to Iona kite-surfing and riding waves. She was the only woman he wanted to hug and kiss.

'There's not much to talk about.' Monty took a seat. 'And I don't have very long before I have to be back in the office.'

'There's plenty of time.' His mother sat beside him. 'You promised me at least an hour.' She looked between him and Sophie. 'Your relationship is important. The two of you are simply made for each other. You've had a blip, but you can get through this.'

Monty glanced at Sophie, and she smiled.

'It was considerably more than a blip.' Monty lifted the menu, wishing it was bigger, so he could hide behind it. This conversation was awkward enough, but having his mother here made it so much worse. Her mediating was more like meddling.

'Monty, I really am sorry,' Sophie said. 'It was a stressful time, and I said some stupid things.'

'It's fine.' He kept his eyes on the menu. 'I don't mind what you said. None of it's an issue anymore.'

'You forgive me?'

'If that's what you want, then yes.'

'Wonderful.' His mother clapped her hands. 'That was easy.'

'So...' Sophie gave him a little grin. 'You want to get back together?'

He placed the menu down and pushed his glasses further up his nose. 'No, I don't.'

'But...'

'I hold no ill will against you, but I... I don't love you.'

'Oh Monty.' His mother frowned.

'It's fine. I understand.' Sophie's smiled had faded. 'But under the circumstances...' She picked up her bag. 'I think I'll leave. It's probably for the best. No point dragging this out.'

Perhaps she expected him to say something to change her mind, but he didn't. She gave a little shrug and stalked out.

'Was that really necessary?' his mother asked.

'Actually yes. Because it's the truth. There's no point building a relationship on a lie. You, of all people, should know that.'

She let out a snort of a laugh. 'Very true. Still, she's a nice girl and you're actually well suited to each other.'

'Maybe. But I don't love her.'

'So you said. But love can be hard to find.'

'Sometimes you find it when you're not looking for it.'

She let out a sigh. 'That's leaving a lot to chance.'

'I've already met someone else. Someone that I love.'

'Really?' His mother goggled. 'That's wonderful. Who is she?'

'Iona McKenzie.'

'Can I meet her?'

He shook his head. 'That won't be easy, but I can show you a picture of her and a film.' He pulled out his phone and found a film of her kite-surfing. Tilting his hand so his mum could see it, he pressed play.

She peered at it, a frown growing. 'This woman on the parachute thingy?'

'Yes.'

'And do you even know her? Or do you just have a crush on this film?'

Monty laughed and stopped the film. 'I know her, but she lives on Barra.'

'What? Oh, goodness gracious. Not that bloody island. Your father was fixated on it, obsessed, and now you.'

'He was right about us having family there. I discovered we're related to the family I stayed with.'

'Really?'

'Yes. I share a great-great-grandfather with Catriona, who owned the guesthouse. Dad never got the chance to do all the research he wanted and to go and meet the people he was connected to. He worked himself to the bone and into an early grave.' Monty didn't want history to repeat itself. It was a wake-up call for him. 'You should go visit yourself one day. It'll surprise you. It surprised me.'

'But you're not seriously thinking about having a love affair with this woman, are you? How would that work?'

'I really don't know. If I can find a way, I will.'

His mum cupped her hands on the table and gave him a quizzical once over. 'There's always a way. If you're serious about her, you'll find it. It might mean change, upheaval...'

He covered his mouth to stifle a grin. The word had reminded him of going 'up Heaval', the hill he'd climbed with Iona.

'What is so funny?'

'Nothing, Mum. You're right. If I want this, I can make it happen, but it'll mean changes.'

'Just don't do anything rash, will you?'

'Are you kidding? In the last few weeks, I've been on a plane that landed on a beach, I've swum in the sea, been bodyboarding, tried surfing...' Not to mention some of the other things he'd done with Iona that he wasn't going to mention to his mother... 'My whole life on Barra was rash compared to here. I learned to be a different version of myself. And I enjoyed it. I've played it safe up until now and I'm ready to do something else.'

'Such as? I mean, you can't leave your job.'

'I need my job, yes, but there might be something I can do. Let's eat. Then I'm going back for a chat with my boss.'

Monty ate lunch with his mother, but his mind was racing ahead. Nothing was guaranteed. Roles couldn't be invented just to suit him. But unless he tried, he'd never know.

'Just be sensible.' His mother patted his hand as he tapped his card to pay for the meal. 'You can be adventurous without being crazy.'

'I'm not sure I know what that means.' He gave her a hug. 'But I want to follow my heart. I've got a feeling it'll see me right this time.'

———————— ♥ ————————

Back in the office, Monty knocked on Mr Robertson's office door and entered when he called him in. 'Ah, hello, Monty. Is everything ok?'

'I don't suppose you have time for a quick chat?'

'Sure, I do. Take a seat.' Mr Robertson pointed to a seat.

'Thanks.' Monty sat opposite.

'What's on your mind?'

'Well, you'll be aware that my father died last month.'

'Indeed.'

'It's shaken me, but also put things in perspective for me, and while I'm happy in my job and with my role here, I wonder if there's a possibility of making it more flexible.'

Mr Robertson folded his hands on the desk. 'In what way?'

'I'm considering moving. Perhaps to somewhere more remote.' Monty began carefully. 'I wonder if there are any opportunities to work from home, perhaps based out of the Glasgow office, as that would be easier to reach.' He might even get used to that landing on the sand. 'This is all just thoughts at the moment, nothing concrete. I just want to test the water.' He was getting good at that.

His boss tapped his pen with a measured look on his face. 'You've always been a solid performer. Reliable and diligent. And I certainly understand the need for flexibility.'

'I appreciate that,' Monty said.

Mr Robertson leaned back in his chair. 'Let me look into it. I can't promise anything immediate, but I'll see what arrangements we can make.'

'Thank you. I'll be ready to discuss any possibilities that arise.'

'Good man.' Mr Robertson reached out to shake Monty's hand.

This was the first step, and there was still a long way to go, but a glimmer of hope shimmered on the horizon.

Chapter Twenty-Eight

♥ ♥ ♥ ♥ ♥

Iona

Iona lifted the boards out of the container. The beach was quiet this morning, but the waves rolled in with their steady rhythm. She loved the calm so much. It steadied her brain and kept her sane. Without this beautiful island to comfort her, she'd have gone insane the last few weeks. Because getting over Monty really wasn't happening for her.

As she went to put her phone away, she glanced at it, and a text notification caught her eye.

Speak of the devil.

MONTY: How are you? Missing you. Hope to see you soon. X

Her heart did a little flip. She read the message again, trying to decipher any hidden meaning in his words. Was it just a casual sign-off? Did he really mean it? Was he coming back? What a tease sending a message like that... Or was it his way of asking her to come and visit him?

She wanted to see him too, but the thought of leaving Barra, her sanctuary, filled her with dread. A visit would be ok, but what about the long term? Was there even a long term? Had she already cut off the avenue? It wasn't something she'd wanted or considered for a long time. She'd lived in Edinburgh before and had no desire to do so again. Would this be any different?

But this was Monty... Could she make the sacrifice for him? Maybe it would be worth it. Because anything might be better than the constant cutting pain in her chest. Choosing between him and her beloved island seemed a cruel choice. One she couldn't even make unless she knew for sure that was what he wanted to.

She looked out at the Atlantic crashing against the shore. Could she give this up?

She thumbed out a message.

IONA: Are you hoping to see me here? Or are you hoping I'll come visit? Not sure I'd cope in Edinburgh these days, but I do want to see you. A LOT! Wish I knew what to do. Do we have a future??? X

She held her breath. Should she delete it? Was it too needy? Oh hell. This was impossible and part of the reason long-term relationships scared her. She put down the phone and collected another set of surfboards. Her students for the day would be arriving soon, and she needed to be ready. No reply came in from Monty before the class and she left her phone in the container as she taught the lesson.

When she finally got back to it, she found a message.

MONTY: I'd love for us to have a future, but I'm acutely aware of the difficulties. As I always have been. You didn't seem interested in a long-term relationship before and my work commitments make our situations difficult. Whatever happens, you belong in Barra. It's as much a part of you as you are of it. Need to talk soon x

That looked almost ominous. He could call her and talk if he wanted, but she suspected he wouldn't. This sounded like a face-to-face chat was needed, or she at least had to explain herself. He was right. She'd fobbed off the idea of a long-term relationship, but now she wanted that more than anything. Any time she had with Monty would always be too short.

IONA: I never wanted long term... Until I met you. We can talk anytime x

There. She'd said it, put it in writing, and she wasn't taking it back. Monty reacted to the message with a heart, but said no more. Even after her surf class was done for the day, she hadn't received any messages.

She returned to the farmhouse and went looking for Catriona. She didn't really want to talk to her about anything in particular, but she didn't want to be on her own. Resolving the turmoil in her heart was something she had to do herself, but she didn't want to be alone. Catriona was in the kitchen prepping meals, looking somewhat frazzled, and Iona felt bad about disturbing her.

'Do you need a hand?' Iona asked.

'If you like peeling tatties, then be my guest.'

Iona pulled a face indicating that she wished she'd never asked but washed her hands and located the potato peeler.

'How was the surfing?' Catriona stirred one pan, then another.

'Yeah, fine. They were all pretty good today.'

'What time is your class tomorrow?'

'Afternoon, why?'

Catriona kept her eyes on the food and gave a weird little shrug. 'I, um, just wondered if you'd be able to pick up some people from the ferry tomorrow evening. It would help me, but if you're busy, it's fine.'

'Sure.'

'Thanks, that'd be great. I'll give you the details tomorrow when I get them.'

'No worries.' Iona frowned at her. Usually, Catriona got Alex to do jobs like that, but it was possible they'd fallen out. Catriona seemed to resent Alex's being on the farm more and more every day, and she never wanted to talk about it. Iona thought it better just to do what she asked and not question it.

———————— ♥ ————————

The following day, Iona finished up the surf class sharply and headed back towards the farm. On the beach, she spotted a lone figure with a dog. Both dog and man were easily recognisable. Scamp was bounding towards her at a hundred miles an hour while Ruaridh jogged along behind. He was so tall and muscly he looked like he should be a rugby player.

'How's it going?' he called as he got closer.

Iona patted Scamp as he jumped around like he hadn't seen her for days rather than just a few hours.

'Ok. You?'

'Ah, you know.' He slowed and stopped, leaning his hands on his knees as he caught his breath, then straightened up. 'Training hard.'

Iona tightened her ponytail. 'For what exactly?'

He gave a little shrug. 'Just like to keep fit.'

Iona kept fit too, but she wasn't as obsessive as him. He seemed to spend every free second working out.

'I hope you're holding up ok. You really had a thing for that Monty guy, didn't you?' Ruaridh caught her eye, and his expression was commiserative.

How could she even reply to that?

'I guess I did. But we wanted different things, you know?'

'I hear you loud and clear.' He ran his hand through his hair, watching her. 'The lack of single people on this island is probably the only reason I'd ever leave, which is sad, because I love it here.'

Iona smiled. 'Well, there are usually quite a few travelling through. See if you can grab yourself a holiday fling.'

'I'll have to think about it.'

Iona patted him on the arm. 'Someone will come along for you, I'm sure. Just have some fun while you wait.' She checked her phone. 'I need to get going. Catriona asked me to pick up some guests coming in on the ferry.'

'Did she?' Ruaridh frowned. 'Dunno why she didn't ask me. I was around to walk Scamp anyway.'

'No idea, but I better head. See you later.'

'Yeah, see you.' He gave her a little wave, whistled to Scamp and ran off. When he did meet the right person, it'd hopefully be someone who loved sport and fitness as much as him.

Iona collected the car from the farmhouse and headed to Castlebay when the ferry was due. She watched it ease into the bay and go through the docking sequence. People who arrived this way had enjoyed – or endured – a four-and-a-half-hour sail from Oban. While the flight was dramatic, Iona preferred the sail. Well, she was a boat lover, after all. She'd not done it often since coming to live on the island, because she didn't have much desire to leave, though she'd occasionally left to visit her parents. They, of course, never visited her. Barra was the edge of the world as far as they were concerned. Sometimes it felt like that, but Iona only saw joy in that fact.

She waited by the ferry terminal, scanning the crowd for anyone who resembled the description Catriona had given her. People bustled off the boat, greeting loved ones or hurrying off hauling cases or carrying backpacks. She tapped her foot, glancing at the castle in the bay. The sea glittered around it, making it look quite magical. What beautiful times she'd spent there with Monty. If only that sparkle was magic dust, and she could use its power to summon him. Perhaps he would rise from the sea like Neptune and wade forward, casting off his foam mantle to head straight for her arms. She almost laughed at the thought. Since when had she been into romantasy? Like never!

The crowd thinned, and still no sign of the guests. Seriously where were they? Surely if they'd missed the boat, they'd have contacted Catriona before now. Iona sighed and pulled out her phone.

The call connected to Catriona almost immediately. 'I don't see anyone who fits the description. Are you sure they're on this ferry?'

'Oh, um, they just called,' Catriona said. 'They're waiting near the seat on the path. Can you head that way?'

Iona frowned. Why would they go there? 'Ok, I'll find them.'

She hung up and made her way along the path, wondering what had possessed them to wander off and how she'd missed them. As she walked, she took in the view of the castle again, and a pang of longing stabbed at her chest like a very pointy trident. What was with these bloody sea gods? If they existed, they should be delivering miracles, not sending her on a wild goose chase, and tormenting her with memories.

Scanning the area for any sign of the guests, she approached the seat. A memory surfaced like a message in a bottle bobbing on top of the waves. This was where she first met Monty and he'd stumbled, knocking her off her bike. She rubbed her shoulder absentmindedly. That had been bloody sore. What a dafty. She'd been so cross with him, thinking he was a crazy, clueless tourist, knowing nothing about the ashes, of course. She winced. How awful would it have been if he'd accidentally dropped the urn? His clothes had looked far too posh for a place like this, and he'd made her drop her chips. She quite fancied some of them right now... Though she'd much prefer him.

Even from here, she could see no one was at the seat. She frowned. Had she misunderstood Catriona's directions? Or had Catriona misunderstood the guests? Maybe they were at a different seat. She scanned around. Was there another one close by? As her eyes drifted over the village towards the bay, they settled on a man walking towards her. For a second, her heart stilled. He looked just like Monty... But no way could it be him. Like really couldn't. Because he couldn't have got here. A plane hadn't arrived. Unless he'd been on the boat. But Monty didn't do boats. The man continued to walk towards her, and her heart leapt into action like it had been shocked. It was Monty alright, and he was heading straight for her.

Chapter Twenty-Nine

Monty

Monty made his way up the grassy path, his pulse beating in his ear like a drum.

And there she was. Iona. Beautiful as ever, her long hair dancing in the wind as she stood near the bench, Kisimul Castle in the background. Her eyes were wide, and she gaped at him as if she couldn't believe he was real. He could hardly believe it himself. Or at least the fact that he was here.

He stopped a little distance away, unsure how to approach this. 'Hi.' That was the best his mind could do for now.

She continued to stare, her mouth slightly open, her eyes searching his face. So many questions flashed in those dark blue orbs.

He smiled gently. 'Are you ok? I see you don't have your bike or chips this time, so am I safe to come nearer?'

A smile broke on her face, and she closed the distance between them, throwing herself into his arms. He caught her, holding her tightly and rocking with her as he enjoyed the full force of the hug. Her warmth, her scent, everything about her was exactly as he remembered, and his heart was fit to burst.

'Oh my god.' She pulled back and stared at him. 'I have a million questions.'

He stroked her hair off her face with both his hands and clutched it, taking a moment just to reacquaint himself with her.

'What are you doing here?' Her eyes darted around. 'Though maybe you should hang fire on that. I'm supposed to be on the lookout for two guests who I think have wandered off.'

He let out a little laugh. 'There are no wandering guests.'

'Wait... What?'

'It's just me. I asked Catriona to send you to meet me, but not to say it was me. I wanted to surprise you.'

'Seriously? She's in on this?'

'She certainly is.'

Iona shook her head and clenched a fist. 'Duh. I didn't even question her, even though I thought it was a bit odd that she didn't ask Alex or Ruaridh. I can't believe I fell for it.'

'Me neither.' He grinned. 'You're slipping.'

'I must be. But does that mean you came on the boat?'

'I did. With my car.'

'And you survived a four-and-a-half-hour boat trip?'

'As you see. These little bands work wonders.' He waggled his wrists to show off the pair of travel bands he'd bought for himself. 'I actually enjoyed it. Such beautiful scenery, and just watching the sea is so calming. I thought I might see a whale. Some people on the boat said they'd seen porpoises, but I missed all that.'

Iona shook her head and slow blinked. 'Well, you coming on the ferry is possibly even more unexpected than you being here at all.'

'Are you impressed?'

'I am, but I'm also curious. Why are you here?'

'For you. For us. For a new start... If that's what you want.' Monty held his breath, waiting for Iona's response. Had he read this right? Or perhaps wanting to make this a surprise wasn't a smart move.

Her eyes held his, then she ran her fingers around his jawline. 'A new start,' she repeated softly. 'With me?'

'If that's what you want.'

'Hell yes.' She grinned, and a huge wave of calm rolled over him. 'You're the first person I've ever struggled to live without. I can't stand not having you in my life.'

'Same. I'll do anything to be with you.' He pulled her into a hug, and she wrapped her arms around his neck, tightening her hold on him.

'I don't want you to sacrifice anything for me,' she murmured in his ear.

'I'm not. Just finding a way to make it work for us.' He took her face in his hands, gazing into those beautiful blue eyes. 'Nothing I do here will ever be a sacrifice.' Dipping in, he covered her mouth with his, sealing his lips on hers in a long, warm kiss. This was where he belonged. It had always been in his blood, even if he hadn't been aware of it. Now it was in his heart.

When they broke apart, Iona rested her forehead against his, her breath coming in soft gasps. 'But what about your job? How long can you stay?'

Monty smiled, brushing a strand of hair behind her ear. 'I've negotiated a new role. I can work from home and travel to the Glasgow office every so often. The flights will be good for that. So I can stay as long as you want me.'

Her eyes widened, and her smile lit her face. 'Really?'

'Yes. As long as we're happy together, which I hope is a very long time.'

'Me too.' She hugged him again. 'Though god knows where you're going to live. You can stay with me, of course, but I only have a little room at the farmhouse.'

'That'll do for now, assuming you're ok with it.'

'More than.'

'Then let's go with that. We can worry about long-term living arrangements another time.'

Iona's eyes sparkled, and it looked like she couldn't stop smiling. Monty could relate. His body and soul had never felt more relaxed.

'You have no idea how much this means to me.' Iona almost crushed him in a hug.

'I think I do,' he whispered, pulling her close again. 'I really do.'

He held her, letting the warmth of her embrace seep into his bones. He'd never tire of this. They stood together, wrapped in each other's arms for what felt like forever, neither wanting to break the moment.

Eventually, Iona pulled back slightly. 'We should probably head back to the farmhouse.'

'Yeah, let's do that. It's not like there's any time limit on these hugs now.'

His plan to surprise her meant they both had their own cars but had randomly parked not far from each other.

Iona gave his BMW the once over. 'That's such a wanker-banker-mobile.'

He smirked. 'Well, you can make an island man out of a banker, but you can't take the banker out of the island man.'

She leaned up and kissed him. 'I wouldn't have it any other way.'

He followed her out of the village and back along the single-track road towards the farmhouse. Waves rushed up and broke against the rocks as the road cut close to the sea. The island looked as rugged and beautiful as ever. This wonderful island that had brought them both together.

As Monty parked in the driveway, Catriona was waiting outside the farmhouse with little Eilidh. Even from this distance, he could see Catriona's smile.

As soon as Eilidh spotted Iona, she ran over and wrapped her arms around her legs.

'You're back!' Eilidh squealed. 'Did you find him?'

Iona ruffled her hair and turned around. 'Sure did.' She winked at Monty. He popped the boot and took out a bag.

Catriona folded her arms. 'Did you not find the guests, then?'

Monty closed the boot in time to see Iona's glare. 'You sent me on a wild goose chase. I can't believe I fell for it.'

Catriona laughed, then turned to Monty. 'Everything go to plan?'

'Definitely. Thank you for helping me pull that off.'

Catriona approached him and gave him a little hug. 'No problem. It was fun. I can't believe Iona fell for it.'

'You're never going to let me live this down, are you?'

'No,' both Catriona and Monty said at the same time.

They all laughed.

'Come on,' Catriona said. 'Why don't you pop your bags upstairs, Monty, then we can sit out at the picnic table and enjoy the view. I'll get us some drinks.'

Monty headed up with Iona. 'You'll have to excuse the messy room. I didn't know I'd be getting a guest.'

'I hope this is ok. I probably should have warned you about it, but the idea of surprising you seemed like fun. If you'd rather I find accommodation elsewhere for the time being—'

She stopped on the stairs, turned around and put her finger on his lips. 'I don't want you anywhere but with me.'

That was all he needed to hear. He popped his bags in a corner of the room while Iona had a quick tidy around. When she was done, she came over and gave him a quick kiss.

'Shame we have to go downstairs really,' she said.

'There's no rush to do anything. I'm not going anywhere.'

She smiled, and they headed downstairs and took their seats at the picnic table. The sea sparkled behind the dunes in the distance. Iona put her hand in his, and their fingers entwined. 'What does your mum make of this?'

'She thought I was mad at first,' Monty said. 'But she's come round to the idea. She might even visit one day. You never know.'

'My parents might too if they discover I'm dating a banker. They'll love you.'

'Why? Because I have the right job?'

'Exactly.'

He shook his head. 'You need to show them some kite surfing. If that doesn't impress them, I don't know what will.'

She squeezed his hand. 'Maybe. We'll see.'

Catriona returned with a tray of drinks, setting it down on the table, and Eilidh added a tray of heart-shaped biscuits with various icing designs and sprinkles.

'Did you do these?' Monty asked.

'Yes.' She smiled at him. 'I like that one best.' She pointed at one covered in pink sugar beads.

'It does look good, but you better eat it, if it's your favourite.'

Catriona handed out napkins. 'If you two can survive the summer season in Iona's room, you can rent the annex for the rest of the year, if you like. Possibly indefinitely if I get the glamping pods up and running.'

Iona flicked her gaze to Monty. 'Really?'

'Really,' Catriona confirmed.

Monty squeezed Iona's hand. 'That sounds great. Thank you so much.'

'Yes, thank you. That would be so great.' Iona leaned over and hugged her.

Catriona sat beside Eilidh and lifted a biscuit. 'No trouble. And I hope you'll be able to give me some more help with the business if I need it.'

'Of course.' Monty chose a biscuit for himself, smiling his approval at Eilidh, who was watching him. 'I'd be happy to.'

'Such a beautiful day.' Iona let out a contented sigh.

'Stunning.' Monty kept his eyes on her as he sipped his drink. The sea washed up beyond, its soothing music like the stuff of dreams. A dream Monty was going to live for a very long time. This was where he belonged, on Barra, beside Iona, ready to face whatever came their way.

Chapter Thirty

Iona

Iona's boat cut smoothly through the water as she steered towards Kisimul Castle. She turned around and smiled at Monty. He'd found his sea legs... Or close enough. He'd never make a sailor, but with the armbands and a bit of practise, he was able to stand up and watch rather than sit clinging to the sides. Sunlight caught the waves, scattering the surface with hundreds of diamonds. The perfect late summer day.

Monty strolled up behind her and put his arms around her as she steered. 'I'm so happy.' He nuzzled his nose against her neck. 'You're just the best.'

'Monty, you're such a sap.' A smile tugged at her lips. 'But I love you.' She still couldn't believe he was here with her, not just for a visit, but as part of her life. This was a better version of her life than she could ever have predicted. No half-measures, no doubts.

'Almost there.' She cut the engine.

'Don't go getting any injuries or anything today.'

'I'll try my best, though if I do, you're welcome to kiss me better.'

'With pleasure.'

She smiled and relaxed into his hold for a moment. They'd shared so much in this place, and returning together just for the sake of it was something she hoped they'd make a tradition. She guided the boat to the small slipway, the castle's imposing silhouette casting a long shadow over them.

They drifted the last few feet, the boat bumping gently against the side. Monty hopped out, and Iona passed him the rope. 'I'll make you a seaman yet.'

'I doubt that, but it's definitely more fun than it used to be.'

'Have you missed this place? Your ancient stronghold.'

He smirked. 'Ha! I definitely don't look at it like that, but it's always going to be a special place for me.'

'It is a special place. I kind of took it for granted before, but there really is something magical about it. All the stories that have happened here over the years.'

'Maybe we can add our own.'

'Oh yeah.' Iona took his hand. 'We can definitely do that.'

They scrambled around the rocks at the edge of the castle to the place where Monty had scattered his father's ashes all those weeks ago.

Seabirds circled a fishing boat a little way off and waves gently lapped the shore. Such a perfect sanctuary; a place where the rest of the world fell away, leaving only the two of them.

'I'm sure Dad would approve.' Monty shielded his eyes, scanning the place he'd scattered the ashes.

Iona slung her ponytail over her shoulder as the breeze picked up. 'He definitely would. And you've ended up living in the place he wanted you to visit.'

'Yeah. That bit is bizarre, but he'd love it.'

Iona wrapped her arms around his neck. 'Just like I love you.'

He brought his lips to hers and kissed her. Softly at first, then deeper, more urgently. 'And I'll always love you,' he breathed.

'One day, I'll get you paddleboarding over here.' Iona squinted back across the water to the village.

'I'm not sure I'm that brave yet,' Monty said with a smile.

'Oh, I don't know. Look at all the things you've done this summer already.'

'Crazy, isn't it?' They headed down the rocks, and Monty knelt down and picked up some stones.

'Are you making another tower?'

'I never was very good at it.'

'Here, let me.' Iona crouched beside him and picked up some more loose stones. 'These ones first.' She placed some flat ones at the bottom, and Monty added some more. She got to her feet and pulled out her phone. 'It looks good. Let's get a picture.'

'I think I can make it even better.'

'Can you? And just how do you propose to do that?'

'Like this.' Monty reached into his pocket and pulled out a small box, placing it on top of the newly fixed sculpture. Iona's heart skipped a beat. That wasn't a ring box, was it? He wasn't...

'Iona.' He gazed up at her. 'You've made me happier than I ever thought possible. Every moment with you is an adventure, and I can't imagine my life without you. Will you marry me?'

She gasped, staring at him, utterly speechless, her mind racing. Was this really happening? She clutched her hand to her mouth. So soon, and yet exactly right, because she absolutely wanted to. Weird visions of herself kite surfing in a wedding dress made her laugh, and she glanced from the ring box to Monty's confused face.

'Yes,' she breathed, tears welling in her eyes. 'A thousand times, yes! I will.'

Monty's face lit up, and he stood, pulling her into a tight embrace. The ring sparkled in the sunlight as he slipped it onto her finger. 'It can be adjusted of course, or if you'd like to choose your own.'

'No. I like this one. I know nothing about jewellery, and this looks stunning.' She held up her hand, admiring how it looked. 'It's gorgeous.'

'Not as gorgeous as you, but I'm so glad you like it. You had me worried there for a moment, when you laughed.'

'I was imagining my preferred mode of transport for the wedding.'

'Which is what? Dare I ask?'

'On my kite board, of course.'

Monty chuckled and pulled her into a warm embrace. 'You are hilarious. And actually, I might be disappointed if you don't arrive like that. It seems like the only way suitable for you.'

'You really are my kind of guy.' She slipped her hand around his cheek and kissed him.

'And you're my girl. And this is our place,' he murmured as she carried on kissing him. 'No matter where we go, we'll always have this.'

'Always and forever.'

With the light breeze ruffling their hair, and the ancient stones of the great fortress of Kisimul as silent witnesses, Iona and Monty held each other close. Even the cry of the seabirds now sounded joyous. With their bodies entwined and lips locked, their hearts and souls aligned. Iona had discovered something rare and beautiful on the wild island.

She'd come here to escape her old life and found something infinitely better. She tightened her hold on Monty, at the same time embracing a future that promised to be the most exciting adventure of her life.

The End

More Books by Margaret Amatt

Scottish Island Escapes

1. A Winter Haven

2. A Spring Retreat

3. A Summer Sanctuary

4. An Autumn Hideaway

5. A Christmas Bluff

6. A Flight of Fancy

7. A Hidden Gem

8. A Striking Result

9. A Perfect Discovery

10. A Festive Surprise

The Glenbriar Series

1. Stolen Kisses at the Loch View Hotel

2. Just Friends at Thistle Lodge

3. Pitching up at Heather Glen

4. Two's Company at the Forest Light Show

5. Highland Fling on the Whisky Trail

6. Snowdown at the Old Schoolhouse

7. Starting Over at the Crafty Bee Barn

8. A Surprise Proposal in the Rose Garden

9. Cutting it Neat for the Wedding

10. A Classy Affair in the Country

11. Mix Up under the Mistletoe

12. A Fresh Start on the Bridle Path

13. Last First Kiss at the Village Church

Love on the Edge – Barra Series

1. The Castle in the Bay

2. The Lighthouse by the Sea

About the Author

Margaret Amatt

Margaret has told and written stories for as long as she can remember. During her formative years, she spent time on long walks inventing characters and stories to pass the time.

Writing books is Margaret's passion and when she's not doing that, she's often found eating chocolate, walking and taking photographs in the hills around Highland Perthshire. Those long walks still frequently bring inspiration!

It's Margaret's pleasure to bring you the Scottish Island Escapes series and The Glenbriar Series. These books are linked (both the two series have crossovers!) for those who enjoy inhabiting Margaret's world of stories but each book can be read as a standalone if you'd rather dip in and out.

You can find more information about Margaret on her website or by signing up for her newsletter.

www.margaretamatt.com

Acknowledgments

Thanks goes to my adorable husband for supporting my dreams and putting up with my writing talk 24/7. Also to my son, whose interest in my writing always makes me smile. It's precious to know I've passed the bug to him – he's currently writing his own fantasy novel and instruction books on how to build Lego!

Throughout the writing process, I have gleaned help from many sources and met some fabulous people. I'd like to give a special mention to Stéphanie Ronckier, my beta reader extraordinaire. Stéphanie's continued support with my writing is invaluable and I love the fact that I need someone French to correct my grammar! Stéphanie, you rock. To my lovely friend, Lyn Williamson, thank you for your continued support and encouragement with all my projects. And to my fellow authors, Evie Alexander and Lyndsey Gallagher – you girls are the best! I love it that you always have my back and are there to help when I need you.

Also, a thanks to the editors at Leannan Press for their work on this novel.

Of course a huge thank you goes to the readers who continue to support me in so many ways. I appreciate each and every one of you and hope that I can keep bringing you more books to enjoy! Big love.

Margaret XX

www.ingramcontent.com/pod-product-compliance
Ingram Content Group UK Ltd.
Pitfield, Milton Keynes, MK11 3LW, UK
UKHW040650270425
457920UK00001B/6